memoir
of a
good death

memoir
of a
good death

anne sorbie

thistledown press

Thistledown Press Ltd.
633 Main Street
Saskatoon, Saskatchewan, S7H 0J8
www.thistledownpress.com

Library and Archives Canada Cataloguing in Publication
Sorbie, Anne, 1960–
Memoir of a good death / Anne Sorbie.
ISBN 978-1-897235-81-2

I. Title.
PS8637.O625M44 2010   C813'.6   C2010-905536-5

Cover photograph (detail), *Flutter Kick* by Barbara Cole, Toronto, Canada
Cover and book design by Jackie Forrie
Printed and bound in Canada

Mixed Sources
Cert no. SW-COC-001271
© 1996 FSC
FSC

Canada Council for the Arts   Conseil des Arts du Canada   SASKATCHEWAN ARTS BOARD   Canadian Heritage   Patrimoine canadien

Thistledown Press gratefully acknowledges the financial assistance of the Canada Council for the Arts, the Saskatchewan Arts Board, and the Government of Canada through the Canada Book Fund for its publishing program.

memoir
of a
good death

for RDH: my love, my life

We made our speech from moving water
a sound that seems to ache
—Al Purdy, "In the Beginning was the Word"

1

Have you ever wondered about the moment of your own death? I rarely did, but in the months that preceded mine I felt as if I'd been severely wounded.

My father died on January 27, 2001, and my own life came to an abrupt end exactly six months later. In retrospect, it was as if his passing foreshadowed my own.

My father's name was Edward Flett and mine was Rhegan. After him, I was the last in a long line of landlocked islanders. My father's family came from Orkney where my great-grandmother's great-grandmother had lived with a bear. The animal was a gift, given to her by the Norseman who stayed in her croft for ten years avoiding war. During that time, my ancestral grandmother gave birth to a daughter. Her contemporaries assumed the obvious, but somewhere in the gap that exists between legend and life is a family trait that hints otherwise: my father, Ed, had vertical ridges on his tongue. His mother passed them on to him, and he gave them to me.

When I entered my parents' home the day Ed died, I imagined his staccato voice, its deep brogue, as it was when he told me the story of my Orkney grandmother. Then I thought I heard him talking about books with his own father the way they always had, and I remember feeling comforted by the lull of their voices. What I saw when I got to my parents' bedroom was the elegant curve of my mother's back. She'd tried to perform cardio-pulmonary resuscitation off and on for one hour and ten minutes before I arrived. "A heart attack," she whispered between breaths into my father's mouth as I moved to the other side of their double bed.

I listened to the story that Stan, the next-door neighbour, repeated for the attending police officer. It wafted down the hallway between my mother's sobs and my aunt's endearments. Ed had been carrying a box to the recycling bins. Stan saw him fall, ran outside, and then called 911 after realizing that my father was unconscious. He and some other neighbours carried Ed from the driveway in front of my parents' villa-style condo, and laid him on their bed. My mother, Sarah, tried to call me, then gave up and phoned my friend Nemit, asked her to find me and bring me home. The emergency response team arrived. Ed stopped breathing. They couldn't revive him. Sarah, refused to give up and started CPR again.

The paramedics stood by at a respectful distance while they waited for me. One stayed in the kitchen and the other by the bedroom door. My mother could not be comforted. The idea of consolation was unfamiliar to Sarah Flett. Her small body was rigid, and convulsive movements punctuated her usual fluidity when she was taken gently from the room.

I knelt and cradled my father's stiffening fingers in my hands and kissed his knuckles.

The paramedic came back after taking Sarah away. "I'll stay," I told him, remembering what my granny told me: some souls linger for three days near the place where their body died. The paramedic moved into the hallway again. I thought I saw my father standing in the corner of the room, but when I looked too hard, he disappeared.

His body seemed deflated as it lay on its back on Sarah's side of their bed. The toes of his stained workboots pointed towards ten and two o'clock. He wore his navy blue coveralls over a plaid flannel shirt and a pair of muted green work pants. He must have just had the coveralls cleaned. They were spotless. My father was only a few inches over five feet, but at that moment he seemed taller. His cheeks were stretched and his mouth was open as if beginning an *Oh*. I smoothed his fingers against the surface of the bed.

I wondered what the dying knew and the living did not, if our perceptions changed as our bodies shut down, if we adapted as if sightless or deaf, if we accepted the loss of what we had known. I wondered if dying forced us to let go of anger and love, or if death was a like a form of impotence. I didn't realize then that I would learn the answers to those questions before the short, Alberta summer came to an end.

I lay on my side next to my father and placed my hand on his chest. My knees were level with his shins, my head was on the pillow above his broad shoulders, and my long, red hair was bunched under my neck. I waited expectantly, but there was no resonance or reverberation from the vocal chords next to my ear. Digestion and respiration were arrested, blood and lymph immobilized, bladder and bowel toothless. No more voiding or avoiding, I thought.

Then I heard a sigh. The sound startled me.

"Natural occurrence," the paramedic said from the hallway.

My father's body seemed to sigh with relief. I shifted my weight, leaned on my elbow, and looked for the gaze that had held me all my life. But his eyes were dull, the lids half opened, the pupils shrunken, the retinas denying reflection. The vivid blue seemed colourless, and the flecks that he passed on to me, were vague. I noticed the wedding ring he rarely wore standing dust-free on the inlaid mahogany table next to the bed. Sarah cleaned that ring weekly as if it were one of her Lladro figurines. Ed had insisted it was dangerous to wear a ring in his line of work. He was a craftsman, and the table was a replica made for Sarah. It was as beautiful as the original that stood on the other side of their bed. The seventeenth-century version was an heirloom, the only thing my mother owned, still owns, that belonged to her English parents.

I sat up and placed my hand, palm down next to the wedding band. The dark table surface felt warm. I examined the third finger of my left hand, which had been collapsed by the weight of five wedding rings by then. I turned slightly and skimmed my fingertip along the edge of my father's ear; it was a gesture he repeated tirelessly on mine when I couldn't sleep as a child.

I stood heavily as the priest's black frock invaded my peripheral vision, and let go when Nemit came into the room with my mother and my Aunt Jane. I leaned against her as Sarah wept through The Prayer for the Dead.

It had been an unseasonably warm January, even for Chinook-blessed Calgary. There was little snow left on the ground, and the smell of brown grass permeated the air. The wind began blowing from the mountains to the city the week before Ed died. Whenever that happened, I experienced a sudden flood of phone calls from affected property seekers. I was showing a home on an acreage, a large river lot just south of the city, to the ninth interested couple when the doorbell rang.

"Expecting another buyer?" the purchaser had asked me. "My wife and I called you because we thought you were exclusive."

"I can't imagine who that could be," I'd replied clutching the bottom edge of the suit jacket I'd worn.

The same expensive navy wool blend occupied my fists as I stood swaying in my parents' bedroom. I remember Nemit's hands stroking my upper arms; I couldn't speak the Hail Marys when the priest began a decade of the rosary.

I'd left my clients looking across the sloping property that ended on a cliff fifty feet above the Bow River and met Nemit at the door of the Dunbow Road house. She stood there, feet apart, hands on the doorjamb. "It's Ed," she'd managed. Her brown face was streaked with tears. "Your mother called me." What she'd said made little sense to me because Sarah often refused to speak with Nemit. Sometimes unpleasantness was all she could manage. "You have to come," Nemit had whispered.

I shook my head slowly from side to side, and smelled my mother's fear when she asked for the Last Rites. Her sobs were harmonized by a low growl. I remember staring at her newly coloured, shoulder-length, blonde hair, and her blue and white tracksuit. Her bare feet were bleeding on the antique rug. She had run outside without her shoes, through the shattered contents of the box my father had dropped on the ground. She wouldn't let the paramedics attend to her until after his body had been taken to the funeral home.

The priest performed Extreme Unction and I heard him say something about anointing — then his words faded into an unnatural sound track. That's when I realized that the growling sound was emanating from my own chest. I felt weighed down and disconnected from the kind of words that Ed had invested with so much authority. I loved my father, was devoted to him, but I never understood his stoic belief in the Catholic Church.

I watched the priest anoint my father's forehead and hands with oil and wondered why the deep lines on Ed's face had disappeared. When the priest slipped communion through the gap in my father's lips and offered my mother a large crucifix, she kissed its metal feet.

I moved away from Nemit and left the room. I felt skinned and exposed.

2

My life hadn't always been about loss. It used to focus on gain. I was always interested in property. From the moment of my conception, I wondered who owned the womb I grew in, wondered at five years of age why Sarah and Ed called me *their* child, wondered at fourteen when I towered over my parents, why they thought I was a commodity they would eventually trade. That's when I began calling them by their first names. My English mother thought it was charming. My father, the rough Scottish-Catholic, never got used to the idea, or so he said, but he usually feigned horror whenever I slipped and called him, Dad.

I spent my adult life exchanging houses for money and money for houses. I traded real estate, but I was never the sort whose photograph appeared in the weekend paper. I didn't want my appearance to hinder or help my sales. I was like my father: I liked to do things the hard way.

I operated a private exchange for owners of waterfront properties on the Bow River. That was my focus, my niche. I was licensed to trade from Banff National Park to the place one hundred miles west of Medicine Hat where the Bow comes together with the Oldman River to shape the South Saskatchewan. Those lands were my territory.

The properties I traded during my life included houses, an apartment building, a nursing home, condominiums, a private school, restaurants, single-family dwellings, farms, ranches, cottages, and cabins. I concocted arrangements and ministered betrothals between Bow Terra Firma and people from around the globe, local millionaires, newlyweds, and couples of all kinds. Once, I even followed through on the registration of land to a horse.

I was a bit of an oddity, even for Calgary, where the sudden changes in atmospheric pressure are matched only by the ebb and flow of oil-inspired fortunes. Maybe I hadn't been unlike my ancient grandmother. People came to me for a specific remedy. They wanted land next to running water in the middle of Western Canada and they thought I was the best person to get it for them.

My parents and relatives thought me contrary. Perhaps in some ways I was. I had legally married and divorced five men before I died at the age of thirty-seven. Sarah and Ed were married for forty-three years. I married for the first time at twenty-one and that merger ended before a year had gone by.

The first time I married, I resisted the practise of the father *giving* his daughter away. The tradition implies ownership, and when I was twenty-one, I believed that no one had the power to own me. I walked down the aisle in the Longview Catholic Church, alone. I wore a pale-blue skirt, Western boots, and a white cotton eyelet, off-the-shoulder top. My only traditional wedding accoutrement, a headpiece. Sarah thought I had looked like a Stampede Princess in that veil-less tiara.

The first man I married was barely an adult. Domenic Wynn was eighteen, three years younger than I was and already hard at work ranching to pay off the property he'd arranged, at age fourteen, to purchase from his father. When we met at a rodeo party, I thought he was my match. By my twenty-second birthday, I realized that he was just a counterpart. I divorced him and left his dry, worn-out land intact. I moved back to Calgary and my parents' home on the Bow River.

I *thought* I was married a second time for seven days. However, the charming Justice of the Peace who went to great lengths to marry me to Liam Richards at Assiniboine Lodge had not registered the marriage before Liam advised me he wanted to make a quitclaim. I can't blame the event on a Chinook, wrong season. The foehn wind didn't blow the day he told me to leave, but the weight of the thunderhead that had been building from the early morning finally burst into magnificent sheets of purple lightning when he unburdened himself.

The JP had taken her time; she was a certified Alberta official, but Assiniboine Provincial Park is in British Columbia, situated on the Great Divide. After a five-and-a-half year relationship and seven days of what I assumed was marriage, Liam asked me to remove all my belongings from the house I owned in Inglewood. "Go home to your mother," he said to me, as if we lived in another century and he could cast me off, legitimately, because I was barren. It was September, 1992. I was twenty-eight. I was not barren. I had been pregnant with his child and decided not to carry it to term. I left immediately and walked along the river to my parents' home.

"Does that break any Calgary Stampede records?" I asked Sarah at the time. For ten days in July, the City of Calgary and the City of Las Vegas are statistical rivals. Both register a similar number of marriages and corresponding divorces.

According to Sarah, to make sure — absolutely sure — that he had no legal connection to me, Liam went to Saint Bernard's Catholic Church in Bowness, the church in the neighbourhood I lived in most of my life. He spoke to the nun in charge of annulments. She said he should go to a registry office because a priest hadn't married us. He wrote a cheque for four hundred dollars and insisted that she rush the process.

"A rush?" the nun had apparently asked him.

Then he added a four hundred dollar donation to the Sisters of the Perpetual Virgin kick-the-habit fund. The nun searched the Alberta and British Columbia registries on the spot and found out that the marriage was not registered. A call to the JP was all it took. She had not registered the indenture. We had *not* been married. I was cut to the bone by coincidence, felt as if my heart and gallbladder had been taken, and was too numb to be sad or angry.

I legally married and divorced four husbands after Liam, but I don't ever think about Jack, Raj, Lynn, or Thomas. They don't inhabit me.

3

I CARRY CLEAR MEMORIES OF LIAM, and our wedding ceremony at Assiniboine Lodge. They roll backward and fold in on themselves, soothing me like the river water that ran over my torn skin on the day I died.

From the top of the hewn log staircase, the main floor great-room of Assiniboine Lodge looked crowded. I made my way down carefully and took Ed's outstretched hand. My parents were amazed that I asked them to accompany me that day. I walked between them over wide, creaking planks to where Liam stood with the JP. Sarah's eyes and lips were parched. Her fingers fluttered on my empty belly while Ed kissed me through his tears.

"Proud of ye," he whispered before standing next to Sarah and resting his head on her sharp shoulder. I wondered through the whole ceremony why he said that.

The JP was married to a local sports announcer. She was vital and loud and looked as strong as a horse in her pointed boots. Her cowboy hat was a Smithbuilt that had a feathered band, and the same plumes decorated and extended the length of her thick, grey braid. Her long dress was loose at the waist and whiter than mine was.

"Welcome!" she boomed, extending her arms. Her voice forced its way through the chinks in the log walls and rushed out the open windows. For an instant, I wanted to follow, but the stays in my strapless dress kept me in place.

"Look about you," she continued. "The Ktunaxa people inhabited this area for thousands of years before us. Take in the spirit of this sacred place! Internalize its power! Now look inside yourself and join me in commemoration of the unity matrimony brings."

On that day, I imagined I was beginning a marriage that would last. But instead of hiding something old, something new, something borrowed or something blue under my dress and cloak — I kept a secret.

My mother helped me veil my vacant body and together we put the finishing touches on my costume. I stepped into crinolines that expanded the folds of my extensive skirt. Then Sarah laced the back of my fitted bodice and draped me, shoulder to floor, in my husband's tartan.

When the JP asked those present to circle Liam and me with their intent, their strength, and their love, my Auntie Jane, my cousin, Reed, Liam's mother, and sister, Nemit, and her partner, Joy, and the group of Spanish seminarians who were staying in Assiniboine Lodge surrounded us.

Now I often think I feel the brush of Liam's fingers the way I had when he raised my chin that day.

"Don't be afraid," he'd said, as he stood there in front of me tall and sure in his grandfather's Black Watch kilt. He mistook my behaviour for nerves. He thought I was overcome with emotion, which I was, but it wasn't wedding-induced.

He removed the wool cloak from my shoulders and exposed my guilt-laden skin. When he kissed the fingertips of my free hand, I looked past his shoulder and saw Nemit's forehead touch

Joy's. They were very much in love at the time and enthralled with their baby son.

The rest of the words intended to bring us legally together had been of the usual kind — promises, assurances, undertakings, warnings, and guarantees.

Ed had shared an overused passage from the Old Testament outlining why man leaves his family and takes up with woman. He quoted phrases such as, *two become one,* and, *she is bone of his bone and flesh of his flesh.*

Then we began our vows. Only sheer luck disrupted the overpowering solemnity that hung in the air. Ed and one of the soon-to-be priests screamed when the bad-tempered cook roared outside the north windows. She'd frightened off a grizzly bear with a high-powered boat horn that threatened to rupture my eardrums, and I was never really sure if Liam said, "I do."

4

THE NIGHT BEFORE I MET LIAM was thunderous and wet. Freezing rain poured ice on the aluminum roof of his tent trailer. It sounded like a chorus of tin bashers using ball-peen hammers.

I'd been riding back from Takakkaw Falls after visiting Nemit at the Whiskey Jack Hostel when the storm blew in. The freezing rain had made me take cover. It was too treacherous to pedal for Field, which was only five kilometres away, or back up the Yoho Valley Road. So, I got off my bike at the Kicking Horse Campground.

I had been surprised when the tent trailer was empty, but I knew someone was in the nearby van. Its windows were fogged. I looked in and saw a sleeping shape. I decided to explain myself in the morning, tucked my bike under one of the wing-like trailer ends, and went inside. I found a down jacket and sleeping bag on the bed, quickly using them to replace my wet clothes.

I still feel comforted when I recall the dampness of that place, the smell of the red cedar and hemlock, the collage of dripping fall colours that greeted me the next morning.

Before I arrived, a bear had pawed at Liam through the trailer canvas, marked the tent with rancid pee, and ripped the lid off the metal cooler he'd stored outside, underneath the picnic table. "Banana bread, eggs, cheese, marmalade, bacon, a pitcher of orange Tang, and two gel freezer packs, completely consumed," he said.

I remember the rest of the story as Liam told it to me. He was travelling home from the west coast and had stopped for the night in Yoho National Park at the Kicking Horse Campground. After the bear rambled away, he decided that his van was a safer place to sleep. He ran to the rear doors, unlocked them, climbed inside, and stayed there even after he realized that he'd forgotten his sleeping bag and jacket.

He said that he slept on the corrugated floor of the van until he was startled by a thudding noise. Until he looked through the blurred windows and saw his tent trailer shaking.

I was moving about inside it.

He started shouting and honking the van horn. Then he opened the window and yelled, "Get out! Get out of there! Yah — yah!" and clapped his hands as if slap-running a horse.

I laughed at the guttural sounds that seemed to stick in his dry morning throat.

He threw the van door open and saw me waving a red shirt through the open tent trailer door. That was when he scrambled to his feet, ran the short distance from the van, and stopped outside, in front of me.

"Rhegan Flett," I said, extending my hand.

He was still as his eyes searched the trailer behind me.

I was naked inside his sleeping bag — except for a pair of his thick wool socks. The hood of the mummy bag gaped behind me. I held the top across my chest, while my feet protruded from the section I'd unzipped at the bottom. I stood there motionless staring at the peak in the front of his shorts.

I picked up the down jacket I'd taken off and used as a pillow. "I was biking when the storm blew in," I continued, sitting on the edge of the bed. "You're the only cover for miles, not many people come out here in October." I smoothed the jacket across my lap.

Liam's bare feet made a sucking sound when they left the ground and entered the trailer. He took the jacket, put it on, and stood there arms out. Then he leaned his six-foot three-inch frame on the edge of the green sink and smiled at me as if I was a regular guest.

"My bike is tucked under that end," I said, pointing.

He hadn't noticed it, but he gestured at my helmet and still-damp clothes, which were strewn across the bed.

I said, "Sorry about your clothes," took his socks off, and bundled them in my free hand before holding them out like a peace offering.

"Liam," he said, taking the socks and putting them in the sink. "Richards." He smoothed his hands down the front of his shorts, and held them there one over the other.

I told him that I lived in Calgary.

"Cypress Hills," he said, "quiet and dry."

I'd laughed again, while noticing his ponytail and the small print below the logo on his well-worn, University of Dalhousie sweatshirt that read, *Faculty of Architecture and Planning*. I felt his eyes on my skin, an inch below the notch between my clavicle bones.

"My family runs an outfitter's cabin on the Highwood," he went on, crouching until his eyes, which were almost black, were looking up at mine.

I shook my head. "Thought you were from Cypress Hills."

"You asked where I was from — now we ranch between Longview and Kananaskis," he said.

I wondered why he wasn't more cautious about bears, but apologized for intruding through the distraction of his hair. It smelled like mint and an herb that I still can't name.

"That fridge behind me has a pack of coffee, a carton of cigarettes, and a jar of my mother's jam in it," he said.

I nodded at Liam's offer of breakfast and looked at the faded avocado door. I stood, clutched my clothes to my chest, lifted the bottom of the sleeping bag, and squeezed through the doorway, back exposed.

When I came back from the log-framed outhouse, he was humming Dvořák's, *Furiant*, one of the Slavonic dances. I was unsure if it was number one or number eight. I felt nervous and underdressed in my padded cycling shorts and fitted neoprene shirt. I knocked on the metal body of the ancient trailer and stuck my head through the door.

He'd made coffee. The aroma was uninviting, but I accepted a hot mug when he offered it and let it brand my palms red. As I raised the mug, I pictured my hair mixed with his on a damp pillow.

Liam called three weeks later. I was at home, reading about a property for sale in Inglewood, a neighborhood which at the time was one of the least sought after in Calgary. My mother, who sometimes arrived at my apartment unannounced, pretended to rearrange dishes in my kitchen cupboards while we spoke. Forty minutes later, when the call was over, I asked her, "Is that one of Jane's outfits?"

Sarah ignored my question. It was late in the afternoon and she'd already suggested, several times, that I get out of my pajamas. She was wearing wide, brown gabardine trousers and a matching vest over a coffee coloured silk blouse. The clothes meant that rather than spend hours coaxing Ed out of his workshop to dye her hair for her, Sarah had driven out to my auntie's place. Her hair was ginger-red. She constantly tried to reproduce my dark auburn version, but I could tell from her scalp that there was too much purple in the mix.

"Who telephoned?" Sarah asked while closing the cupboard doors gently, a sign that she was trying to practice restraint.

I set down the November 1987 *Real Estate News* and stretched out on the chaise in front of the ceiling-to-floor windows. Snow whirled in the air. "Someone I met when I visited Nemit at the Whiskey Jack Hostel," I said.

She looked at me over the frame of her silver glasses. "Was the caller female?" She trailed her left hand along the breakfast bar and climbed onto one of four tall stools that sat in front of it.

"Male," I said, fascinated by the snow that rose on gentle updrafts. I was looking west from the twenty-first floor of Tower One at Point McKay on the Bow River. The mountains were obscured by cloud. I lived on the edge of Bowness, my parents' neighborhood, in a community called Parkdale. My apartment was about five and a half kilometres west of downtown Calgary.

Sarah sat on the stool with her feet on its horizontal bar, her knees jutting out like butterfly wings. She gripped the front edge of the seat and forced her arms straight. This is an image of my mother that I love. There are thousands of others in my flow of memories but many of those are unpleasant.

She wanted to know all about Liam. Instead, I told her that I was thinking about using more of my trust money from Granny Flett to invest in a house. She moved her hands to the sides of her body, gripped the edge of the seat again, and held her legs straight out. Then she slipped off the stool and strode into the living room where she stood uncomfortably close to me. Sarah hated that I didn't answer her questions.

She declared that she loved me when I introduced her to Liam, and pretended to be horrified when we told her the story of how we met.

Five years later my parents were both pleased and disappointed when I told them that Liam and I were going to be married. I was nearly twenty-eight at the time and still concerned about what my parents thought.

"Liam and I have decided," I said. I wore an imaginary track in their living room carpet, swung my body round at each end, and took in the view of the Bow River from the house that I still think of as my granny's.

"Decided what, darling?" Sarah had asked.

I remember the smell of her spring clothes; it enveloped the conversation. She used to air her light jackets and coats, dresses and pants, blouses and walking shorts every year.

"To get married," I said, while my eyes were fixed on the whirlpool the river made at the bottom of their property.

"Lovely! I knew you would come to your senses! I'll call Auntie and let her know, she can call Reed and of course we'll have to have his girlfriend and her family."

"His girlfriend and her family aren't invited." I had baited her.

"Not invited?" Sarah jerked her body off the flowered settee.

"Not invited. The location we've chosen isn't very accessible." I had known she wouldn't have trouble searching out words for a reply.

"Not accessible?"

"We want to get married at Assiniboine Lodge."

"In the mountains?" The colour on her face deepened as she circled the room.

"Ed!" I called from the doorway. "Can you please get Mum to stop repeating everything I say?"

"Girls! — Sarah," he said. I had loved the way my father's tongue pulsed against the hard 'r'. "Sit yourself doon — and you, Princess Rhegan, give your mother a chance. Would you please? If you canny dae that, then I just don't know."

I remember watching the reflection of my mother's face in the mirror behind the wet bar. She touched her palm to the back of her ear-length bob, pressing it against the stiff surface.

I had sat in Ed's wingback chair and waited for his squat body to negotiate its way behind the bar.

"Breathe in, breathe out," Sarah muttered.

"We just want to keep it simple." My feet hung off the footstool.

"Simple!"

"Sarah."

"Rhegan! How do you expect people — expect us to get in there?" She couldn't stay still. "I will not hike for two days, fight off bears, or sleep in a tent to watch you get married in a pair of hiking boots!" She retraced my track in front of the French doors that opened on to the garden.

"Calm yourself, lovey." Ed's voice was laboured as he came back into the centre of the room. At the bar, he'd poured Glenfiddich into heavy glasses. He handed me a tumbler and downed his own, before wiping the back of his hand across his mouth. "An' you," he'd said, pointing, "call me *Dad* or I'll not be riding in any helicopter."

"Helicopter?" Sarah's look reminded us both that she loathed being the last to know. "God above," she crossed herself.

"September long weekend. We've booked the lodge. You two, Auntie Jane and Reed, Liam's mum and his sister, Christine, chopper in on the Friday afternoon. I'll send some things with you, the cake, my dress, and Liam's clothes. The JP will fly in Saturday." That's when the wheels came off, so to speak.

"A J-fucking-P?" Ed spat. "I'll have nae part in a wedding that's not recognized by the church." The tumbler waved about in his left hand.

Sarah took the glass from him. "My Edinburgh crystal," she said voice rising, before looking at me with a satisfied smirk.

"I'm your effing dad, and by God this time I'm on your mother's side!"

"Ed, sit down." Sarah lengthened her neck and tilted her head to one side as they sat together on the settee.

"I'm willing tae hold ma tongue for a lot a' things, but you know how I feel about heathen weddings. It's a bloody sin not tae be joined in holy wedlock by a priest who is — "

"God's agent on earth. Yes, dear," Sarah said, ruffling his salt-and-pepper hair. "Breathe in, breathe out." She pulled on a tuft.

"Maybe I should come back when you've had time to digest the idea," I said, standing.

"Digest the idea?"

"You're doing what she does!" I said.

"She! — that's your mother and don't you bloody well forget it, young lady!"

I leaned against the oak bar, touched the flowers and vines carved into the panels on its front, called him Daddy, but I knew he wouldn't be pacified.

"Bloody hell — at least tell me the JP's a man."

"She's a woman."

"That's it! I'm going tae the shop!" Ed had left through the French doors. I watched him walk across the lawn.

"Just give him a while, okay?" Sarah said. "You have made a choice and we will respect it the best we can — even if we do not *like* it."

"Don't like my groom?" I sat next to her, back straight, knees together.

"Silly girl." She patted my hand.

"It's a beautiful place — "

"Next to what?" She got up and filled the small sink behind the bar. My parents had gone to Saint Mary's Cathedral once a month and Saint Bernard's every other Sunday for Mass. I could have married Liam in either church.

I turned and put my feet on the settee, told Sarah to think of Assiniboine as another one of God's places, and reminded her that the mountain was as grand as the Matterhorn.

She washed the glasses, drained the sink, and rinsed the crystal in water that sent steam into the air.

"I'm wearing a dress," I'd said.

The glasses clinked as she set them on the ceramic counter. "A wedding dress? What do you think you want to wear? Long? Short? Mid-length? A veil? A headdress? I still have the hat I wore. A hat with a veil!"

I stood up and turned to face her. "Sarah . . . I'm . . . I . . . "

"No need to panic." She came towards me, reached up, placed her wet hands on my cheeks, and then on my shoulders.

I felt stiff and expectant.

She had embraced me, something that she rarely did when I was growing up. "It will be lovely," she said. "And I will need a mother-of-the-bride outfit. A coat dress — with a hat!"

And so it went with my parents. Sarah had always sided with either my father or me. Our family discussions were triangular, always two-against-one situations, and my father was always stubborn and loud.

I called Liam at work and asked him to speak to Ed. After Liam arrived, I walked with him from the house to the shop and stood beside the lilac bushes near the open door while he and Ed spoke. Ed knew I was there, but neither of us ever broached the topic. That way he didn't lose face.

"Hi, Ed."

"Li-am." Ed's arms were out for balance. His workboots, the front one-third of which were always covered in sawdust, sat on the floor. "I like pacing on this beam. It's the first piece of equipment I ever got for Rhegan. Got it when the Mount Royal Gym Club was upgrading."

Liam sat on the workbench next to Ed's toolbox. I watched Ed transfer his weight from one foot to the other.

"Listen, son, I know that we all like tae please our women, but I just canny imagine you not getting married in a church."

"I'm okay with marrying at Assiniboine."

Ed executed a slow spin on the ball of his left foot, planted the right in front. The leg of his oldest overalls billowed slightly. "You're okay wi' that? Well that's just grand. Insult tae injury, man. Insult tae injury."

I practiced on that four-inch beam every day when I was twelve. Ed placed it in the middle of the lawn and watched me prance, cartwheel, and break my ankle trying to land a back somersault. He let the grass grow knee-deep, told Sarah it would soften my landings.

"We'll still be legal."

"No' in the eyes of God."

"You're upset because the JP is a woman."

Managing Ed's reactions had always been a delicate balancing act, an act that Sarah perfected and performed often until Ed died. Liam and I were her understudies.

"Good God, man. Where's your sense of integrity? The Pope doesn't see fit tae put women in the priesthood. Far too emotional. So what does this thing you're doing say aboot that?"

"It says we're progressive."

"Progressive my arse. I might as well just bend over an' let you give me the what for." Ed stepped off the beam and circled a pool of sawdust in the middle of the shop floor.

"We hope you can find your way to respect our choices," Liam said.

"That's the trouble with you lot, too many bloody choices. That's why the Catholic Church is successful world-wide — it preaches restraint."

"It preaches guilt."

"Careful, boy-o." He pulled his socks out of his boots, sat on the beam, and pulled them on before slipping his feet into the boots and tying a double bow in each lace.

Ed strode across the floor, raised the hood of the Rover, and checked the oil. He pulled the dipstick out of its casing and cleaned it with a remnant of an old tablecloth. "Rhegan locked me in here once, you know," he said, replacing the wavering length of metal.

"What?"

"Aye, she did that. Paid for it dearly as well. Did she not tell you?

"No." Liam laughed when Ed told him what happened, but at the time, it had been no laughing matter. My father was furious.

Ed refused to let me miss Mass when I was ten. I wanted to go to Brownie camp. He helped me get ready, even helped me design a box-kite frame so that I could earn a wood-crafting badge. Then he found out I'd be away Saturday night and all day on a Sunday, so he said I couldn't go, said I'd be cast out by the Lord, that I'd burn up in the fires of Hell. So I locked him in the shop. He didn't know until he tried to go in for supper two hours later. The only access to the shop at that time was the side door — and it had a padlock on the outside. I went into the house, told Sarah that Ed was lacquering and that he'd be a while, convinced her that the two of us should go to my Auntie Jane's to get away from the smell.

"There I was screaming like a banshee until Rhegan's granny let me out," Ed told Liam. "The old windae was too small for me tae get through."

"And Rhegan?" Liam asked him.

"The conniving wee bugger stayed with her cousin, Reed."

The whole point was, I'd made him miss the Wednesday night Knights of Columbus Mass.

Liam slipped off the workbench and they stood next to each other, arms crossed, while my father told him the rest of the story.

Granny told Sarah to leave me at Jane's for the week when she found out. When I came home, I wasn't the least bit sorry. So Ed made me miss Brownies on the following Monday, made me write lines for two and a half hours. I scribbled, *I will not lock Ed in the shop*, the whole time I should have been in my Pixie group. I was the group leader, the Sixer.

"Did she do it?" Liam had asked Ed.

"Aye," he said. "And at the end was a wee prayer that thanked God for sparing her Daddy from the burning fires o' Hell."

"You were a bad kid," Liam told me later that night as we sat on the floor at the top of the spiral staircase in the Inglewood house. The end of his forefinger traced the length my clavicle, stroked the hollow at the base of my throat.

"He did miss Mass," I managed before he kissed me.

I had a point to make with Ed when I was ten. I couldn't tell my father then, or even when I was an adult that I thought he was wrong. So I learned from Granny Flett and my mother how to calm Ed, how to avoid confrontation with him. Thereafter I repeated the kind of placating routines they used — except when it came to property.

As much as Ed loved me, he never believed that I could manage or exchange land. He waited daily for me to get into financial trouble. I disgraced him when I divorced Domenic and dishonored him when I married Liam outside the church. He never understood that autonomy was important to me, and I didn't want to buy into the shame or guilt that the church preached, especially the kind that he seemed to embrace.

Weeks after I told my parents that Liam and I were getting married, Ed made a single request — that he share a reading from the Catholic wedding liturgy at the civil ceremony. I conceded. He came to the wedding. It was the last one of mine he attended.

5

ED HAD BEEN FLABBERGASTED WHEN LIAM cast me off. He thought it was because I bought a house on the north side of the Bow, a run-down two-storey that faced the river on Memorial Drive in Parkdale.

Just four weeks before the wedding, I bartered and the vendor reduced the price to compensate for the ailing furnace, the damaged plaster and exposed lath, the ancient electrical, and the rusted five-gallon hot-water tank, which was a luxury in its day. I bought the house and added it to my holding company. I restored the kitchen cabinets, installed a new furnace and hot-water tank, resurfaced the claw-foot tub, exposed the hardwood floors, added insulation, upgraded the wiring, and repaired the walls. Then I put up a *For Lease* sign. The same man has been in that house ever since. He loves the proximity to downtown, walks the four and a half kilometres to and from work every day, and has no desire to own the place.

I owned the house that Liam and I had lived in. I also owned four apartments, which were rented. I didn't buy stock or invest in mutual funds. I didn't register money for retirement. I invested in property; doing so was a natural part of my family's matrilineal heritage. I began buying property when my granny broke my father's heart and sold her land near John O' Groats.

Mathea Flett, the daughter of my ancestral grandmother Gudrin, moved to the Scottish mainland from Orkney after the old bear mauled her mother to death eight centuries before I was born. After that, Mathea's land passed from mother to daughter — until my granny gave birth to Ed.

Granny owned Mathea's land near John O' Groats when she married my grandfather. Despite what the law said, he agreed that her land would always be her land. They lived on it until 1942 when they immigrated to Calgary with my father in tow. When my granny sold that property in 1980, she had been in Canada for thirty-eight years and during that time, she'd collected rent from Mathea's place. When the family died out, she decided to let the land go.

After the sale was completed, and because she had given birth to one son and no daughters, my granny gifted me forty thousand pounds, keeping the money in trust until she thought I was old enough to understand the intricacies of proprietorship. While the sale symbolized a break from the past, her actions also represented the continuity of a centuries-old tradition.

I used some of the money to buy two apartments in Bowness after I finished university. Granny advised me to mortgage them and provided collateral when Ed wouldn't. I rented the apartments to a divorced couple in 1988. The wife lived in the third-floor suite. The husband lived in the second-floor suite. They each paid three hundred and fifty dollars a month. I was twenty-four and had just earned my real estate license. Four years later, I owned twelve hundred square feet in a three-storey concrete building. I used one of the apartments as collateral, doubled down and bought two more. Two paid me income and two contributed to my growing equity. I was self-employed. I was hard working, and from then on, I made an exceptional living selling Bow River properties.

Ed said I hadn't an ounce of good sense, taking chances like that — without a man to back me up. "What happens," he asked, "when the interest rates go up?" He worried about Granny having to bail me out when mortgages flew up to fifteen percent. I was locked in at eight-and-a-half.

My father hadn't shared the same penchant for property. Sarah and Ed never built or owned their own home until after Ed retired. They had always lived with my grandparents, Astrid and Harold. My parents held some land. They owned the lot immediately west of Granny's, but it had only my father's carpentry shop within its boundaries.

When Granny died in 1990, she left me her home, and bequeathed an equal amount of money to Ed. He tore at his hair; he didn't understand her need to keep her ancestral tradition alive. I told him that he could live in the old house as long as he and Sarah wished, and they stayed there until 1993, one year after Liam and I split up. Ed retired then and wanted to cut costs, so I made him an offer for the shop land. Sarah held her breath and forced a smile. She'd always felt resentful because they never built their own home. I told Ed he could use the shop whenever he wanted, for as long as he was able. He dropped the price and shook my hand. My parents moved to a brand-new villa-style condo a few kilometres downstream, and parked their old Rover in the attached garage. I moved home.

Ed rode his bike from Bowness to Inglewood the day I signed the papers for the Parkdale place. He wanted to know why Liam wasn't party to the deal, wanted to know what I thought I could really own without my man, wanted to know if I'd heard what he said. I didn't answer. Instead, I focused on the rushing sound the river made, planned and arranged.

Sarah knew that the deadlock between Liam and me had roots in an expenditure of another kind, one I made while on a trip to Montana with her a few months before Liam and I got married.

I had told Liam I was going on a trip with Sarah.

"I'm okay with that," he said, assuming I was still looking for a wedding dress.

When we left, I drove. As the city haze faded behind us, I let Sarah do the talking. For one hour and twenty-two minutes, she described and embellished, railed about Ed, complained about Ed, and laughed about their latest golf trip to Cranbrook before she looked at me, really looked at me. Then there was silence.

I thought about how silence was constructed in the womb. Through the umbilical cord — the noise — was it loud? Was it magnified or muted by the surrounding viscosity? Surely the mother was heard, sensed. Foetal ears functioned in the womb. Heard the constant transference from mother to child. Watery exchange, changing amniotic fluid, digestion, respiration, heart pumping, blood beating, lymph cleansing, kidneys processing, bowels bulging, mother voiding and avoiding.

The small town of Longview was framed in the rear-view mirror, the southwest flank of Kananaskis Country and the Highwood Range were across the plateau on the right side of the car. The Chanel fragrance Sarah wore filled my nostrils and the bananas she stored in the snack-pack made me nauseous.

Liam had insisted on cleaning my car before I left. He dusted the dashboard, washed the windows, cleaned the chrome — no streaks, no spotting allowed.

"Would you like me to drive?" Sarah asked when we reached the Frank Slide. Boulders, some bigger than houses, lined the highway.

"Thanks," I said, pulling over. The idea of lives flattened and sealed under the mounds of rock was daunting. I wondered if death was quick, if there was a lot of blood.

I got out of the car and met Sarah by the trunk. Low blood pressure and the move to standing after sitting for so long made me light-headed.

"Breathe in, breathe out," she muttered as her fingers floated over my rounded abdomen. Her feet seemed to dance the same way mine did. I resisted her help as she walked with me to the passenger door.

"Are you all right, darling?" she asked.

"Fine," I said as I sank into the reclined seat, closed my eyes so that I didn't have to watch her squat-pee in the ditch.

As I dozed, each town we drove through was complemented by sounds and smells. Crow's Nest Pass: engine hum, and mother hum, and the burn of my own drool. Frank: cooked ham; Coleman: pickles and gherkins; Blairmore: roasted garlic and freshly-turned vegetable gardens.

We stopped in Sparwood at the Golden Dragon and sat in a vinyl booth. The smell of the semi-red sauce smothering Sarah's lunch assaulted me. I drank water and ordered plain rice when Sarah finished. She spoke — spoke about my *poor* Auntie Jane and her son, Reed, spoke about his drinking and the fact that he was dependant at twenty-eight. I pretended to listen but I'd heard about my cousin's habits numerous times in the same context. When she was finished, I decided not to balk at the ritual I knew she'd insist on before we continued.

Before we got back on the highway, I took pictures of Sarah. She was a dwarf next to the incomprehensible rubber of the world's largest dump truck, which stands quietly in a flat parking lot at the edge of Highway Three. Carefully placed boulders native to the region encircle the area, which is marked by a brown and white tourist attraction sign.

She stood under the ladder that was fixed to a strip of fender behind the front wheel on the driver's side. Ladder and fender were perpendicular to the body of the truck. Both stopped about four feet off the ground.

"Boost me!" she demanded.

I braced myself, one foot slightly behind the other, hands clasped at knee height. She stepped onto them with one foot, put a hand on my shoulder, and reached up. That was one of the few times in my life I was glad my mother was smaller and much lighter than I was.

"Ta-da!" she sang, easing her weight from my hands. She climbed onto the Titan's fixed ladder, posed on the first rung. "Come on! Let's climb this monster!"

After she began climbing, I held onto the third rung, reached up for the fourth, fifth, and sixth, legs dangling until I got a foot on the ladder. Then I followed her until we stood on the fenced platform in front of the windshield and stared through the rear cab windows at the huge box.

She grabbed my hand and raised it over her head, heels lifting like a pumped up jogger. "See, darling," she said, "in the grand scheme of things how insignificant some things are?"

"Ma'am! Miss!" Neither of us had noticed the white, crossbar-lit car pulling into the parking lot next to the highway. "I'll have to write you up," the officer said. "Ah — Mrs. Flett. Trespassing again? That will be two hundred and fifty each."

"Five hundred dollars! Last time it was less! We want a photograph! Darling, give him the camera." She took the small automatic from her fanny pack.

I dropped it toward the officer who wore a turban and single bee-stripes on his legs. Sarah put her scrawny arm around my rib cage, but managed to keep her body detached from mine. I stared at the pink of my mother's clothes and couldn't imagine her without me.

I thought about the weight of the unformed child in my belly, about my decision to have an abortion. My mother was not particularly maternal. I had convinced myself that I was made the same way. I felt an interest when it came to Adam, Nemit's son, but I could never imagine surrendering my life to a child the way she had, the way Ed did. My father was the one who always heard and responded to my nighttime cries. He read to me before bed while Sarah watched from the doorway, and cradled me in his arms when I felt bad. The shop was the first place I went for solace. Sarah didn't often like to touch me or to be touched by me. The organic changes that initiate mothering in the female body had been incomplete in Sarah, sometimes didn't exist. She hadn't wanted to nurse me and fought with my granny about feeding me formula instead of breast milk. When Granny taught Sarah how to drive, she had to convince her that it wasn't a good idea to leave me at home, alone in my bassinet.

Ed needed my granny after I was born; perhaps that was the real reason that they never built their own place. Sarah managed to do what was required of a mother, but according to Ed, that was only because my granny told her what to do and when to do it. I'm not sure that Sarah ever felt the incessant pull of motherhood the way that other women seem to, but I know that she cared for me.

When my physician decided not to support my choice to abort my pregnancy, it was my mother who suggested that we drive south. "That way," she said, "there would be less chance of anyone finding out."

After we turned towards the U.S. border at Roosevelt, the landscape began to widen and the mountains receded. The sides of the highway were lined with white crosses, each one a memorial to a quick death. They stayed in my peripheral vision for a long time and made me think about the flow of blood from mother to child, the foetus engorging and gorging itself. For a moment, I felt as if I might lose the possibility of something. Then the thought vanished, like a salmon jumping upstream, and then disappearing under the surface of a fast-moving river. I focused on the road, couldn't look at Sarah at all.

I was animated when I walked into the clinic in Kalispell, drained when Sarah held my elbow as we walked out. I wanted to scream.

I fell asleep as she drove north and woke when the engine stopped.

"Whitefish," Sarah said softly, as I struggled to open my eyes. "Wait here." Before she checked in, her hand traced a line from my temple to my chin; it was a gesture she made on rare occasions.

The lake was behind the row of cabins that were part of the Bayshore Inn, and the road that steeply snaked up to Big Mountain Ski Resort was across the highway about two miles ahead.

"All right, darling," Sarah said, when she came back with the key.

I had never before seen so much compassion in my mother. I wanted to yell, *Stop patronizing me!*

Inside the cabin, I settled on the recliner in front of the huge windows. Sarah covered me with a blanket and I dreamt that when I lifted my head my long hair stayed behind, that the thickness and length of my life was cut away.

"Good morning, Rapunzel!" a voice sang.

I turned my head toward the sound, tears streaming.

"Shshshshshshsh," a voice whispered.

I remember placing my feet on cold metal.

"Shshshshsh," Sarah crooned.

I dreamt that a thumb crossed a switch, that a flexible tube rippled.

"Rhegan," my mother's voice whispered.

I felt her warm hand caressing my forehead, and I clenched my fists. My breath came in spasms. I opened my eyes, looked out over the lake, and could see patches of ice on its surface. My eyelids drooped. A rod jigged in my hand. I wound a metal handle. A fish swam away.

I thought about the beauty in the lines on my mother's face. They made me want to cry. I dreamt, saw red silk skimming bare feet catching my mother's attention.

"Knight — to Queen." Sarah slid the piece across the chessboard. The next day we sat at a green Formica kitchen table near the windows overlooking the lake.

"You can't take advantage of me like this," I said.

"Why not?"

"I'm defenceless."

"Darling — it is not my fault if you did not pay attention when Ed taught you how to play." My mother was devious when she played games, and that always made me want to laugh.

I took her Knight with my Rook.

She advanced her Bishop. "Checkmate!" she said.

Later the same day I decided to go for a walk. I made my way carefully down the long flight of wooden stairs that led to the rocky beach. My quads shook and I wondered how they'd feel when I had to go up. I stopped at the bottom listening, thought I heard a flute. I decided that the sound was coming from the south and turned in that direction. Sarah stood outside on the deck.

Until then I had stayed in the cabin letting her be the uncharacteristic nurse. The temperature plummeted soon after we checked in. The man at the front desk called to say that it was minus fifty at the top of Big Mountain, in case we were thinking about spring skiing; but there was no snow by the lake.

I marvelled at the noise the water made when it broke ice and lapped the beach in tiny waves. The lake moved below its late skin, forcing pure sound through blowholes. I pulled my wool hat lower on my forehead and leaned against a huge log. I'm not sure how long I was there before I detected a plop-hiss between notes. I lifted my head and saw a sheepskin-clad man wearing lace-up ropers. The coat was the same colour as his sandy hair. He syncopated the lake's rhythm, raised his hand, waited for a note, and then threw a stone.

"*That* is the Phillips boy," Sarah said breaking the strange cadence.

My mother always snuck up on me when I least expected her. I didn't scream. I let her hug me.

"The Phillips *boy*?"

"The family came here every year at the same time we did for twelve years of spring skiing and you do not recognize him?"

"Don't know." I looked at his lined face.

"Well, he is quite a bit older than you are," she whispered.

He reached us a couple of minutes later.

"Mrs. Flett! And — Rhegan?"

"Yes. Rhegan," I said.

"Tho-mas!" a tall woman called from the door of a cabin. Smoke spiralled into the air above its roof.

"My mother," he said. "Nice to see you both."

I watched him lope over the uneven ground. I saw him again six years later in a lobby with Nemit, and married him next to Bow Falls a few months after that.

My mother, strange as it may seem, kept the details of our trip to herself — until a week after my wedding at Assiniboine Lodge. Although, we never discussed it, I assumed that she understood why I wanted to abort the child. I imagined that she knew and accepted the idea that I might be just like her. In a moment of what she called clarity, she told Liam about Kalispell. To me, she said that our relationship, if it was to last, should be based on honesty. For the next nine years, I rarely spent time with my mother, and hardly spoke to her until Ed died.

Six months after that, I took the things that mattered with me to my grave, leaving her hurtful indiscretion behind.

6

YOU THINK ABOUT THE GRANDCHILD WHO never was and
wonder if he/she could have helped ease the pain you feel
now, the pain that your daughter wants you to ignore. You
decide not. Far too much to expect of an imaginary eight-year-
old. Your daughter seems to love being alone, goes into heat
in the spring summer season and gets rid of her mate when
the temperature drops. Each time your daughter discards a
husband she hibernates. You were Ed's wife for four decades.
His death is your death.

You are puzzled after your husband dies; you do not know
how your day should go. You cannot get used to cooking for
one, so you try to cook for your daughter. She is uninterested
in a daily sojourn to your home. You suggest a weekly event. In
time you give up, and your next-door neighbour, the one who
helped carry your husband inside when his heart failed, takes
the foul-smelling leftovers from the driveway in front of your
garage to the large bin, which is concealed in its own tasteful
structure near the entrance to your condominium complex.
The bags contain main courses of quail, tenderloin, duck, and
bison. You refuse to trace Ed's last steps. Instead, you wear a

path in the lawn between the back of your villa-style home and the river. The sound of the flowing water is a small comfort. You also know that your daughter is just a few kilometres upstream and that you could see her — see your mother-in-law's old house, the one she lives in now — if the lush banks curved west instead of northwest.

Soon after Ed's death, you wrapped yourself in your fur coat and sat outside in your father-in-law's old teak deck chair at the bottom of the garden near the whirlpool. You could not see it then, but you could hear it moving under the ice. You watched the thin, open strip of the Bow River rush past your garden — sometimes the water was grey, sometimes navy blue. You felt disconnected. Ed and his family, despite its unusual history, grounded you, gave you roots. Your own parents were both dead by the time you met your husband. He came to stay in the rooming house in Millarville where you cleaned and cooked and served meals in exchange for a place to live. You had been there since the age of ten. Your sister was also in service — to a prominent family in Banff: the Bengel's. You only saw her at Easter and Christmas between 1948 and 1957. In fifty-eight, you met your husband. You were twenty; he was thirty-four. Ed was building a guest cabin for the McKay family father. You cannot remember the man's first name. You do remember that he thought he was the boss of the women who ran the restaurant and house in which you worked.

The first time you heard Ed speak about planes, you imagined flight. He had an old car and after a few months, he invited you to Calgary. Mrs. McKay would not let you go when she saw that the junker did not have a floor on the passenger side, just a rust-encrusted hole. Ed's mother came with him the next week, drove you to Calgary herself. Your feet rested on thin, smooth boards that fit together so well not a drop of air stirred under your skirt. You felt as if you'd finally been rescued.

Two months after Ed died, you had to move the deck chair away from the water because the ground was getting soft and you felt the melting snow inside your leather shoes. You decided it was time. You turned the knob on the only louvered door in the basement and walked inside the storage room. Your husband's sharp smell infuriated you. You gripped the handle of his golf bag and dragged it out. You pushed it through the too-small opening in the patio doors and enjoyed the sound of the steel shafts clinking against each other, smiled at the dull thud the club heads made when they landed on the deck. You threw off your lightest winter jacket, teed up ball after ball in an exposed section of lawn, went through sleeve after sleeve that he collected and never used, laughed when each small globe disappeared under the surface of the river, and felt frustrated by those that rolled about on the surface of the remaining ice. You tried every club. When you tired of each, became bored with its angle and length, you walked closer to the river's edge and javelined the shiny shafts into the water. You dumped the bag on the driveway in front of your home, right next to the garbage. You yelled, "WHAT?" at the group of neighbours who stared at you. "You are welcome to the shoes, the windbreaker, the glove and the ball retriever, and the stroke counter, and the pencils, and the ball markers," you said to no one in particular. You heard zippers and pouches opening; you recognized the feet of the vultures before the garage door met the cement.

Spring arrived and you took two more months to deliberate before deciding which of Ed's clothes should go to the Salvation Army and which you wanted to keep.

Your tall, slender daughter comes through the front door, eyes big. She wades through piles of your husband's clothes, makes her way into your room and sits on your bed. Your daughter runs her hand up and down the coverlet as if rubbing your husband's back. You hated the way she did that to Ed and despised the fact that he let her. You thought that particular gesture bordered on impropriety.

You rip the bedspread off, and then you try to pull it out from under her, tell her that she is just in time to help you flip the mattress.

Your daughter asks why Ed's clothes are all over the house.

You tell her that you are categorizing, being methodical. You tell her that you are using the same principle your husband used for organizing his magazines.

Your daughter stands, looking pained. You want her to cry and you feel deprived because you have not been privy to her grief.

You throw the bedding on the floor. For years, your husband stacked magazine issues all over the house: *Car and Driver, Popular Mechanics,* and *Woodworking* were his favourites, *Reader's Digest* and its accompanying condensed books as well. Your daughter forgets about the system Ed developed over the years. One or two titles per room. Oldest issues near the door. Piles arranged so that the newest copies were always on top. Your daughter forgets that you *let* Ed build his library this way, even after you moved. You let him pile magazines in neat stacks, in the entranceway, in his bathroom, under the wet bar, under the bow window in the kitchen, in the window seat in your bedroom, under your bed, at the end of your bed.

Your daughter thinks your home is unsightly and says you should recycle the lot and keep Ed's books, especially the books that his father left him. And. Your daughter would like, *like* to have your husband's best white shirt. Your daughter wants something to remember him by. She tells you this as she picks up your husband's wedding ring, kisses it, and puts it back on the bedside table.

You ask your daughter, *Why?* You ask again because your husband's tools fill one end of your daughter's three car garage.

You position yourself at the foot of the bed. You work with your daughter, slide the mattress off one side of the bed. Together you stand the mattress on its long edge. You both lift and walk counter clockwise so that the just-used surface is parallel to the box spring. You give a light push and the mattress lands, unused surface exposed.

Your daughter decides to leave, telling you that she has an appointment with a potential client.

You make the bed with linen that you rip from vacuum-sealed packages.

Today you kneel in front of the urn containing your husband's ashes. Your hands caress the sides of the hard vessel. Your husband, a man who was a broad, five-feet-four inches tall has been reduced to one hundred eighteen and a half cubic inches. Your daughter is not the only one who knows something about the measure of things. You realize that you were distraught when you chose cremation. You think that your daughter must have been devastated as well, because she never once contradicted your instructions at the funeral home.

You lift the blinds behind the Jacuzzi tub where the urn sits. The neighbours are on their patio drinking coffee. You back away and sit on the closed lid of the commode, elbows on your knees, hands under your chin. You move your hands to your thighs and rake your nails across your red corduroy pants. You palm your breasts in a circular motion. The starched fabric of your husband's best white shirt grazes your skin. Your hands slap your thighs.

"Sarah!" Betty and Stan call between sips. "How are you today, sweetie?"

"Lovely." You get up from your squat in front of the chimney, lean for a moment on the grey siding, and then walk quickly over the small green space between your home and the neighbours'. Despite the fact they are English, you find their Sheffield singsong mildly irritating most of the time.

"Cleaning out the fireplace trap then, are we?"

"Yes."

"Stan, why don't you do that for her?"

"Here, let me help you, luv."

"Oh, my. Oh, my," Betty bursts out. Stan is motionless. Your husband's white shirt is transparent in the sun. You pause so that the man from the Midlands has time to appreciate your alabaster skin.

"Here, ducks, you sit and I'll take care of that for you. Won't take me but a mo—ment" Stan's voice falters just enough to delight you.

You stretch your arms up and yawn, reward the man for staring. You give him a peck on the cheek. "Thank you, Stan," you say, before you sit in his chair and lift his coffee cup.

"Wait, luvey, let me get you a fresh one," Betty says, but you have already taken a sip. "That warm enough for you? Would you like anything else? A doughnut? A bagel? A Bismarck?"

"No, thank you, Betty."

"You're getting awfully thin, Sarah. Are you eating right? Rhegan cooking for you?"

You sneer. "Rhegan does not cook."

"You could always go to Meals on Wheels. Victoria, three doors down, did. She says it's not too bad."

You watch Stan and decide to tell Rhegan later how graceful his long fingers are. Your husband's were always rough, his prints accentuated by Castrol motor oil, and sawdust.

"Says she's used to taking her hot meal at noon now," Betty continues. "Sandwich for supper."

You lean forward.

"I said sand-wich for supper, dear. Stan! Are you nearly done over there?"

"Oh, do not rush him, Betty. I will have coffee and a bagel. Cream cheese too, thank you."

"All right, lovey, then. Have you seen my dahlias this year? Double doubles. I can't understand it, dear. I mean look at this then."

You stare at the bent-over Stan.

"Look, would you? It's a freak of nature it is. I mean the colour is wonderful. All right, lovey, I'll be right back with your coffee and bagel." Betty calls over to Stan, " — right back I will!"

You stand and walk down the imaginary line between your place and theirs. A train trundles past, across the river on the far side of Bowness Road. You recall the old streetcar that used to cross the John Hextal Bridge and then follow the river to Calgary when Bowness was a village. The river is swollen at the bottom of your property. Especially near the whirlpool, which forms a small vortex that makes a sucking noise as it flattens out and repeats itself. The willow bushes seem to reach out to the sound.

"Stan?" The noise of the shovel scraping is gone. "Stan!" You call. He walks away, metal pail half-full of cinders. "Let me," you say softly, hands on your chest just above your breasts as you jog toward him.

"Don't worry at all, ducks. I won't drop dead."

"Stan-ley, how could you say such a thing?" Betty sets the coffee and bagel on the table. "Here, lovey. Don't pay him any mind."

You seize the opportunity, relieve Stan of the pail, and walk away.

"Stan Smith. Well, I never — "

You glance over your shoulder. Stan bites into the bagel and sips the fresh coffee while he watches you carry the cinders toward the front of your home.

Inside your kitchen, a fine mist dusts the air. You cover the yellow ceramic countertop with newspaper and set the pail next to the urn containing your husband's remains. Pail and urn stand side by side like pre-measured ingredients. You line up your utensils: trowel, then ladle, then slotted spoon, then sieve. You hesitate, but your hands are steady and gentle as you place the lid on the newspaper. You peer inside. You notice a few calcified lumps and poke the surface of one with your forefinger. You ease the ladle into the urn, bend your wrist, and fill the wide, metal reservoir usually reserved for gravy. Your movements are slow and deliberate.

You open a re-sealable plastic bag using your free hand and your teeth. The sandwich bag opens wider when you snap it in the air. You let the dust line the bottom of the small sack and then set it down. You breathe loudly, palm in the middle of your chest. You maneuver the ladle in and out of the first bag six times, then quickly wash away the moisture that builds up on your palms. You fill three more bags. When you fill the last bag you are careful while pouring the residue from the urn. It does not contain quite as much as the other four. You place each bag inside another so that the five individual pouches of ash are secured within a double wall of plastic. Then you line the bags up in a sun-lit section of the counter.

You retrieve an empty ice cream container from the garage and go back to work, humming. You dip the trowel in the bucket of fireplace ash, and empty its contents into the sieve. You pat the side with your hand, encourage the finer bits to pass through the mesh like flour for your best piecrust. The lumps you reserve in a pile on the newspaper.

You fill the small container, massage the back of your neck with both hands, and decide on a glass of lemonade. After pouring, you sit at the table and look at the empty urn. It is truly hideous. Wide at the top, narrow at the bottom, the base colour almost matches the fixtures in your lilac ensuite. The lid is edged in gold-coloured paint and crowned by a gold knob. Yellow, pink, and orange gerbera daisies blur the embossed surface.

You could have chosen a statue with a hollow base, topped by two dolphins jumping glass waves, a ceramic angel holding a small steel ball, or a miniature of the CN Tower. Briefly, you wish you had chosen a memento chest, compressed sawdust finished to look like mahogany, the inside lined with simulated velvet. You could have used the box to organize Ed's favourite fishing flies, to hide the extra keys to the Rover, or to keep small cuttings from his best overalls, his favourite suit, and his pajamas. Rhegan could have used the little chest to store her numerous wedding rings.

You read an advertisement on an exposed corner of the newspaper. It is for a ceramicist in Red Deer who makes custom urns; her name is Suzanne LeBeau. You tear the name and telephone number carefully from the page and set the piece of paper aside. You fill the urn with sifted fireplace ash and set it in the middle of your kitchen table. "Jesus Christ Almighty!" you say aloud. The five double-layered bags on the counter are swollen. Moisture beads the insides. Hands shaking, you open and deflate each bag. They sigh.

You rarely drive; you trundle your bike out of the garage when you go to see your daughter. Before wrenching the door shut you take a look at the hard plastic helmet she insists you wear. You hate electric garage door openers and do not trust them.

You step through the bike frame, place a foot on a pedal, and lift your rear to the gel seat, which is one cycling innovation that you do approve of. You make your way to the end of the cul-de-sac near the Shouldice and Hextal Bridges. Forty years ago your block and the one next to it were open space. Now the same few acres house a collection of attractive, semi-detached bungalow homes for mature adults. They are well built. Rhegan chose the complex herself. The dividing and outer walls are brick, not wood.

You cross the refurbished plank floor of the Hextal Bridge, which is closed to traffic now, and you note that your bike tires echo the rhythmic sound of metal wheels on tracks. You turn right onto the rough surface of Bow Crescent and negotiate your way through a series of tar patches and construction barricades. It seems as if the river has been rediscovered. What were once overgrown lots hiding the homes of blue-collar workers are now much sought after properties. They are being tamed and manicured, colonized by a generation of oil-invested families. Small, clapboard homes and yards that were sometimes filled with decaying vehicles are being replaced by houses designed by firms in Toronto and New York. Replicas of Mount Royal mansions are being situated to give the occupants privacy *and* unobstructed views of the river. Initially you thought that the renovations Rhegan made to your mother-in-law's old house were excessive, but those changes pale when compared with what you see now. You look across the lot nearest to you and note the level of the water in the newly formed basement. You focus across the river on your home and observe your neighbours, Betty and Stan, tussling on the surface of their king-sized bed. "Old people," you say, as you pedal along the straightest section of the Crescent.

You leave the construction behind and bump cautiously onto the paved bike path that curves and then continues parallel to the Bow River. You ride on the wrong side of the yellow line recently painted in the middle of the path by City maintenance crews. While you pedal, you watch for the cracked molehills that disguise poplar roots, carefully avoid bumps that might threaten the contents of your pannier bag. There is a slight incline before the bend in the river where you like to stop, where you and your Eddie liked to sit on the bench and stare across the water at the northwest wilderness. Your chest heaves when you reach the top. You brake, put your foot down, and steady yourself. A young couple sits on the bench.

"Good morning!" they say together.

You force a token smile, swallow a lump, push off, and keep going.

You and Ed bought a big lot backing onto the Bow while you lived in your mother-in-law's house on the property next door. At the time, you did not know that your husband saved money. You thought that he gave all his earnings to you. Bowness was trying to become a new part of Calgary back then. The path you ride on now was non-existent years ago; overgrown bushes and trees made the riverside a lovely refuge.

You spent a year clearing the lot with your husband before you helped him build a woodworking shop on the property. It was a building big enough to hold four cars. He filled it with tools and built cabinets. In the summer, when the weather allowed, you took your lunch together on the bank of the river and made love in the seclusion offered by the bushes at the bottom of the property. Afterwards, you liked to watch your husband swim naked in the frigid water. Then you napped together on a thick travel rug. Your daughter was conceived next to the Bow on July twenty seventh, 1963. That was years before a popular local politician proposed what became the Bow River Pathway system.

When your husband exchanged his old junker for an ancient set of brass-handled planes, you imagined flight. Your husband restored two bicycles, which he said he found at the edge of the city landfill. You turned up your nose until he told you they were Raleighs, which were made by one of England's best bicycle manufacturers. After that, you rode your bike all over Bowness and carted groceries home in the woven basket in front of the handlebars. When you were pregnant, you pedaled about against the advice of your mother-in-law. She tried to feed you disgusting concoctions of herbs and weeds to keep you strong. You threw them down the drain when she was not looking and you continued to ride your bike, until one day your husband took you in a taxi to the Canadian Pacific train depot, which was downtown near the future site of the Husky Tower. You drove home together in a silent car with cracked leather seats. You cradled your tummy in your hands and smiled. A brand new, dark-green pram, its chrome frame folded and concealed in the boot, had surprised you.

Your husband had the Rover shipped from Clyde Bank in Glasgow. Six months after that, in May 1964, your mother-in-law taught you how to drive while your tiny daughter slept on the back seat. That same year, Bowness became a Calgary neighborhood. Almost thirty years later, your daughter bought the lot you and your husband owned, and renovated the shop and your mother-in-law's house so that she appeared to have a single, large property. Then your daughter parked her car where the Rover used to sit.

You stop your bike and walk off the path to the low, one-rung fence that edges the properties now. You look at the house Rhegan constructed around the original. It has two floors and the shop is now a four-car garage with two double doors. Your daughter has equity in nearly three thousand square feet of boxed air. You grip the handlebars, breathe in, breathe out, and imagine peals of eight-year-old laughter. Your daughter thinks you need to let go, wants to take you travelling again, but you are resisting. The trip you made together right after Ed died is a blur. You wonder if it is legal to transport ashes across the International Date Line.

You pat a double-layered zip-lock bag through the thickness of your fanny pack, rest your bike against the garage wall, unlock the door, and welcome the sight of Ed's toolbox. You walk toward the workbench and gently set the pannier bag on top. You open the lid of the worn wooden toolbox with the heavy-duty hinges and remove the tray that holds screwdrivers and hammers. You know that there is significant room underneath, more than enough for the bone of your bone.

7

I REALIZED TOO LATE HOW MUCH my mother suffered. I thought she just needed to let go and I thought I could teach her how simple it could be to do that. I had experience. I had divorced five men: Domenic, Jack, Raj, Lynn, and Thomas, one before Liam and four after. The trouble was, divorcing those men was nothing like losing my father.

I suggested to Sarah that we take a trip together, so we went to England in the month immediately following Ed's heart attack. My mother had never "gone home" and I thought she would feel better if she got away. It was an awkward, cold, and rainy two weeks. There was a pronounced silence between my mother and me. We went through our travel motions like robots, had little to say to each other beyond what we would do on a given day. I had confided nothing to her since she told Liam about my abortion nine years before. Ed had been so disturbed by my visit to Kalispell, and by the fact that Liam had ended our relationship, that he wouldn't be in the same room with me. It took months before he would have a conversation with me. At the time, I was completely devastated by the absence of my father in my life; I felt as if my thumbs had been cut off. The only thing worse was his death. In typical Sarah fashion, my mother tried to appease him while sympathizing with me. Her behaviour did nothing but make the situation worse. When Ed finally spoke to me, he told me that I should try to understand what my mother had done, that she wouldn't always be around. I interpreted his approach as the administration of a liberal dose of Catholic guilt. My father never mentioned the words abortion or betrayal. He relied absolutely on Sarah's balancing act. As for me, instead of trying to comprehend Sarah's actions, I built a wall between my mother and me. I imagined that it was the same kind of barrier that had existed for her from the day I was born. After that, the distance between us was doubled and we were both unwilling to be the first to show the other her vulnerability. So we ignored each other — until Ed died.

After we returned to Calgary from England, she refused to talk about anything else that involved travel or flying. It was strange and incomprehensible to me, as if she had finally settled. When I was a teenager, I always had the feeling that my mother would rather have been somewhere else. When we returned from London, she stayed home, rarely tore herself away, as if she'd come home for good. I began to worry. Each time I dropped in at my parents' house Sarah seemed to be in the middle of a cleaning binge. She sorted my father's clothes; cleaned out the attached garage; got rid of every cracked plate, glass, and cup; thinned her collection of ceramic angels; and cleared out the overflowing file cabinets in the office. She even made arrangements to go out to my Auntie Jane's, invited me to go along and watch her incinerate thirty boxes of business records. I declined.

In hindsight, I didn't need to teach my mother about letting go. By degrees, she separated herself from her life as she knew it. I should have recognized what kind of strength it took to achieve that, instead of imagining that she was simply out of her mind with grief. In May, nearly four months to the day after Ed died, when I found Sarah sitting calmly by the Bow River, I suggested that we paddle a stretch of my terrain. She agreed. I bought a canoe, planned and arranged.

I agonized over which tent to pack, the three-man, or the two. The three-man, purchased at a local hardware store, was a domed affair with lots of headroom. It still held the thick smell of the paraffin bug repellent that Thomas swore by. The two-man carried an expensive brand name, and demanded closeness; it was wide at the door, narrow toward the foot end. Liam had to cock his head when he sat up in it. What bothered me most was the fact that they both had only one door.

"Hell-oo! I'm here," Sarah called. The screen door in the kitchen slid back so hard that it bounced out of its track. "Sorry, darling. I never do get that right."

I felt the muscle on the back of my arm jump as I watched her place the small plastic wheels in the track and demonstrate just how slowly she could close the screen. My mother loved to torment me. She wore Ed's white shirt tied at the waist and a pair of golf shorts that looked like a skirt from the front. Both were extremely loose. Her fanny pack was slung over her shoulder like a purse.

"Decided?" she asked. She strode across the tiled floor and jumped the three steps down into the carpeted family room. Her behaviour was odd and I instantly felt as if I should keep up my guard.

"No." I sat on the tan leather couch, the tents spread out on the floor in front of me.

"We are paddling in seven weeks."

"I know." I stared, remembered the footprint each tent made, especially the one I had shared with Liam.

"What's the problem?"

"No problem." I stood up. "I'm going to buy another tent."

"Another tent?"

"Another tent."

"You have four."

"I'm wrestling with these two. The others are too heavy. I want something that's more — adaptable."

"I thought weight wasn't an issue in a canoe."

"I saw one yesterday with two doors." I had found a tent that allowed for escape. As much as I wanted to take my mother on a trip that I thought would be good for her, I was apprehensive about us being in such close proximity. We'd be on the river most of the time, but the thought of spending several nights with her made me claustrophobic.

"Two doors?"

"So that when you get up in the middle of the night you don't have to crawl over me. It has two vestibules and lots of gear space. It's very practical and I know I'll use it again."

"That is exactly what you said about your last wedding dress."

I ignored the slight and asked her to help me stuff the tents back in their bags. We avoided speaking about what was really on both of our minds: my father. Instead, we knelt together, rolling fabric homes into pack-away bundles. I noticed that Ed's smell was gone from his shirt, which meant Sarah had washed his clothes. My breath forced its way out of my nostrils. As I stood, the heat of the sun left my back and I saw the threatening rain clouds through the open window; I felt as if I needed to retreat to my cave.

I heard the rush of the river despite the hundred or so feet of lawn between us and the water. The utility company claimed it wasn't increasing the flow and the Lakes and Rivers engineer

I spoke with the day before, said that spring run-off hadn't yet reached its peak. But the river was bloated. Engorged. I began to notice a surge in the flow a week before Sarah came over to discuss equipment. My neighbours had told me that Sarah was fussing about in the garage, that she was there while I was out meeting a new client. I didn't realize at the time that the increasing water flow coincided with her garage expedition. I assumed that she just needed a wrench or screwdriver or something of the kind.

I climbed the curved staircase to the second floor. My mother, as always, followed me too closely. Sarah stared around the room that was once Jack's study, a shrine for Raj, an ammunition store for Lynn, and a fly-tying room for Thomas. A tall, antique wardrobe with three panels stood diagonally across the corner farthest from the door; a map rack stood next to it. On the opposite wall five long shelves, about two and a half feet wide and six feet long, held an assortment of outdoor shoes, ground sheets, fishing flies, containers and squeeze tubes, water bottles, a ceramic core filter with an extra carbon layer, a case of iodine drops, and a camouflage vest.

"Good God!" she said, "I will never get over the clutter in this room!"

I grinned. Her whole house was untidy. "All useful," I replied, looking at the inventory: climbing ropes, crampons, freeze-dried food, a set of twelve stainless steel forks, bottles of Aspirin, several courses of antibiotics in brown plastic containers, a case of jasmine-scented candles, three jumbo boxes of panty-liners, and a six-month supply of birth control pills. Sleeping bags of varying loft were spread out on the bottom shelf. On the floor under them, a series of light backpacking mattresses were stacked one on top of the other according to length.

"Could we use the bags that zip together?"

"I don't think so, Sarah." I was flabbergasted by her question, perhaps I was even hurt. When I was a child, I would have jumped at the idea of being that close to my mother.

In the other corner of the room was an old coat stand that looked like a banana tree after a heavy rain — forty-three nylon stuff sacks hung from its hooks.

"May I?" Sarah asked slipping two fingers into the wardrobe handle.

My skin crawled as she turned the key in the old lock. "These dresses should be in bags, darling."

I returned the tents to the appropriate shelf, arranged an assortment of lifejackets in the middle of the floor, and hid behind my long hair. "Put the fanny pack down and try this one," I said. I held up a purple jacket with bright-red cinch straps and a long belt that went from the back to the front, through the legs.

"It would never fit me," Sarah said, then gently hung the fanny pack on the coat stand.

"Not the dress, the jacket."

"In a minute, darling. Which is your favourite?"

"Don't have one. You know that."

"You spent — what — minutes deciding on these, remember?"

I had been meticulous, coordinated each with the match I'd made, dressing in a way that I thought would enthrall each particular man.

"*This* is my favourite." Sarah carefully pushed three dresses aside and reached in to extract a full-skirted, vapoury version that was like an ankle-length tutu. I had worn it when I married Thomas. Her arm circled the skirt, caressed it, and guided it toward the open door. She removed her arm and the skirt expanded as if the fabric had a life of its own. "Pull Granny's dress form over here," she said.

I adjusted the shrunken shape until it matched my height. I hadn't looked at the dress for quite a while. Sarah told me that it would "yellow" if I didn't wrap it up. The dress was never white. It was the colour of a manila envelope.

Sarah removed the long, thin straps from the covered hanger. Instead of slipping the skirt over the form, she held the beaded bodice against herself. "Maybe I should get married again," she said. "Do you think I'm too old? Unattractive? There is a young retiree in my Tai Chi class every Thursday who just might be suitable. I'm quite serious. He is trim, intelligent, and apparently financially stable." She zipped the dress onto the form, expanded the chest panels so that the dress wouldn't fall to the floor, and looked at me. "You must have felt like a princess in this."

I asked her if the man owned any land.

Sarah ignored me and tried on the tiara. The seed and teardrop pearls had framed my hair when I piled it on top of my head. She struck a pose. I held out the purple jacket. She turned and hooked her arms through, said, "The jacket feels fine."

"Nope," I replied. "Too short in the waist, and if I were you," I went on, "I wouldn't waste my time," I watched Sarah reach between her legs for the crotch strap.

"Not everyone is mad about land ownership, darling. This is a child's jacket! My God are you — pregnant? I don't care if you're not getting married this time!"

I ignored that slight as well, helped her out of the lifejacket, and turned to get another.

Sarah disappeared into the wardrobe again. She retrieved a wispy, pearl scarf and wrapped it around her elegant neck — front to back to front, the ends grazing her shins. "Darling, is this how you wore this gorgeous stole?" The material underlined her face and softened the severity of her shorn, white hair. She had cut it that way since just before we left for our trip to England, and stopped colouring it as well.

I held up another lifejacket. "Put your arms in here."

"Perfect."

It was. "Let me see," I said, cinching the three belts and checking the shoulders. It didn't fit me anymore.

"Perfect," she said again.

"It fits, but I'll pick up an approved jacket before I take you on the river. That way, if you fall in you'll be visible in the water. The one you're wearing is just for water skiing."

"Darling, you know I *hate* to get wet!"

"Walk around a bit. See how it feels. Make sure you'll have room to paddle."

Instead, Sarah crouched and opened the drawer in the base of the wardrobe. Then she balanced and slipped on a pair of beaded, square-toed, square-heeled, pearl-coloured sling backs. "Why don't you wear these shoes?" she asked. "They are fantastic."

I admitted to liking the shoes. It took me weeks to find them.

"Are they Italian leather?" She asked. She bent one knee, twisted to look over her shoulder, and examined the shoe, one hand on the wardrobe for support.

"Where are your glasses? They're cloth," I said.

"You bought them in that little village south of Stratford. The costume shop we visited on our trip. It was next to the fishmonger, remember?"

"No. I didn't buy shoes there. I wore these when I married Thomas." That had been three years before Ed died. When we started to prepare for our canoe trip, I had imagined that Sarah was feeling better, that she was less confused.

Her face fell. "A lot of details are missing in the month right after Ed's death. Unnatural, isn't it?"

"Isn't what?"

"Not having someone to do for." She took the shoes off and returned them to the wardrobe.

"Get rid of the scarf," I said. "It's cutting off the blood to your brain."

"I love your father!"

"I loved him too."

"I married him wearing a blue tweed suit and a pillbox hat."

"Blue tweed. I'll wear that next time. Remind me."

"Your trouble, darling, is that no one is as perfect as you are."

I reached past Sarah and retrieved a shoebox from the shelf above the dresses. "Here," I said. "This will cheer you up. Your favourite part of the trousseau, milady."

She threw the lid on the floor. "Lovely! The rings! So selfish to keep them locked up."

"I can't wear them." The truth was, I didn't *need* to wear them.

"That does not make any sense. Imagine the cost — they should be in a safety deposit box." Her fingers floated over the contents.

"No one will look in an old shoebox in a wardrobe in a house at the end of a street in Bowness."

"Rhegan, let me put them somewhere for you. By the way, who gets these in the event that you — ?"

"I'm giving them back." I lied to torment my mother; I had willed the rings to her.

"Giving them back? Why do you think those men want old rings? You could have done that right away instead of shutting them up in this rotten old wardrobe." Sarah knelt on the floor and opened a silver, bell-shaped container that revealed a half-carat, emerald-cut ruby. The stone was the colour of old blood. She stood and set it reverently on the top shelf near the birth control pills. A square box ornately carved with elephants opened to reveal an unadorned wedding band and fifteen, twenty-four carat gold bangles of varying widths. She placed the box next to the silver bell, and executed a bowing motion. She opened a small square of tissue paper, disclosing a wide ring made of white gold worked in a filigree pattern. As she placed the ring next to the carved box she said, "White gold makes the twenty-four carat look dull. Where are the others?"

I told her that I had lost one and that the other had recently ruined my blender.

We managed to stay away from any real discussion of our canoe trip, what we would need to bring, how long each segment would take. Instead, Sarah helped me return the contents to the wardrobe and we went outside. She walked toward my garage, changed direction suddenly, and then sat on a glider rocker under the willow that my granny had planted halfway between the house and the river.

I plopped down on a redwood chaise. "I just made another woman's day," I said.

"How did you do that?" Sarah asked. Her motions took the chair back and forth between both ends of the glider frame.

"Sold her a house with a river view."

"What will you do with the cash this time?"

"I want to be sainted."

"Sainted?" She crossed her legs but slowed only a little, pushed off with one foot.

"Sainted. You know — "

"Like Mary or Veronica or Bernadette?"

"Somewhat like Bernadette."

She continued to rock and her hands punctuated her sentences, fingers splayed for effect. "Ah, you will have visions. Your past and now-martyred husbands will speak to you from the gazebo. The spores on the lilies surrounding it will bleed, and Bowness will be denoted on the tourist map of Calgary by an image of a flashing Sacred Heart."

"You're getting carried away, Sarah."

"I wish I could be carried away." She moved forward, planted both feet on the ground immediately in front of the rocker and put her chin in her hands.

I resisted the urge to touch her shoulder. Instead, I went into the house to start brunch. I watched Sarah from the kitchen window as she looked toward the June swell of the Bow River, wondered if she noticed how close the waterline was to my garden. She got up and walked toward the garage. Her steps seemed to quicken the closer she got to the side door. As she disappeared inside I remember wondering why she was drawn to the building.

I began cooking despite the fact that I hadn't seen her consume a complete meal in almost five months. About ten minutes later, I padded across the patio toward my mother. "I'll have to put all that away sometime," I said at the door to the garage. "I rarely use the stuff Ed put in there."

Sarah closed the lid of Ed's old toolbox, and caressed the clasp of the fanny pack that encircled her waist. Her shoulders shook.

"I loved the way Ed was so neat," I continued, pointing at the pegboard over the bench. "Look at the spanners and the screwdrivers and the levels and the hammers and the saws and the planes. I love the way Dad planes, the rhythm of his movements — loved watching him."

She sniffed. "Darling, don't put it all away." Her voice was small. "It looks as if you have a man about the place."

"I need to talk to you about Jack," I said turning.

"You know Ed hates him."

"Hated him." I went through the door, hoping she would hang her sorrow on the pegboard next to the tools and follow me.

"Every mention of the man's name makes your poor dad turn over in his grave."

I hunched my shoulders and stepped in the middle of each carefully-placed piece of flagstone between the garage and the house. "He's not in a grave."

"Mother of God, the man must weigh less than I do and he is at least a foot taller." Sarah hurried her tiny frame, tried to walk next to me.

I knew I could distract her by talking about Jack. He meant nothing to me by then, so I hardly felt as if I was confiding something important in my mother. "He knows how to keep everything in check," I said.

"I don't remember how you met *that* idiot."

Her words made me cringe. "Taking over for Ed, are you?"

"Certainly not, I would have called him an ee-git then!"

My pace quickened as I reached the deck. Sarah placed her hand on my arm. I turned on the first step and looked down. She was too close. "Mother, you're — "

"You never call me mother."

"Well, I'm going to start adding Teresa to that if you don't stop preaching to me."

"I thought saints liked that sort of thing? Get a towel and wipe the bloody sweat from your brow."

"Let's go inside."

And so it went with Sarah in the weeks before we got on the river. Each visit was infected by grief, although neither one of us attempted to disclose to the other what she felt. We clung to what we knew: avoidance, but she came by almost every day. I had felt some sort of need in Sarah that I couldn't quite understand. Ed would have been proud. I tried to make her feel welcome, attended church with her on Sundays and, after Mass, I watched her play with her food.

At breakfast, six weeks before the July canoe trip, I brought up a topic I had avoided for months. "Have you decided about Ed?" I asked.

Her egg whites stared up at me like a face without eyes. The yolks pooled and hardened near the rim of the plate; she had nibbled the edge of one slice of toast. "You don't have to push me."

"Sorry."

"No, Rhegan, you are not." She suspended one of the eggs on the end of her fork.

"He can't live in the bathroom forever."

"Why not? The urn looks lovely on the edge of the Jacuzzi."

"You told me you hate that thing."

"The bathroom was Ed's favourite room. He spent hours in it." She dropped the fork.

I began gathering the dishes. "Put the woodworking magazines away yet?"

"No — but his clothes are gone — "

"Except for his best shirt." It was the only thing I'd asked her for and I didn't understand why she kept it. I think she wore it to torture me. I pushed the remnants of her meal into the composting bin and watched her fidget in her chair.

"I did move the *Car and Driver* issues. Must have been ten years worth stacked on either side of the pedestal sink." She swept the crumbs off the glass table onto the floor.

I cringed. "You humoured him far too much."

"You can never humour a husband too much! What are you thinking? I let him pile magazines in the loo — "

"And in the kitchen, the living room, the laundry room, and the entranceway. I thought things would be different when you moved to the condo."

She put her face in her hands, scrubbed her fingers in her hair.

"You're right, Sarah." I closed the dishwasher, set the two-hour delay, and sat down again. We turned toward the window, stared at the steep banks on the other side of the Bow.

"Did I mention that I haven't fertilized and I have the greenest lawn on the block?" I looked at my mother's reflection in the window; her eyes were moist and fixed on the glass. "Did I tell you that I saw Jack?"

"I have decided that Ed should be interred," she said.

I was surprised.

"Saw him when?" she asked. "Last I heard he moved to Montreal."

"I met him when Nemit had nude photos taken. He moved back. Interred where, Queen's Park?"

"I am not interested in Queen's Park. The lesbian woman? Nude?" she asked.

"Completely." My line of sight had been interrupted by groups of runners on the path at the bottom of my property, each bunched together as if drafting its leader.

"Well! — I think Edenbrook is better. Scenic. Mountain views."

"Not as if he'll see anything, Mum." I didn't look at her but I covered her hand with mine, ignoring an impulse to disregard her feelings. "Cheaper?"

"Yes." She withdrew, and rubbed her hands on her thighs. "But we will when we visit. Does it not bother you that a man you are now dating — if that is what you call seeing an ex-husband — was taking nude photographs of your, ahem, friend?"

I sat back. "We're not dating. I have some unfinished business with him — and as far as Nemit goes, he's a professional photographer, she happens to have chosen one of the best in the city — "

"Don't you feel betrayed? You'll come to the interment?"

"No, I don't. You've already had a funeral Mass and you know how I feel about monuments to the dead." My grandmother taught me that we hold our past and our future, that which is important to us, in our hearts. She said that we didn't need memorials and I believed her. That philosophy had allowed her to sell her land near John O'Groats. "I don't think there's any point," I went on. "Why aren't we sprinkling him?" The members of the slowest group of runners were all wearing coloured jackets with fluorescent stripes that came together in a 'V' just below their hips. They looked like a swarm of bees lost in the rain.

"Where would we do that?"

"Over the mountains. I thought he loved the helicopter trip into Assiniboine." I pictured my mother and I holding the urn next to the stream that runs into Lake Magog.

"He threw up. Besides, he would end up in our faces if we tried to empty him over a ledge. Even I know something about updrafts, Rhegan."

"What about the river?" I imagined us standing together above the elegant arches of the Louise Bridge —

"The river?"

"The Bow," — on the suspension bridge that connects Memorial Drive to Prince's Island —

"No."

"Why not?" or — next to the lions on the Centre Street Bridge.

"Were you turned on?"

"What?" I glanced at her for a moment then looked back at her reflection in the window, imagined my mother and father, bodies touching as they sat together in my backyard gazebo. Water ran off its roof like tears.

"Watching Jack take pictures of the naked lesbian."

"Why can't we sprinkle Ed in the Bow?"

"He would be washed away. *Well, were you?*"

"What do you think?" I turned slightly, looked at the furniture under the willow, and was glad that I'd taken the cushions off the glider and the redwood furniture the night before.

"I don't want to think about it. I just wish you could understand my need to — keep him."

"Keep him?" I looked across the table at my mother.

"Remember him. You know how men are about things that last."

"Blowhard?"

The moisture that filled her eyes earlier was gone. "I knew you'd get tired of men sooner or later and go through a transformation. That would explain Jack! You say you are not dating. He is just a front, isn't he?"

I couldn't make up my mind if she was distraught or if she was angry. It took me a long time to realize that she was both. "Okay, I'll come to the interment! But don't expect me to visit a buried urn." This time when I covered her hand with mine, I held on.

She squeezed. "I'm planning for the fourteenth of July." Her voice softened and her eyes held mine.

"That's just seven days before we leave."

"I want a procession."

I let go of her hand. "The city is parade-mad that week." I wanted to disagree, kept sparring with her instead. "I was turned on, okay?"

"I don't care. You are going to be in one, headlights on, and hazards flashing — Were you really?"

I decided to give in to my mother, to attend the interment. I didn't want to hurt her. She was on a grief-stricken rollercoaster ride and I thought that maybe I could stop it from careening out of control.

8 ———————————————————

YOU GO WITH YOUR DAUGHTER TO Barotto Sports and humour her decision to buy the tent with two vestibules. When you arrive, you see Liam, the man that you always thought of as your Liam, in the middle of a display. He is surrounded by what looks like a group of collapsed scarecrows, their clothes stuffed with wads of paper and plastic bags. One of them is "holding" what is apparently the last campfire pie-maker in the shop. You watch as he tries to detach the long-handled contraption from the arm of a plaid shirt and succeeds in knocking down a group of hunter-mannequins in bright orange vests.

You laugh; your steps are light as you make your way around the display. You hug and hold onto the man who, technically, was never your son-in-law. You drink in the smile of surprise on his face.

"Let me help you with that," a salesperson of about twenty-five says to him, as she fusses over the display.

"I hate hunters," you hear him say to her. "I don't usually come here because your store sells guns. And I don't usually knock stuff over. This thing is a gift for my sister."

A pregnant woman walks by carrying a long box to the cashier. You see her roll her eyes and give Liam a *puh-lease* look. You lengthen your neck, hold your head up, and take his arm. He is your ward.

"What's in there, a shotgun?" he asks the salesperson.

"A folding crib," she replies.

You watch as a man with toddler legs wrapped around his neck joins the baby woman and circles her shoulder with a protective arm.

You run your fingers lightly down Liam's arm and ask him what he is doing in Calgary again. You are perturbed by the way the salesperson grins at Liam when she hands him the pie-maker; you feel annoyed while her hands linger too long on his.

"The wife of a close friend is dying," he says. "Joan, an old friend of Rhegan's and mine — " His lips knit a straight line and you note the way he pulls in a breath when he sees your daughter milling about the tents.

"Does Rhegan know?"

"Yes — but she hasn't stayed in touch with them over the years."

You tell Liam about the canoe trip that your daughter is planning on four sections of the Bow: Lake Louise to Banff, Banff to Seebe, Seebe to Calgary, and Calgary to Carseland. You explain that your daughter thinks you need to let go; you note the way he moves his eyebrows as he listens.

You are concerned when he says, "Seebe to Calgary — a lot of hazards there — Rhegan must think you'll be okay with that."

Your daughter gives the man a distant and perfunctory, *Hello,* before disappearing into a display tent with two vestibules. You are embarrassed because your daughter seems to hide until Liam leaves the store.

Later, your daughter divulges that she knew Liam would be in town, and then admits that Barotto's was not where she had expected to see him. You do not understand why your daughter wants to discuss Jack or why she keeps her thoughts about Liam to herself.

9

I STRUGGLED TO HAVE WHOLE CONVERSATIONS with Sarah, but we always got off track. I tried to tell her about Jack the day she opened the wardrobe, tell her that he wanted to sue me. I tried to tell her again when she spoke about interring Ed's ashes, tell her that he intended to take half of my holdings, but we didn't get that far. Jack's idea gave a completely new meaning to being sought after: I felt both hunted and haunted.

Five weeks before the trip, I tried to talk to her about Jack again. "Have you ever met a man who is completely in love with himself?" I asked Sarah.

"In love with himself?" Sarah gestured as if she was rolling something back and forth between her open palms.

"I mean self-love, as in taking absolute care of the body — "

"All men are like that, Rhegan. Five husbands and you still don't know that the penis — "

"I'm talking about physicality."

"So am I!"

"I'm *trying* to tell you about Jack." I had just finished pitching the new tent; it stood outside on the grass below the deck. I stared at it from the open patio doors.

Sarah stood in front of my deep kitchen sink; her arms were three-quarters submerged in soapy water. "Look, Rhegan," she continued. "All those times that you thought men were turned on by your natural beauty," her voice rose, "they were just turned on."

I came inside and stood beside her. "Have I ever told you how many times you twist — ?"

"The story before you even get the chance to — "

"Let me tell it, then!" We were shoulder to shoulder. "Don't wring the sleeping bag like that! You'll ruin the loft." Water spilled over the edge of the marble counter, ran down the maple cabinet, and drenched the front of our pants. I used a mop to soak up the puddles on the tiled floor, stood on a towel, took off my jeans, and padded across the floor to the patio door in my T-shirt and thong underwear.

Sarah watched me go outside and throw the jeans over the clothes dryer. When I came back, she handed over her striped cotton trousers. "So you said you were turned on when you met Jack." She followed me out, stood on the deck, and stared at my bare buttocks as I retraced my steps.

"Are you finished squeezing the water out?" I asked, over my shoulder. "No. Sorry." Sarah snapped the elastic on the leg of her Lycra underwear, and said, "I'll go back in. Squeeze softly." She was trying to make fun of me. I noticed the hollows in the sides of her buttocks and thighs.

I was walking across wet flagstone when the Lakes and Rivers man from Alberta Environment coughed to announce his arrival. "Looks like the seepage is up another foot or so since yesterday," he said.

I turned slowly to face him, and crossed my arms. He stared toward the Bow. "What's your department going to do about this?" I moved toward him, wiping my feet on a small section of dry stone near the garage door. "It's Earl, isn't it?" He backed up, eyes fixed on something about six inches to the left of my hips.

"Ah — yep. I came to drop this off." He stretched his arm toward me.

I took a thick, perfect-bound government booklet entitled, *Erosion Control Programs*.

"Kind of dry," he said. "Lots about compensation if it comes to that." He turned around completely as I headed toward the house. "Read the Policies section!" he yelled. His shoulders shook with laughter.

"Who was that, darling?"

"Earl," I said when I went back inside.

"Earl?"

"Haven't you noticed how high the water is? The Department of Lakes and Rivers has been around almost daily." I slipped on the tile. "Sarah! You've already soaked everything within a ten-foot radius." The counter surrounding the sink, the ledge in the bow window, and the floor were drenched. She had both sleeping bags in the sink. Each time she pressed her hands into their bulk, water coursed up over the lip. I reached in and pulled the plug.

"I will clean it up this time," she said. "What about out there?" She pointed the dripping mop at the gazebo. "By the way, darling, I have not rinsed the bags in clear water yet — has Earl spoken about sandbagging?"

"All Earl has talked about in detail is my garden." I began squeezing fabric gently, while cool water blurred the skin on my hands.

"I do not understand why you refused to let me send the sleeping bags to the dry cleaner," Sarah said.

"Come on." I turned the tap off and scooped the dripping bags into a plastic tub, soaking the front of my legs. "Help me take them outside."

"But I have no trousers on."

"Don't worry, he's gone!"

Water dribbled up our arms as we hoisted the bags and stretched them across the clothes dryer.

"I thought you were going to take my whirligig out when you moved in here. Not very sophisticated, you said."

"I'm sentimental." Since then I'd added the gazebo and the rock garden to the area between the willow and the river; the whirligig couldn't be seen from the path.

"Sentimental?"

"I used to peg the clean sheets together, stake them out like a tent."

"How could I forget? You stopped the thing from turning in the wind the way it should have."

Now flagstones, rather than Ed's too-tall grass, covered the area under the dryer. We walked the hundred and thirty feet to the bottom of the garden, past the willow, the gazebo, the rock garden, and the climbing rose that I was trying to encourage up over the arbour with its double seat. We looked toward the opposite side of the garden. Years ago, the neighbours had planted a row of blue spruce on their side of the property line between the shop and the river. The trees afforded us a significant amount of privacy, and made a beautiful backdrop for the beds of perennials I'd carved out and edged with curving new lawn. We stopped. The last twelve and a half feet of my property was underwater.

"What I don't understand about this," I said to Sarah, "is that my neighbours' lawns aren't showing any signs of seepage."

"This water is warm," she said, swishing her toes from side to side as if she was wading on a beach.

"Look at the ground a little way along the bike path."

She looked in both directions. The water seemed to fan out from the bottom of my yard. "Rhegan, surely the city must be able to do something." Three houses downstream the river no longer lapped over the bank, and grass stuck out of large patches of dry ground here and there.

My mother and I spent that entire Saturday afternoon together, dipping in and out of water like a couple of playful cubs. I still hadn't made any connection between the water level and Ed's ashes, and despite my efforts, Sarah hadn't let me tell her the whole story about Jack. I was attempting to get close to her but she was still distant.

The next day at Mass, I was determined. I began one of our family's infamous behind-the-missal conversations, the kind that my mother and father always conducted with whomever had the misfortune to sit next to them in church.

"Jactitation," I said, leaning toward Sarah.

"You cannot say ejaculation in church!" she hissed.

"Jactitation," I repeated. I wanted to explain.

"Jack-tit-ation?" she whispered. "He is in love with your — sorry darling — droopy breasts?"

Communion was being served and the Saint Bernard choir was singing a guitar-laden version of the "Prayer to Saint Francis". We were kneeling, elbows on the wooden pew in front.

"No — It's another word for twitching."

Sarah just stared at me.

"Limbs or muscles," I said.

"And this connects to?"

"The day I met Jack again." I smiled as I spoke, nodded at the communicants returning to the altar with chalices of unredeemed host. We waited for the priest to complete his post-sacramental prayers. He finally sat after returning the communion to the tabernacle. The congregation followed him, moving as one from the kneelers to their seats.

We didn't move until after Sarah whispered, "So the day you met Jack — "

A young child in the row in front turned and laughed out loud. His mother grabbed his arm, glared at me, and turned him back.

We sat. I lowered my voice. "I experimented — with the blender."

"What were you concocting? A veggie shake of some sort?" She lifted herself off the pew momentarily and smoothed the back of her pink dress against her thighs before sitting again.

"Not exactly. I was trying to get rid of something — "

The priest rose and moved to the pulpit. "Let us give thanks to the Lord our God for the gift of his sacrament."

"You have never been able to make a straight point with me," Sarah whispered.

"It's no wonder," I said. "I wanted to get rid of the ring Jack gave me. I'll never wear another one as long as I live."

"Please," Sarah said. She adjusted the small cross that she wore at the end of a ridiculously long gold chain and shushed me, finger against her lips.

"This week's announcements begin with prayers for the sick of our parish — "

"I tried leaving it in a coffee shop when I met Nemit before the photo session. I left it in the sugar bowl on our table."

Sarah made sure that the straps of her navy sling-back shoes were on the right part of her heels.

"I was getting into my car when the busboy ran up and gave it back, must have seen the edge sticking out, thought it was a coin."

"Please stand for the final blessing. Lord God, look down upon your servants — "

We stood. "I've never seen you like this," she said. She bowed her head and screwed up her face as if she was in pain.

"Mass is ended. Go forth to love and serve the Lord!"

"Thanks be to God," we said with the congregation.

"So then you went home and put the ring in the blender?" she asked. "Quickly, let's leave before the final hymn."

"Please turn to number 433 in your hymnals: 'The Lord is My Shepherd'."

"Too late. No — I put it in the blender before I met Nemit for coffee. I listened to the thing jump around while I crushed ice for a drink. Very satisfying."

"Christ almighty, Rhegan! Where is it now?"

"Embedded in my car tire."

"Let me guess."

"I don't think you could."

Her voice went up an octave. "You've intentionally driven over a one-and-a-half carat diamond and embedded it in the tire of your sport utility vehicle?"

The people around us sang louder.

"I sold that two days ago."

She threw up her hands and looked at the recently restored ceiling. I leaned into her, enjoying my newly allowed proximity. She picked up her keys.

"It's embedded in the tire of my new car."

The woman from the pew in front glared at us, grabbed her son by the hand, pushed past her neighbours, and marched up the aisle followed by two other children.

"Car?"

"A 1968 MG Midget."

"Lord God in heaven," she said.

The congregation's voice tapered off at the end of the second verse and the choir sang the chorus again by itself. The priest, celebrants, and altar boys began their procession out.

"A month ago I walked to Shouldice Park to see Nemit's son play baseball."

"Ah, yes the lesbian's son. What's his name again?" A man in the pew behind us coughed. "You know, darling, technically it is summer now. You can put your black clothes away and wear colours." She looped the bag that matched her shoes over her bent arm.

"Adam. You know that, and you can wear black all year. I was just sitting there, cooling off after the long walk, fingering the platinum setting when Adam asked me to help him warm up."

We moved to the end of the pew, genuflected, and made the sign of the cross before turning to leave.

"What position does he play?"

"Pitcher."

"Adam, pitcher on the Bowness community junior baseball team. Son of Nemit, the woman in the nude Jack photographs." The crowd around us dissipated.

"So I caught for him," I continued. "When the coach yelled, *Balls in!* I let the ring fly."

"To the pitching mound?"

"No. I wanted to show off so I tossed the ball out to the kid in right field. I felt — " We pulled on our coats, skirted the outer edge of the crowd, avoiding Father Joe's sweaty Sunday palm. "Satisfied," I said as the crowd surged through the arched front doors. Outside the Scotch mist engulfed us.

"Your hair is a frizzy mess," Sarah said. "Rhegan, you do know that there are numerous taming products available — "

I ignored her and continued. I felt strangely light as we walked arm-in-arm through the graveled parking lot, and revelled in the fact that she really was letting me tell her the whole story. "The kid was busy digging the toes of his brand-new cleats into the red dirt. He let the ball go by and looked as if he completely misjudged its direction. The coach yelled at him to get the ball that I had thrown from in front of the team dugout. At the same time, his mother was screaming at him about his white shoes. He left the ball where it landed and ran in, windmilling his arms. Three days later, Nemit called and said the coach had asked all the parents if someone had lost a ring, and showed the thing off on his pinky at the next game. Nemit recognized the setting and called me. What can I say? I phoned the coach and gave a description. Nemit picked it up for me."

"That is unbelievable," she said pulling us away from a puddle-filled pothole.

"Some kid speared the ring with a cleat — about five feet in front of the dugout."

"I think you should pray."

"We were just in church."

"To Saint Jude."

"Saint Jude?"

"The Prayer to Saint Jude. Say it faithfully for seven days. Favours are given if public recognition is promised."

"As in the, *thank you Saint Jude for prayers answered*, lines in the paper, next to the legal and judicial notices?"

"As in, *Prayer Corner*."

"I don't believe it. What do these people pray for? Miracles? Money? Love?"

"Death," she said.

I stopped walking, puzzled. I should have paid more attention to what she said, but she tugged at my arm and went on, "I mean, I suppose you could pray for death, probably peace of mind, the safety of a loved one, or the return of a treasured item."

"Rain."

"You would do that," she laughed.

We stood on opposite sides of the Rover. The woman who'd been upset by our conversation during Mass spun gravel and almost crashed into a passing car.

Sarah fiddled with the keys. "What do you think upset her most, us talking, or us discussing the destruction of a perfectly good wedding ring?" she asked.

"Ring."

"Why?" Sarah mouthed from inside the grey car as she reached for my door handle.

"She was at Mass with her kids but not her husband," I said, sitting on the front seat.

Sarah turned the key in the ignition and backed out of the stall. She steered the car away from the church, and made her way east along Bowness Road.

"Where are we going? I thought we were going to visit Auntie."

"I want to show you the procession route," she said.

I sighed. "Ed's been gone for five months. Don't people only do that kind of thing the day of the funeral?"

"It is important to me." She stopped the car at a four-way, waited for the vehicle on the right to go through the intersection, then turned left and drove up the hill toward the Trans-Canada Highway.

"He would be mortified."

"He is upset that I never did that after his funeral Mass."

"His ghost? I don't believe that, Sarah. I think it's just your imagination. I think what you are feeling is just good old Catholic guilt."

"Is there a difference between regular guilt and Catholic guilt?" She stopped the car again at the intersection opposite the entrance to Canada Olympic Park.

I stared up at the ninety-metre ski-jump and decided I'd rather whoosh down its slope and soar into oblivion than discuss religion with my mother, but I did anyway. "Of course! Catholicism depends on guilt. Priests are conditioned to make people feel bad about deviating even slightly from established rituals. Reason I never married in a church."

"Oh, but you did — the first time, darling. This is a conversation you should be having with Ed." Sarah turned left onto the highway, merged into the far right lane.

I put my hand gently on her arm. "He's dead, Mum."

"Not to me. Not to me."

The silent car glided along, eased up the steep pitch of Sarcee Trail. I took in the panoramic view of the northwest hills, the University, the river valley with its green foliage. My eyes followed the Bow south-southeast toward downtown. I took in the smattering of tall buildings, the dinosaur-like silhouettes of construction cranes. I opened and closed the zipper on my purse. The noise seemed to echo off the teak dashboard.

"Pay attention," was the next thing Sarah managed to say. "You always get lost and refuse to look at a map. You are just like your dad."

"He asked for directions. I know where Edenbrook is."

"*You* do not seem to know how to follow them."

"I'm like you, then." I noticed that she wasn't using the cushion Ed thought she needed to see over the steering wheel.

She maneuvered the car onto Seventeenth Avenue, and we went west up another hill, gaining speed without the lurches that accompanied automatic gear changes in domestic vehicles.

"How much did Ed pay to bring the Rover from Glasgow?" I asked.

"About as much as I paid for his funeral."

"That's all?"

Sarah braked hard and stopped at the last set of traffic lights before we left the city. "I knew you thought I should have spent more!"

"That's not what I mean and you know it." I looked ahead at the narrow, rolling tarmac. "I don't know why you're upset." The giddy feeling I'd had walking arm and arm with her as we left the church was gone.

"Upset?" Sarah stomped her foot on the accelerator when the light turned green.

"Why can't we discuss Ed without — "

"You are being completely disrespectful now," she said, voice quivering.

"Of you?" I asked.

"Of the whole process."

"Well, it makes you strange." My stomach churned as the Rover crested the first hill. I worried about acreage owners pulling out of driveways hidden by tall hedges as we plunged down the next slope. "You're driving too fast!"

"Mother of God." She eased her foot off the pedal as we drove over the next crest and passed the driveway to the private school Adam attended. Its flat roof was rimmed by a wide, bright yellow stripe.

"What are you thinking? What makes you like this?" I was pulled to one side as she took a curve. The road headed south.

"I have not had an orgasm in nine months, three weeks, two days, and eleven hours," she said.

"But Ed died five months ago. You're still going too fast."

"I am not. What did you expect? He was seventy-seven."

"Sarah, your mood has nothing to do with that."

She glared at me. "How do you know? You just go from man to man to man!"

"Keep your eyes on the road! I think we should leave this discussion for another time." I held on to the chrome strip at the base of the passenger window with the fingertips of my right hand, clutched the edge of the seat with my left.

"We cannot. You are probably already *with* that Jack again and I have sent out invitations for a luncheon."

"You want me to help you?"

"No, I do not *need* your help, Rhegan." We approached the intersection that led into the cemetery. Sarah brought the car to a quick stop. "I suppose you'll be bringing *Jack*?" she asked looking at me again.

"You're getting carried away. I'm not seeing him."

"Oh, so he is not the kind who is respectful of family rites."

"Family rites?" I grabbed the dash as she sped across the road and drove into the cemetery.

"Of passage." She took a deep breath. "There's the Catholic area." She drove toward it slowly.

"Segregated dead people?"

"Come now, get out and look," she said pointing. "That is the Garden of Remembrance. I want to show you the plot."

"It's not exactly a plot is it? I mean it's only a foot square." I remember wondering why people were so enthralled by memorials. I opened the door and swung my legs to the ground.

"Close the door, would you, darling?"

I closed it gently, and walked across the grass, trying not to let the cube heels of my new Italian shoes sink in the softness. In front of me was a white marble monument, twelve feet wide and five feet high. In an alcove, at its centre, a bronze statue of the Virgin Mary spread her arms, palms open, head slightly bowed. I bent to read the commemorative prayer; it was flanked by panels listing the carved names of the garden dwellers. When I realized the prayer was in Latin, I lifted my head. The roof of the Rover entered my line of vision. I straightened up and watched Sarah circle to the gate and drive off.

I walked to the ornate bench positioned for visitors to preside over the small field of ground-level plaques. I stood on it. No sign of the car on any of the roads leading away from the gate, just a huddle of people a couple of gardens over. I decided that the Novena to Saint Jude was not such a bad idea. I wondered if I could remember all the words to the Hail Mary and the Our Father, which were supposed to precede it.

The hope I'd felt, after spending the previous day and that particular Sunday morning with Sarah, quickly faded. I realized two things: I should have been careful about letting my guard down with my mother, and I should have prayed the day I met Jack again.

10

I ARRIVED AT JACK BENNETT'S STUDIO three-quarters of an hour before Nemit, and went inside. Outlook Photography had an excellent reputation. Jack had photographed numerous Calgary personalities, from the mayor who became premier, to university presidents, and homegrown actors and singers. He was good at what he did and I wasn't upset at all by her choice of photographer.

Jack expected me and didn't flinch when I took the stairs to the second floor loft. From there I leaned on the metal railing and observed the main floor studio. I hadn't told Nemit anything about his telephone calls, the ones he made repeatedly after he returned to Calgary from Montreal. On that particular day, I wanted to see him at work, and to assess his habitat. I was in a predatory mood and I knew that when he worked he was absorbed, shutting out everything except his subject and the technical details required for the best shot.

I watched. Was the unmistakable reverberation of the automatic shutter the only sound Jack heard? I imagined that he ignored the bass drawl of the stereo and the chatter between the model and her manager. His focus was so intent it made me salivate. I was sure about the kind of intimacy he sought with the woman swaying in the simulated wind. She was a bag of thin bones straining against a translucent cover, hardly adequate enough to satisfy even a small appetite. But I knew Jack, and I understood how disappointed he was that she hadn't come alone. When the music stopped, he killed the lights.

Jack had half an hour before Nemit would arrive. I observed. He shut off the oscillating blades and changed the backdrop to black. He dragged a patterned, green chaise across the room and set it about two feet in front of the backdrop. It was rosewood, with Queen Anne legs. In the kitchen, he watched from the large window as the model slid onto the front seat of her manager's car. He pointed, looked up at me, and said, "Great idea." The last time he'd called he told me he was supplementing his income by turning the yard behind his Fifteenth Avenue home into paid parking.

When Jack had arrived from Montreal, he'd called to ask if I'd help him find a place. I'd declined, "Unless it's on the river, it's outside my territory." Nevertheless, I did inspect the property for him *after* he purchased it, thinking it might appease him. He expected to hear that the property was worth more than he paid. I hoped secretly to find flaws. I didn't.

Most of the main floor of the house was studio. The second floor, half of which was open to the lower level, housed his bedroom, bathroom, and living room, reminding me somewhat of my Inglewood house. The basement contained his office, darkroom, and photo stock. Every room paralleled his Spartan look.

I continued to watch Jack as he examined his hollow cheeks in the glass door of the wall oven, moving his head to admire his own symmetry. He sniffed twice before snipping the top off a pink pack of Aspartame sweetener and emptying its contents under his tongue. I imagined that his routine was the same as it had been when we were together: he ingested solids Friday, Saturday, and Sunday, purged Monday, Tuesday, and Wednesday. Thursday he rested.

I danced downstairs from the loft when Nemit arrived. She swung a paper bag oozing the aroma of burgers and plastic cheese. Jack said, "No food," his voice higher in person than it was on the phone.

I took the bag from Nemit and retreated outside, sat on the hood of my MG. Jack stared at me through the kitchen window as I chewed and swallowed. In my mind's eye I saw him holding back the urge to scream as the smell settled on his upper lip.

He moved away from the window. I knew he would wait for Nemit in the studio, and I pictured him fussing with his camera and film while she undressed. I gave in to an urge to be cruel. I went inside and threw the half-eaten fast food in the kitchen bin.

"I'm doing this as a gift," Nemit said as I reached the columned archway between the kitchen and the studio.

"You explained that when you called," Jack replied.

"For my new partner," she continued.

"That her?" he sneered.

"Not funny, Jack. I want something artistic. Something tasteful."

He positioned her on the chaise. "Put your elbow there. Arm — yes that's right. Hand on your head. Look past the camera."

I watched Jack back away while Nemit stood up.

"This isn't it. Not what I want. Shoot my back." She turned her body so that he could examine the subject.

Jack dragged the chaise away and replaced it with a square table, which he draped with black cloth. "Sit." Nemit sat. "Turn."

She turned slightly. "Hands there and there." She gripped the edge of the table on either side of her knees. "Elbows straight." She pushed up through her palms. "Look to the left." She looked left. "Gaze at the ceiling." She lifted her chin. Bluish shades strained over the shape of her spine, her square chin, and the powerful wings that formed her shoulder blades. I admired her strength, understood her distress when Joy cheated, and held her up each time their relationship had crumbled.

"Look right," Jack said. She looked right. "Stare at your *friend*." She stared hard over her shoulder.

The shutter ricocheted off the brick walls and harmonized her low laugh. She turned toward the camera; the loose skin that covered her stomach was pleated like a Roman shade.

Jack changed the light. He dragged the covered table away and replaced it with the chaise. "Lie on your side this time," he said. "Other hand toward your thigh. Knees slightly bent. Good."

"Good?" she said, straining to look over her shoulder at me.

"Look up," he said.

"Looking up."

As I watched, I combed my hand through my long hair, raking loose strands to the floor, something else that I knew would annoy Jack. He spun the camera toward me as if he was a poacher looking through a riflescope. I hid behind a column.

"Sit for the last few shots," he said.

Nemit moved to the open end of the chaise while Jack changed the film. I felt his mood lift.

"Right hand at the nape of your neck. Left stretched out to the side. Reach! Look at your thumb. Good!"

"Great," I said.

Jack abhorred interruption unless it was of his own making. "That's it," he said as the shutter ground to a full stop.

I wrapped Nemit in a robe. The shutter made one last leap. I pursed my lips at Jack's thin frame.

While I waited for Nemit to dress, Jack moved back and forth between camera and kitchen. Retrieved a canister. Unloaded a film. Found a pen. Applied a label. Wrote a name. Marched to the fridge. Opened the stainless door.

"No food?" I asked.

"You know my routine," he said.

I crossed my arms and leaned against the end of the kitchen counter. "Roommates?" I asked. I saw cheese and bread and wine before the door closed completely.

"You're kidding."

"Just making conversation. A friend? A woman?"

"A man," he said, evaluating my body.

Nemit emerged from the bathroom where she had dressed, trailing her coat. "I'm high, my arms feel light."

"Probably from holding them up," Jack said.

Nemit scowled at him, threw her coat over her shoulder, said, "Let's go," to me, then turned and murmured, "Thank you, *Mr. Bennett.*"

"Ten days," he said, before she asked.

He watched us, arms joined, heads touching, talk our way back to our cars. We separated. I opened the door to the MG, camouflaged my body behind its mustard frame as I sat in the low seat. Jack was afraid to engage when he thought he was outflanked.

I was ruthless when it came to my marital and professional lives. After Liam, I always tried to maintain absolute control in relationships; if that wasn't possible, I made adjustments, and did whatever I had to in order to feel like the dominant partner. I refused to play small. I had accepted the fact that Sarah, that both my parents, could affect me emotionally, but I refused to let anyone else have power over me or my holdings. I called this determined preservation. My father, when he was alive, thought it perverse and too aggressive for a woman. When he said so, I told him he was unnaturally distrustful of me.

11 _____

I WAS SURPRISED BY MY FEELINGS when I entered Ed's shop on the Wednesday after Sarah left me at Edenbrook. She'd driven off, furious with me because I'd asked why she wanted to inter Ed's ashes. It wasn't the first time she'd left me somewhere. She'd done the same thing at a grocery store when I was four. Later, when I was in school, she rarely ever came to collect me, and as I grew up, only Ed or my granny attended meetings with my teachers.

The sight of my father's fingerprints, the ones he left on the back of the white door when he closed it, made me cry and I was glad that I'd resisted the urge to scrub them away the day after he died. I placed my hand gently over the shadow he'd left.

I backed the MG onto the driveway and left one of the double overhead doors and the side door open to air the building. It always smelled musty after a heavy rainfall.

I was composing myself at Ed's workbench, taking solace from the sight of his tools, when I heard Sarah hop off her bike and set it on the kickstand. She walked up the driveway past the MG, marched across the garage floor, and circled the ski-boat and the canoe before she stood next to me. I turned my head and watched her eyeing Ed's toolbox.

"Hell-ooo!"

I picked up a screwdriver. "Where's your helmet?" I asked turning away from her.

She ignored my comment. She never wore a bike helmet. "Fixing something?" she asked loudly.

I knew that she had ridden her bike along the path, through the water and past my property to the walkway, then looped around to the front. The back of her bike shorts and part of Ed's shirt had a line of spray down the middle.

"Just going out in the sun to tighten the driving mirror."

"That car is pretty small, Rhegan." She moved outside with me, stood next to the MG squinting.

"Pretty small."

"Did you get the ring out of your tire?" Sarah asked. She opened the passenger door and plunked herself down on the bucket seat.

I got in the other side, and focused on the screw head at the base of the mirror.

"You told me I would never guess. So how?"

"How what?" I caught myself being nasty with my mother.

"How did it — the ring, darling — how did the ring become attached to the tire?"

"Damn it, Sarah! Embedded! It was embedded in the tread! Nemit dropped it and I backed over it!"

"I do not understand," she said, leaning closer to me and bending her neck at an awkward angle so that she could see the screw head.

"When she came over to give it back! You're in my way!" I got out of the car and paced back and forth at the end of the hood. "She walked up the driveway as I opened the garage door. She dropped the ring. I backed up before I saw her and stopped on top of it."

"Why did she not just wear it? The whole thing could have been avoided, you know. Is it still there?" she asked. "You are making me dizzy. Stand still."

I stopped. "Nemit had a frightened look on her face when I got out. Then she started laughing. I asked, *What's wrong?* She just pointed and said, *The ring.* I jumped in the car and spun the tires driving forward."

"What about the diamond?"

I had expected her to ask about the diamond. "The pressure forced it out of the setting. It's on the lawn somewhere." I walked to the back of the car, waited to see if she'd start scrounging in the grass. "Look at this." I pointed to the right rear tire with the screwdriver.

Sarah turned in her seat, then got out and stood beside me. The misshapen platinum could've been mistaken for a squashed soft drink tab.

"But why is it still in there, darling?" She put her arm around my shoulders.

I stiffened. "It feels — satisfying!" My voice was still raised.

"That is a feeling *I* know well," Sarah said, with a half-grin.

I walked away from her and threw the screwdriver. It landed with a dull thud on the tray in the toolbox. "I'm sure you do."

"Careful with that!" Her hands came up and covered her mouth.

"It's not going to break, Sarah — coming in?"

"I need to grease the chain on my bicycle, and then I think perhaps I had better ride home — before it rains," she said. Her movements were jerky when she retrieved her bike and took it inside the garage.

I followed, pressed the button to close the overhead door, and left the car with its top down outside.

"The water is still high, darling."

I moved toward the side door and Sarah circled toward the workbench, gripping her handlebars. "You don't need to fuss with that," I said as she stood in front of the toolbox.

She leaned her bike against the bench, and moved the screwdriver. "I'll just close the lid." Instead of holding the handle on the top, she used both hands, one on either side, closing it gently as if it was her Swedish music box.

"You know where Ed hides everything, where to find what you need."

Her voice was a whisper.

"Alberta Environment was out again today."

"On a Saturday?"

"Sarah, it's Wednesday. Look, I have to go in because I'm expecting a call about the Inglewood house at two."

Her body shook as she faced the workbench.

"Earl was here again. He explained the theories behind water tables and aquifers."

"Are they releasing more water west of us?"

"It's not the utility company. It has a modest effect on flow levels. He said that there's little headwater in the Spray Lakes now. Typically, after June fifteenth, run-off ends, and the water level begins to fall. There's the phone." My hand hovered over the shadow print once more before I ran toward the house leaving my mother alone.

It wasn't until the day after the interment that I understood the full effect of my father's death on my mother's psyche. Only then did I figure out her need to make such frequent visits to my home, or why it might be important to repair the gulf that existed between us.

12

WHEN YOU HEAR YOUR DAUGHTER'S REALTOR voice on the telephone, you open your husband's toolbox. Your hands shake; the plastic sacks you hid inside a few weeks ago are intact. The sound of the screwdriver landing on the upper tray echoes in your head. Your right leg begins to spasm, your body jerks, and you step back to shake out your arms and legs. "Breathe in, breathe out," you say.

You decide to move your husband's remains. You look about what was once Ed's shop and decide that it is just as much a place for leftover equipment as the room in your daughter's house. Instead of camping equipment, you see floatation devices and watercraft: a motor boat with a *For Sale* sign in its window, two red kayaks suspended upside down from the rafters by a pulley system. You see a metal dory, about as long as your husband was tall; it hangs on the wall and its motor with its rudder and long handle for steering stand up in a wooden frame that your husband designed and built. Next to that are two long surfboards that your daughter and her friend used to float from here to Edworthy Park where your husband would pick them up, and of course, the O'Brien slalom water-ski that your husband got for Rhegan when she was seventeen. These point skyward in their padded wall attachments. Scattered about are the life jackets that your daughter insisted you try on. Hanging on the wall above them are a marine first-aid kit, coiled ski ropes, a bailer on the end of a length of coloured twine, a throw rope with a yellow bag on the end, boat keys on a key fob that floats, a plastic bag with boat safety manuals in it, and lengths of rope for securing boats to piers. You decide that your daughter is much like her father.

You think it odd that there is an area of the wall where a number of hooks have been removed and you struggle to remember what is missing. The space is covered in a series of maps that show the South Saskatchewan River System, the Upper Bow River, and a detailed angling map of the Bow from Calgary to Carseland. You squint at the blue bands of highlighter that your daughter has used to mark Bow Glacier and sections on the river from Lake Louise to Banff, Banff to Canmore, Canmore to Seebe where the Horseshoe Dam demands portaging, Horseshoe to Calgary, and Calgary to Carseland. You trace them with your finger. You pay special attention to the question marks your daughter has penned over the Banff to Canmore and Seebe to Calgary sections; you tap on each to commit it to memory. You recall Liam's reaction to your story about the canoe trip when you saw him at Barotto Sports and you decide that you will try to call him after you ask Rhegan for his parents' telephone number. You need clarification.

You are not surprised to see your daughter's brand-new canoe standing in the centre of the open section of floor next to the motor boat. Styrofoam supports cradle its hull. You peer inside and catch your breath when you see the highly varnished teak paddles that your husband made. Your daughter and Liam never used them. You pick up the paddle in the bow. Coyotes run from one end of the handle to the other. You take your glasses off to admire the detail. You imagine howls and barks emitting from the open mouth of the leader and the laughter-like yips of the pack that follows her. You decide that you will use the coyote paddle. You replace it gently and pick up the paddle in the stern. It, too, depicts an animal. The same bear is shown in three stances: one at the top of the upright that forms a 'T' with the handle, and two on the handle proper. You know it is the same bear because, in each rendition, the left front paw is missing one claw. In the lower figure, the bear looks curious as it stands sniffing the air. In the second pose, the bear's ears are back, it is gnashing its teeth and it looks ready to run at something. In the third, you recognize the features of a full-on attack: mouth open, teeth and tongue exposed, and one paw ready to strike the unseen prey. You always thought that this paddle, one of the two that constituted your husband's wedding gift the day after Rhegan and Liam came back from Assiniboine Pass, was terribly vicious.

You thought your husband had been turning wooden bases and stems for the various sizes of wine glasses you spent your savings ordering directly from Riedel. You felt comforted by the sound of the new lathe emanating from the shop in the month before your helicopter flight. You were confident that he was doing what you had asked him to do. You look toward the machine now and feel glad that your daughter has left the canvas sheath on and that she has not put a *For Sale* sign on it yet. In the month before Rhegan and Liam were married, you had no idea that the long silences in the shop meant that your husband had decided to begin a carving project.

You drop the bear paddle in the canoe because you want to know if the Kevlar hull will stand up to mistreatment the way you have. You think that where you are concerned, your daughter has a tendency toward complete disrespect.

You lift the yellow case that lies in the middle of the canoe, slide back the two clasps that keep it closed, and expose the foam forms designed to protect camera equipment. You throw the foam in the oversized bin that stands between the two double garage doors. Your body and hands no longer shake.

You circle back to the toolbox and carefully transfer the small sacks to the camera case after you marvel at the hard-bodied shell and the watertight seal. You know that the contents will be inert in the cool darkness of its interior. You put the case back exactly where you found it, take up your bicycle, and ride for home.

13

I DECIDED THAT IT WAS TIME for me to follow my mother's example. As the interment date drew closer, I started to believe that if Sarah could finally bury my father, then it was time for me to let go of the Inglewood house, the home that Liam and I lived in. Even though I owned our home, I had left when he asked me to and went to live with Nemit.

Liam moved away from Calgary about eighteen months after we separated, and took a position with an architectural firm in New York. I never moved back into the house; it was empty for eight years because I couldn't bear the thought of anyone else living there. I had listed it and gone through the motions of selling it once or twice a year, but never found the right buyer. When Sarah seemed to be physically letting go of Ed, I decided to show the house again.

I arranged a meeting with a prospective purchaser, a graphic designer who was thinking of moving her business away from the old Dominion Steel warehouses just off Twenty-Fifth Avenue near the Stampede grounds. I knew that the City zoning policies would allow for the kind of business she wanted to conduct on New Street.

"Can't face another summer downwind of the stockyards," the woman said on the phone. "Your property is closer to downtown, provides easier access — and better air."

I guessed that she hadn't given any thought to New Street's proximity to the Calgary Zoo, which was directly across the Bow River. She said that she'd been in her current location for ten years, that she could handle the Den of Antiquity and its owner, a Scottish antique dealer with notable clients who he sometimes sent her way. But the recent crop of artists who had moved in with their welding gear, kilns, and blaring stereos made her decide to move.

"I just don't want to rent any more," she'd said.

I understood that reason completely; it underlined my decision to show her the house.

After the call, I sat on the couch in the family room rubbing warmth into my bare feet and eyeing the cover of the water management document. I noticed that the side door to the garage was still open, and felt pleased that my mother was shivering inside. I hoped that she put sawdust on the floor before working with the chain grease, thought about checking, then decided it would be easier to clean up after she left.

The woman was late. I waited in front of the Inglewood house and heard her vehicle before I saw her.

"Rhegan Flett," I said as she struggled out of the driver's seat.

"Pauline Kaiser. Nice to meet you, Ree — gan."

"Rhegan."

Her vehicle's wheel wells were level with my underarm. I stood next to it impatiently.

"I'm excited to go through the place and I have to tell you that I'm ready to write the cheque today. So let's talk numbers."

Pauline followed me to the rear of the house. The grass was overgrown at the side, thigh-high clumps interspersed with dry patches of grey dirt.

"I'll have to do something about the yard. I can see it landscaped and terraced."

"That's a possibility," I said.

She followed me to the edge of the property, which bordered the river for about twenty yards. She looked at the top of my head and stared curiously at the collar of my Mandarin-style dress.

"You are not at all what I expected. I got your name from a friend who has some property near Point McKay, which faces out to the water and the bike paths. There isn't one here, is there?"

"Yes. The pathway switches to the south side at Twelfth Street." She looked confused. "The old Zoo Bridge."

"He said you never advertise. He said you don't even carry a cell phone. How can you do business like that?"

I laughed. "I track property and prospective clients."

"You shop for clients?"

"I match people and properties."

"Most matchmakers are only interested in marrying their friends off."

I had married off myself — five times. I suppose that my love of matching people and property compensated for my lack of success in marital relationships.

"The contracts I'm involved in *are* a bit like marriage agreements," I said. "Let's go inside."

"Does no one water right now? This yard feels like cement. I'll definitely have to do something with the outside." The house was covered in aged wood siding.

"I can recommend an individual who specializes in restorations — "

"For the right price I might just raze the thing and start over."

I opened the back door and we stepped into the three-by-four entrance. Stairs led up to the kitchen. I was stung by the suggestion that the house could be demolished.

"Where's the basement?"

"There isn't one. Just a root cellar outside."

"I thought that wood contraption was covering an electrical box."

"No — the house was built in 1918."

"Now, the only reason I'd be interested in keeping it original is if it's a miniature of the Deane House. *That's* an interesting place. Is this house haunted?"

"Haunting," I said. "What do you think of the kitchen?"

"Very European. I certainly wouldn't expect this based on the outside. Oh, I love *that!*" she said, looking at the huge door hanging from a track on the ceiling.

"It's a coat closet. If you'll move into the kitchen, I'll close the outside door and you can see it properly," I said.

The woman moved her bulk up three stairs. "Slide it back for me — exquisite," she said, as the shelves and coat rack were revealed. "Although you'd need a stepladder to get up there."

The bottom of the closet was about two feet above the floor. I reached in and pulled out a four-tier ladder, which folded out in an A-frame.

"Who'd want to climb that all the time? What does the owner do?" she asked.

"He's an architect," I lied. It was a white lie, the kind Sarah taught me to tell, the kind that were supposedly harmless.

"He must have run out of money for sure," Pauline said, looking at the uncovered cement under my feet.

"The front entrance is the same," I said.

Pauline opened a few of the tall kitchen cupboards. The doors extended to the ceiling. "What are these made of?" She asked, admiring a second sliding track door over the pantry.

"Plywood."

"No way! This has to be maple."

"Stained plywood," I said.

She ran her hand across the stainless steel counter top and smiled approvingly at the separate sinks, which angled out from the corner to the left of the kitchen window.

"It's very cold, isn't it?"

"Depends what you like, I suppose," I replied, thinking of how much time Liam and I spent finishing the house.

"The floor is all right," Pauline arced a foot over the dark square panels. "I don't think I've seen these before. Are they a pre-finished product?"

"It's cork. Easy on the legs," I said. "Let's move into the living room."

"Oh, I love that curved wall," Pauline exclaimed. "Now that's architecture."

"The last owner didn't do that," I said. "The owner before did."

"Go figure. Don't like the cement surround on the fireplace either. You're right; it's at the front as well. What kind of furniture did he have in here?"

"Black leather."

"Makes me shiver just thinking about it. This is not at all like the Deane House. What was Andrew thinking about?"

"Perhaps he wanted to play a joke."

"On me? I don't think so. I should call the man right now. What's the upstairs like?"

"Actually there are two more rooms on this floor."

Pauline followed me across gleaming hardwood, past the curved wall. Its inside enclosed a tiny room.

"What'd he use this for?" she asked standing in the middle and obliterating the long window.

"Drawings. He stored them in here in racks."

"And this one?"

"His office." There was a smaller version of the suspended track door between the two rooms, which I slid back.

"I couldn't swing a cat in here! I hope the upstairs is better."

I had decided by then that she wasn't the right buyer for the house, but I led her up the spiral staircase anyway. Pauline moved carefully so that her expensive jeans didn't touch the metal railing, which looked as if it was layered with many coats of paint.

"The colours are good, I'll give him that," she said, surveying the Spanish red living room and the soft sage on the curved wall. She laughed. "And these stairs are the same shade as your little car!" At the top of the stairs was a half wall. The front side was living-room red, top capped with maple-finished plywood. The inside was covered in fabric. "Is this grass cloth?" Pauline ran the back of her hand across the wall. "This damn ring catches on everything." She detached a long thread from the wall covering, as she surveyed the largest and warmest room in the house. "Obviously the former owner once removed put that up." The paper had a cream base with dark-blue, green, and blood-red flecks in it. "Is there a bathroom up here?"

I pointed to the end of the long room at the centre of which was a six-foot-wide section of wall containing a closet with mirrored bi-fold doors nine feet tall. Openings on both sides led to the bathroom.

"Where the hell did he get those?"

"Impressive, aren't they."

"My assistant will spend all day looking at herself and never get anything done," Pauline cackled. She leaned toward the mirrors and examined her nose, moved into the bathroom on the left side of the closet. "A claw-foot tub! I could remove that and take it home! My sixteen year old would just die to have it!"

"The closet doors are from a home the previous owner has in New York State." Another white lie. We got the doors when the matching pair was broken during the renovation of the penthouse suite in the Palliser Hotel. Liam worked for CP Rail and had been contracted to help upgrade the original building at Emerald Lake Lodge. At the time, the manager of the Palliser thought he might be able to use them out there, but they were too tall.

"Okay. I want to buy, despite the fact there is no bathroom door," Pauline said, emerging on the right side of the closet and leaning against the wall there. "This will be interesting. I can use it pretty much the way it is. My assistant can have the lower floor and I'll have the upper. The commode is right behind the closet. Not a problem for either of us. I'll have to do something on the main floor for clients. Why did the architect not do anything about the yard?"

"I believe he wanted to maintain a low profile."

She was already moving down the spiral stairs and heading for the front door. The metal shook. I followed reluctantly. Outside on the sidewalk I felt agitated.

"Do you think the exterior is properly sealed?" Pauline bellowed.

I walked toward her, resisting the urge to cover my ears with my hands.

"I mean how could he just leave it to weather like that?" Her voice reached a higher pitch, making me cringe.

"There are no signs of moisture damage on the inside walls," I said quietly.

"Alarm system?" she yelled over her shoulder as she crossed the lawn to the other side of the house.

I climbed four wooden steps and walked in Pauline's direction on the wrap-around porch. "In the back closet."

"Okay. Let's do supper and talk offers."

I felt like roaring, but lowered my voice instead. "I'm not available for dinner."

She looked up at me, puzzled. "What?"

"And the price is fixed. The owner won't move at all."

"No dinner? A set price? How do you make money? Look, I'm prepared to make an offer, and I'll write a cheque for half right now." She followed me, stumbling on the uneven ground despite the fact that she wore flats.

"Half is too much."

"What?"

"Good faith is demonstrated quite decently by ten percent, exceptionally by fifteen."

I went through the front door but didn't hold it open for the woman. When she came in, she slammed the door hard against the wall. "What is your game?" She was threatening.

"No game. Quite simple really. The price is the price."

I jogged quickly up the spiral stairs and turned off the lights in the bathroom and bedroom. Pauline was blocking the way at the bottom. I imagined my free hand was a giant paw and pictured the damage I could cause if I swiped it across her face.

"Let me through," I said baring my teeth. "I need to lock the front door. We'll leave by the back door after I set the alarm."

Pauline moved but I still had to brush up against her to pass. She cried out when my sharp bones dug into her arm. She kept pace with me. "You've memorized the alarm code? Oh, I get it. Sleeping with the owner?"

"Every night."

"I knew it! When Andrew told me about you I thought you couldn't possibly be genuine."

I moved through the kitchen. She followed me, pulled the oven door open and let it slam back into place.

"Can you step outside please?" I asked.

She picked up her briefcase. "I want this property. I'll deal only with the owner. I want his name."

"Her."

"I want *her* name, then."

I stood on the bottom rung of the ladder, reached inside the closet. The alarm began to emit a series of short beeps. "Okay, we have approximately fifty-five seconds." I folded the ladder, tucked it in its original place, opened the door, and stepped outside. The beeps were getting closer together. "Pauline — "

The woman moved slowly. A long piercing beep began as I closed the door. I swiped a plastic card through a rectangular box.

Pauline looked up from the grass to where I stood on the back stoop. "Where's the lock box?" she asked.

"I don't need one," I said, "keyless entry system."

"How long is the owner planning to hold on to this house?"

I had shown great restraint despite her aggressive behaviour. She was in my territory. "You aren't right for this place. The owner wants it preserved."

She followed me to the river's-edge, wrinkled her nose.

"What's that smell?" she asked.

"Animal urine." I pointed at the Zoo.

"I don't care! I WANT this house!"

I walked toward the MG with Pauline in tow, looked back at her and saw that she'd lost a shoe. "I'm the owner," I said over my shoulder.

"Come on! Let's just sit down over dinner. Let me invite my husband and we'll work this out. Between the two of us we can pay cash." She was whining now.

"The price is still fixed. Perhaps the two of you need to discuss that before we meet. Now, I really have to run, I'm meeting a renter in Parkdale and, unlike you, I don't keep people waiting."

I stood next to the MG, changed my shoes for runners, and pulled a windbreaker over my dress. "Leave a message for me next week and I'll let you know if the place is still available." I was just baiting her. I had no intention of selling the Inglewood house to her.

I slammed the car door and turned the ignition key. Pauline was speechless. I revved the motor a few times, depressed the clutch, backed up, changed gears, and drove off. I imagined the heave of her substantial chest under her crossed arms.

I realized that I was nothing at all like my mother. I tried on, but never took up, the idea of separating myself from the things that I loved, even though I'd had many chances. I did let go of the house soon after that, but only by default.

14

I was afraid when I didn't see Sarah again until the fourteenth of July. My house felt empty and the water that had been encroaching on the bottom of my property was lapping the base of the willow, occasionally spilling across the flagstones near the garage. I felt soaked and parched at the same time.

Sarah was animated when I arrived at her house for the gathering before the interment. "Here she is!" she sang. "How did the Inglewood sale go? Are you up or down? Jane! Reed! Rhegan is here! Where are they?" she asked as she crushed me in an awkward embrace.

My aunt climbed the stairs from the basement and when she hugged me, she told me that I was gaining weight. Jane was much less feminine than my mother despite the fact that she had white hair cascading down her back. She always wore men's suits, travelled twice a year to a tailor in Lethbridge who custom fit her clothes. That day she wore a summer-weight navy twill three-piece. When she stepped back, she hooked her thumbs in the slit pockets of the waistcoat. I admired her buttercup silk blouse and her tiny burgundy brogues, which I knew she bought where she purchased all her footwear: in a children's shoe shop.

"Did you see Rhegan's new car? New to her, that is," Sarah said to Jane, who immediately went to the window while my mother steered me halfway down the stairs. "Everybody! This is Rhegan. Ed's one and only child."

The small crowd turned briefly toward us then its members resumed their conversations.

"I think they know that, *Mum*." Then I heard someone in the basement say that she didn't think I was coming.

The furniture had been moved away from its usual centre of the room place, and a long table with a black and white checkered cloth stood parallel to the patio doors. Most people were standing but Betty, the next-door neighbour, sat alone on the settee, which was against the wall. A woman in a wheelchair was near her, head turned, looking about as if she desperately wanted to get away. A couple of men were admiring the bar, which Ed had brought from Granny's old house before I began renovations.

"Let me see what you are wearing under that baggy Mackintosh," my mother said. "You are the only young person I know who owns one."

Suddenly I felt like I was ten and she was helping me off with my coat after school. We moved up to the entranceway. "It's Ed's. I bought it at Value Village, or should I say rescued it after you donated all of his things. Look, the initial you embroidered on all his clothes is on the edge of the inside pocket." I showed her the tartan lining and the dark green strip that edged the pocket. There was the single letter in script.

Her eyes grew big when she recognized her own work but she recovered quickly, peeled the coat away to reveal my red knit dress, fitted, boat-neck, no sleeves. "I should have known," she said.

"What did you expect, black?

"Yes, actually."

"You told me weeks ago I should wear colours now." I slipped my shoes off. The front door, which was still slightly ajar, opened wider and Nemit came in.

"Lovely," said Sarah.

"No kidding, Mrs. F. I like the rain!"

Sarah glared at me. "Should I expect anyone else?" She turned to Nemit, smiled. "Where is your son, dear?"

"Ball practice."

"In this sort of weather?"

"The team is inside. Did we miss the food?"

"*We* did not," Sarah said.

I gave Sarah Nemit's coat, slipped my hand through my friend's arm, and we marched downstairs. I cringed. My mother had laid out a buffet of Ed's favourite breakfast food including two huge bowls of the dessert that sends most displaced Brits into fits of nostalgia: trifle.

"Hello, Victoria," I said to Sarah's neighbour. "You're looking well."

"Thank you, dear, but life in a wheelchair is a real challenge some days. As soon as my son tries to move me to that home he's been talking about I'm going to unpack my husband's gun and BANG." She was fully made up and she wore a Chanel suit I'd seen in *Vogue*. The matching shoes, which I coveted, had red leather soles.

"Don't you pay her any never mind, Rhegan; she's getting a bit thick in her old age," Betty whispered to me.

"What did you say, Betty?" Nemit asked, staring at her tiny waist and flowered, fifties frock. Nemit turned toward me. "Is she wearing petticoats?"

"I said she's getting a bit thick, dear, you know," Betty's voice dropped, "senile."

"I'd feel the same if my son wanted to lock me away somewhere," Nemit said, crouching so that she was eye-level with Victoria. "I'd want to blow his silly head off. Have you had anything to eat, Victoria?"

"No — we haven't met — you are — ?"

"Nemit."

"Nee-mit, beautiful. Victoria. I'm very happy to meet you. I would like a potato scone, I see them next to the strawberry preserves, and a bit of trifle too, if you don't mind."

"Of course not. What about the fried bread, the eggs, or the ham and pineapple?"

Victoria lowered her voice, "Terrible when it's cold, and I've never known Sarah to have the talent to serve anything warm."

"How is Stan?" I asked Betty as I sat next to her.

"Oh, he's wonderful, he is. Never could imagine myself with any other. I'm a one-man woman, I am. Don't have an understanding of the divorce craze at all. But maybe you can explain that to me one day. Another day," she said, patting my arm. "Here's Stan now. I just sent him over the back for the big coffee urn — over here Stan," she called, as he came in from the ground-level patio. "Well that's the wrong one! I said the twenty-four-cup, not the twelve! Good thing we need it for after Edenbrook. Excuse me Rhegan, I must go, but you make sure you talk to me later. Stan, I just don't know how you could mistake..." As her voice trailed away, Sarah motioned me over to a group standing in a circle.

"Rhegan, these are the people in my Tai-Chi classes. Mary-Anne from the Tuesday group. Deborah and Flora from Wednesday, Roger, Bob, Kenneth, and Veronica from Thursday — "

"The noon class?" I recognize some of the names.

"The noon class. Bill, Aileen, Walter and May, Andrew and Julie, Allan, from Friday. And this, "she said taking a man's arm, "is Shug — "

"Shug?"

"Hugh, darling, from Thursday, recently retired."

"Where are the Monday people?" I asked, looking past them. Later on I chastised myself for doing that. Why shouldn't my mother have had another love interest?

"Oh, we're all there on a Monday but not all together on the other days," Bill said. "Some of us can't manage too many classes. We're all getting a wee bit older, you know."

"Now don't depress the girl," May said. "Especially no' today."

"Do you have to be Scottish to take these particular classes?" I joked. "I like your kilt, by the way, Bill."

Sarah moved away and I watched her go up the stairs to the kitchen. There was a titter of laughter and Mary-Anne, a woman dressed in a bright sarong topped off with a white, men's shirt tied at the waist, spoke up. I remember thinking that she must have had some influence on Sarah's wardrobe. "He tells us that he wears it in the traditional way."

For a moment I was tempted to ask her to unroll the right sleeve so that I could see if the cuff was decorated with one of Sarah's embroidered "E"s.

"I'm Canadian," she went on. "The one and only!" Her multitude of silver bangles sounded like chimes.

"I'm very pleased to meet you all. Did you know Ed well?"

"Oh, none of us ever met your father," Bill said.

I wasn't surprised.

"We're just here to give your Mum a bit of support. That's what we do the best," he continued.

"Well, I'm sure Sarah appreciates that. I'd better see if she needs help with anything." The circle closed in on the space I left.

I saw Reed across the room, and sashayed towards him, arms out.

"How the hell are *you*?" he asked, hugging me a bit too close. I smelled cologne mixed with the booze that constantly seeped from his pores.

"I'm fine," I said, my voice muffled against his shoulder. My cousin was completely bald and his skin looked as if he had spent most of his life in the sun. He was wearing a bone-coloured linen suit, a black T-shirt with a v-neck, and shoes with no socks. Reed was painfully thin but his stomach was permanently distended. "You can let me go now." One heavy arm stayed around my neck.

"Sad day," he said.

"Not really."

"You're burying your dad." His free hand suddenly covered his mouth. "I always thought you *adored* Ed." His eyes were lightly glazed.

"It's a long story."

"I know! Mum's been telling me the *details*. You know that generation is a lot happier if you just give in to their bents! You're dressed u-up," he sang. "Where are we going after?"

"Back here . . . and . . . I'm meeting Jack later tonight."

"Jac-tit-ation? The restless man behind the lens? My mum tells me *everything*. Yours must be really pissed at you!"

"It's just business." I remember drawing my lips together, biting them on the inside. "I'm going upstairs."

"Take it easy on her!" he called.

The Big-Ben door chimes rang as I reached the first step. Sarah emerged at the top of the staircase. "Okay, everyone!

Can I have your attention? The cars are here." Betty and Stan reappeared at the patio door. He was carrying the twenty-four-cup coffee urn. "Just set that on the table if you would for now, Stan," Sarah said, "and can you manage Victoria round to the Handi-Bus?"

"Never you mind, love. I'll manage that fine," Stan said.

"I'll come too; hold the brolly over the old dear," Betty added.

"I'm not an old dear, Betty. I hear every word you say. Every word!"

"Okay, Vic-toria, not to worry. Stan here is a wonderful driver, aren't you, Stan?"

"Rhegan, could you lock that door after them, please?" Sarah asked.

"I'll get it, Sarah," Nemit hollered.

"Well, could she unplug the warming plates as well then?" Sarah asked me. "We will turn them on again when we return."

"God. I'm on it, Sarah," Nemit called back.

Mary-Anne, Nemit, and I carried food to the refrigerator.

The Tai-Chi group filled the stairs. "Are we in the second car then?" Bill asked.

"The second car," Sarah said quietly.

"Do you have the urn, Sarah?" I asked.

"The urn?"

"The reason all Ed's best friends are here today."

Sarah disappeared down the hall. Auntie Jane turned to me, said, "Do you have to be this sarcastic all the time?" Then she followed her sister.

"It's the stress," Nemit said, from the top step. "Come on. Put your shoes on. Get the Mac. I'm going out. Looks like they're a bit confused."

I slipped on my red sling-back shoes. "I'm coming," I said. I held the Macintosh over my head. "Get under here!" I said to Nemit. "All right! Those of you who won't fit in the second limousine, please join Victoria, Betty, and Stan in the Handi-Bus." I wondered why Sarah arranged for a second car.

"Can I go in there too?" Nemit asked.

"I was hoping you'd come in the first car with me."

"Please?"

"Mary-Anne?"

"Victoria," she said.

"I should have known."

I nodded to the driver, who was gallantly holding a golf umbrella over his head. I signalled toward the doorway where Jane was locking the Scottish oak door that Ed had fought with the condominium association to install. Sarah was bent in a cramp-like embrace around the urn. She wore a black Jackie-O pillbox hat with netting and a black coat over a matching long-sleeved dress.

We stared at each other with open mouths.

"Your hat — "

"Your shoes," she said as she walked past me to the waiting car.

"Ruined already," Reed laughed. When we settled inside the car, he added, "What colour was the pair you wore the last time you were out at Edenbrook?"

I remember thinking I was part of a family that believed saying hurtful things was normal. I usually tried to ignore them, but I said, "Do you have to be this much of an asshole all the time?" before I could stop myself.

"Do *you* really have to be this sarcastic — ?" Jane began before Nemit interrupted.

"It's the stress," Nemit repeated, getting in and sitting close to me. The leather seats were cold, colder because all of us were drenched. "It's damp and miserable," she continued, "and the only people having any fun are the ones in the beer tent on the Stampede grounds."

It occurred to me only when I saw her two-tone cowboy boots on the damp floor, that I had spent every other day for almost a week panning for a lost diamond in the cuttings from my front lawn instead of dressing up with thousands of downtown professionals, and participating in Calgary's answer to Mardi Gras: Stampede. Instead of masks, some people wore three-hundred-dollar cowboy hats made of felt or straw, brims curved in sultry shapes. It was the one week that no one cared who cut or coloured their hair. Piercing eyes and the ability to have stand-up sex in a public place made everyone beautiful. I recall asking myself why I was missing the festivities.

Then I remembered that Nemit had infield seats for the women's barrel racing finals the next day, the last day of the rodeo, and thought that I might still find a blue-jeaned mate. That was when I started to smile and when my mother asked what I was thinking about. "Our trip to England," I lied, as the driver steered the car around Bow Crescent.

"Do you recall the last chauffeured trip we made together?" she went on. She was rubbing the urn tearfully as if trying to make a genie appear. "Up to the pass," she said, sobbing.

I sank back in my seat, leaned on Nemit, and watched the second car and the Handi-Bus circle after us.

Jane's voice penetrated the confines of the long, white car. "Are you with us, Rhegan? You look as if you are in another world. It's okay, Sarah." She patted my mother's arm. "I told you it wouldn't be any easier if you waited."

I wondered how my aunt would know that. Jane never had a husband. She had continued to work for the Bengel family in Banff after Sarah and Ed were married. Even hinted at moving in with my parents. Ed told me how thankful he was that living with my granny had saved them. Not to be outsmarted, Jane somehow *fell* pregnant with Reed a few months after Sarah announced that she was expecting me. The matriarch of the Banff family arranged for Jane to be moved to Calgary — away from her husband and their son. Mrs. Bengel asked Jane to sign a document saying that neither she nor her heir had any legal claim on the Banff properties. Jane did, but not before securing her future. The estate of that Canadian socialite paid her an allowance that was adjusted for inflation every other year until Reed turned twenty-five. That's when she'd received one final balloon payment, and used the money to buy the acreage that they lived on.

"What are you thinking about, darling?" my mother interrupted again. "I was thinking about the helicopter ride into Assiniboine."

"God . . . seven years since that wedding," Nemit added.

"Nine," I said.

"Ed loved that man." Sarah sat back with the urn perched on her lap. Another sob caught in her throat.

I loved that man. I wondered why he hadn't come. I was sure my mother invited Liam. Maybe I was more like my mother than I cared to admit. When I look back, we both liked to be in control. For me it was partners and property, for her it was family and plots of her own design.

When we reached the cemetery, a formally dressed crowd was gathered under a square awning a short distance from the Garden of Remembrance. Four men in tails moved their feet restlessly on the fringe.

"Are they musicians? One of them has a tambourine!" said Jane.

"My friend could have played the pipes if you'd asked, Auntie," Reed offered. Until that moment, he'd been asleep.

"Imagine the pipes out here," Jane said. "Absolutely majestic in the shadow of those mountains," she continued, sniffling. "Ed would have cherished it." All through the interment, I wondered why she said that. There had been no love lost between Ed and Jane.

The cars stopped. The Tai Chi group emerged, umbrellas up. They gathered about the Handi-Bus.

"I'll go help them," Nemit said, opening the door. She joined the huddle. I felt like a voyeur. Through the open door, I watched her watch the electric ramp lower Victoria to the ground. I turned my attention to Betty when Nemit stooped under the umbrella that the driver held over Victoria.

"Well, that wasn't at all a bad drive," Betty said. "I said not bad — was it Vict-oria?"

"I'm not deaf, you clown."

"Well, I never! Stan? Stanley, where are you?" Stan stood next to Mary-Anne. The rain made her sarong cling to her legs.

The driver of the second car motioned the group toward a small hole in the ground. Its edges were draped with bright green indoor-outdoor carpeting.

"How was your drive in the limousine, Reed?" Betty asked, squeezing between Reed and her husband.

"A lot more comfortable than the bloody bus, I'll bet," Stan said. The group stared at him.

"Make room for the family, please."

Jane was still in the car with Sarah and me.

"Here," Sarah said to me. "I think you should carry."

She plunked the urn on my lap. My hands automatically reached and balanced it but I wasn't prepared for the weight. The urn slid forward and the lid bounced on the rubber floor mat. I had thought that burial urns were sealed. It was then that I began feeling suspicious about my mother's motives, but I had no idea why. I watched Sarah take her sister's hand and step out of the car.

"When you're ready," the driver said to me through the open door.

I placed the urn carefully on the floor and reached for the lid. "A moment please."

The driver bent down and lifted the round lid, stared inside the urn for a wide-eyed moment and gently replaced it.

"Well, Ed, I guess you really are gone," I said. *Och naw,* echoed about me. "You don't have a voice," I said. "You're dead."

The driver coughed in front of the car door.

Just think of me as a wee annoyance, pet.

I pulled the Macintosh around me, and wrapped the urn in a grey fabric cocoon. The driver held an umbrella over my head and stumbled with me towards the huddled group.

"Mum," I said at the edge of the tiny hole in the ground, "Mum, where's the priest?"

"What priest?"

"The one who usually says the prayers for the dead, sprinkles the coffin with holy water."

"We said the Prayer for the Dead months ago and there's no coffin, darling. Your red shoes *are* ruined."

As I stood there in disbelief, my attention moved from what I'd just heard to what I saw. Sarah was right about this place. The clouds were high and, although it was raining, we could see the range that included the Kananaskis Mountains. They were cold-grey and fresh snow covered the tops of the highest peaks. I made a mental note to check the price of land bordering the Elbow River and the smaller tributaries that ran through

Priddis and Bragg Creek; both were west of Calgary. I thought that maybe it was time for me to expand my territory.

"Let me take that for you now," the driver said to me, motioning with the umbrella handle.

Bill and May started humming "Amazing Grace"; they harmonized. The tune was syncopated by the dull beat of a tambourine, as if the musician with the other group couldn't resist corrupting the melody.

"No, I'll do it," I replied. I knelt awkwardly, legs covered by the Mac. I lowered the urn into the square. It stood in a few inches of water. I used the small spade that was protruding from the mound next to the opening to scoop dirt while I held on to the lid, making sure that the urn wouldn't tip over. When I straightened up, low blood pressure and the sudden move to standing made me lose my balance. Sarah steadied me.

"Fine?" she asked.

"Fine," I replied.

She took my hands. "Breath in, breathe out."

The driver offered us disposable wipes, and I began to say the Our Father. "Which art in heaven," the group continued. Sarah didn't make a sound. She looked odd, almost as if she'd just remembered something. Throughout the prayer, Betty's voice was the loudest. "And deliver us from evil, Amen," signaled the Catholic ending. "For thine is the kingdom, the power, and the glory," Betty added, before realizing that she was the only one who had carried on.

"Would anyone like to say something about Ed?" I asked. "Mum?"

Sarah stared at the ground in front of my red shoes.

"Mum?" I asked again.

"This is not really a goodbye," she began. "Ed is simply . . . simply . . . " she didn't finish. Her face was filled with the kind of fear it wore on the day Ed died.

While the drivers distributed small plastic trowels, a large procession entered the cemetery. A sax began playing and the members of the group under the nearby awning hummed deeply while they found the right key. The tambourine shook as if coaxing the sound and their voices sang, "Yessss, Jesus loves me . . . mmm . . . "

Sarah looked past the group and watched a white hearse snake forward. Cars followed, circled the main drive, and coiled around the Garden of Remembrance. The last few vehicles parked near the Handi-Bus. Their passengers walked-ran toward the bigger group. The spiritual ended " . . . because the Bi-i-ble tells me soooo!"

"Ready, Sarah?" I asked.

She moved away from Jane, crouched down, scooped up some wet earth, and dropped it into the opening. Once she was seated inside the car, the rest of the group did the same.

"I wonder who that is," Betty said, pointing at the coffin on the metal frame in front of the large crowd. Nemit helped Stan maneuver Victoria close to the opening. She bent and filled the older woman's trowel. Another hearse glided toward us.

"Thank you, dear," Victoria said to Nemit. "What are you doing later?"

I had arranged to meet Jack. The outcome was unsettling but not nearly as disturbing as the secret my mother had been keeping. The next day, my suspicions about Sarah were confirmed. She had manufactured and staged the interment for reasons that are still unexplainable to me except in the context of mind-altering grief.

15

I MET JACK FOR DINNER. NOTHING elaborate. I chose a bistro called Muse in Kensington, the trendy arts-driven neighbourhood on the north side of the Bow near downtown. The area is bordered on the east by Tenth Street, to the north by the Alberta College of Art, and to the west by Fourteenth Street. Its southern boundary is Memorial Drive and the Bow River. My Parkdale property was just minutes west of there, and when I lived in Tower One at Point McKay, I sometimes drove to Kensington and met clients at the family-owned restaurant, Osteria de Medici.

Muse is still on Ten-A Street, perpendicular to the river, entrance on the main floor, lounge in the basement, restaurant on the second floor. The interior uncluttered: stucco walls painted shades of muted green, few *objects d'art* to distract patrons. I sat at a table that overlooked the lounge. I couldn't see people arriving but I could hear them. When the host brought them up to the second floor, I watched them climb the stairs, and tried to guess why they had come based on their attire and how they composed themselves before they sat at a table.

My opponent arrived at exactly seven-thirty. The host recognized his name, flirted with Jack until he gave him his card, and invited him to make an appointment. Jack's shirt looked new, possibly Armani, but I could see that he still bought vintage clothes. His pants were plaid and his shoes were black and beige wing-tips. I once tried on a pair of embroidered mules in a consignment store here in Kensington. As much as I loved them, I couldn't match the previous owner's gait.

Jack had his hair cut since I saw him at Nemit's sitting. The skater flop, which I always thought of as a glorified bowl cut, was much darker, much shinier, and it had been textured. The bangs were still long and had deep-v shapes cut out of them in strategic places. His eyes were camouflaged when he looked at me from the top step. He didn't make any attempt to smooth the hair back.

Before the waiter arrived, Jack said, "I've consulted a lawyer."

I showed him my neutral face, but felt as if my ears were back and burning.

"I intend to sue you for half of the value of your properties: the house you live in, the house in Inglewood, the four apartments, the place in Parkdale, and the new cabin."

I laughed. The cabin wasn't mine. I'd agreed to hold it while a client finalized her divorce. The cabin title was registered to a male, a Mister Findley, a Trojan of sorts. The kind you can't trace in the Alberta registry database — unless you are a veterinarian. The cabin was the property that I'd registered to a horse.

"You won't be successful," I said, when a large plate of Mediterranean ziti was set in front of me. Jack had forgotten that an ambush required surprise.

"But the cabin is an addition since we were married, and your income must be three times what it used to be." He drank low-sodium bottled water, and ate greens. Although it was Saturday, he still didn't have dressing, tomatoes, or bread. "I'm amazed in fact that you haven't added any other new properties to the balance."

I stabbed the ziti with my fork. Then I dropped my cutlery, reached into my document folder, and handed him a copy of the prenuptial agreement he signed before I married him in ninety-three.

"The rules have changed," he said. "Either partner can sue for more alimony, especially when they are under duress."

"Maintenance, in your case. And, you and I never agreed to pay each other anything."

"I think we should."

"Your home certainly doesn't suggest that you're *under duress*. You're wasting your time," I said. "The new law applies to people with children and it's in place so that parents can't deprive their offspring to get back at each other when their incomes go up — significantly."

He engaged. "The law is also in place to protect partners who had no income and who were supported by their spouses. That was me. Those people are entitled to apply for increases in *maintenance* when the supporting spousal income *goes up significantly*."

"If I were you," I said while eating, "I would find a better lawyer. You don't meet the criteria for an appeal in either instance. You lived in my house for less than a year. Is the person you've retained not familiar with the Alberta Statute of Limitations? It's been eight years — clearly you've over, or perhaps, underestimated the situation."

He used his knife and fork to tear up his salad. Nothing passed his lips.

I married Jack soon after Liam. He had just completed a graduate degree at the University of Calgary and hadn't yet begun to build a name for himself. I was on the rebound and he needed a springboard. He had some money, but I think he spent it all on the ring he presented me with when he proposed. He obviously thought that marital dividends would be high.

He left for Quebec within five months. Flew out there to meet with an agency that wanted someone based in the west. Said he'd be away for a month. He consumed the money in the joint account, which thankfully only held enough to cover basic household expenses. I hadn't been paying attention. I can usually smell a parasite at one hundred feet.

When he went to Montreal, he took all his belongings: his camera equipment and the single duffle bag he had when we met, and moved in with the woman who interviewed him seven days after he arrived. The hotel at Place Ville-Marie charged my credit card for a mere six nights.

I reminded him again about the prenuptial. I repeated what I'd said on the phone numerous times: "I paid for all the communications between the Calgary and Montreal law firms; you didn't contest the terms of the divorce when either decree, Nisi, or Absolute, was delivered." If nothing else, I could see from his food play that I was wreaking mental havoc.

Jack left five minutes later, unsatisfied. I stayed and finished my meal, paid the bill, drove home. Only then, in the confines of my car, did I allow myself to wonder if he'd succeed. I remembered the story about an Alberta woman, Irene Murdoch, who got almost nothing after breaking her back on the family farm for twenty-five years. A 1968 judicial decision had taken her lifeblood away.

I was determined that Jack wouldn't get an ounce of mine. I would have undertaken a full-on attack if it had been necessary, perhaps even snapped, and burned my properties to the ground, rather than relinquish any part of them. He was the only ex-partner who tried to attack the very piece of me that I thought I guarded best.

The greatest defence is an offence. Ed taught me that when we played soldier with Reed. I decided that wives should plant thick groves, dig moats, prepare for late attacks.

16

I DIDN'T HAVE TIME TO DIG a moat. A trickle of water ran down the street towards me when I came back from Muse that night. A thin film covered the sloped driveway and, as I parked, the headlights illuminated water glistening between the house and the garage. I took off my red shoes and got out. The lawn immediately behind the deck was soaked, but the water that had accumulated further down the yard was draining in the low area at the side of the garage, flowing over the flagstones to the driveway and out to the street. Most of the yard was submerged in a shallow lake that lapped against the back of the garage. The soil under the line of blue spruce was a sea of mud, the bottom step of the gazebo was covered, and the furniture below the willow was partially underwater. I ran into the house and called Earl's emergency number.

"How was the rest of your night?" Nemit asked, the next morning.

"Frantic. I had to call Alberta Environment. Earl, the guy from the Department of Rivers and Lakes who has been monitoring the water levels, arrived and called the City. My yard looks like a bunker and I feel as if I'm about to drown.

There's a pool of deep water at the back of the garage, and if it gets any worse they'll make me evacuate."

"God. Want me to come over?"

"No. I mean yes." I stood at the bedroom window surveying my waterlogged property.

"What did the enviro-man say? I wasn't listening. Never mind, I'm picking up Adam and I'm coming right over."

As soon as I hung up, the doorbell rang. I waited a few minutes and it rang again. Then I heard Sarah's muted voice interspersed by her palm-style knock on the front door. I hadn't gone to bed until five. It was eight-forty. "I'm coming!" I yelled as I pulled on my robe and ran down the stairs, wondering what she'd done with her key.

"Rhegan, why am I parked in a stream and why are you not dressed for church?" Sarah looked at me over her glasses as she sank into the overstuffed living room sofa. She kicked off her shoes, threw her purse on the seat, and crossed her arms over her chest.

I had one hand on my throat, held out the other, and waggled my fingers, "Come with me to the back," I managed.

"What is wrong with you? Are you crying?"

I grabbed her hand. I knew if I could swallow the lump in my throat, my tears would be few. It was what I did as a kid when she asked me the same questions.

When we reached the patio door, she was dumfounded. I opened it and we went out. Water shimmered under the planks of wood we stood on despite the fact that there was a low wall of sandbags around the deck. The City crew that came out the night before had also stacked bags, four high, the length of the yard on both sides so that the neighbours' gardens weren't affected too much, but that meant the pool was deeper in the middle of my own. The bottom of my property was open to the

river but the water wasn't coming from there, it was draining
out toward the Bow.

My mother crushed my hand, "What . . . what is it?"

"Earl thinks it's an unmapped aquifer. He should be here
shortly."

"Oh, God! Wh — what about the garage?" She wrung her
hands. I held one as she stepped over the sandbags. She let go
and made her way to the side door. She rattled the handle.
"I . . . can't get it to open, darling."

"It's not locked." I held out one arm, motioned for her to
come back. "You'd better come in and change before we do
anything in there."

She tried to look through the window but the lilac was too
tall. She came back and stood next to me, eyes wet.

I held onto her. "We'll get through," I said, repeating a
phrase my father often used.

She pushed me away, balanced, reached up inside her flared
skirt and took her stockings off one at a time, rolled them, and
threw them on the deck near the door. A car pulled up on
the driveway. "Who the hell is that, Rhegan?" Sarah left me
standing on the deck and walked in the water flowing between
the house and the garage, as if defending our trench. "Good
God!" she said, squinting back at me in the glare the water
caused. "It's Nemit."

"She's worried about me."

"Do up your belt. The boy is with her. Do you know where
she stayed last night? That woman — "

"Victoria invited *that woman*."

Sarah sucked in her breath and, holding her arms out for
balance, crossed back to the deck. The water was up to her
knees. Her fingers bruised my forearm as she came back over

the sandbags. The hem of her skirt was wet. She started inside then turned and stood in the doorway.

Adam ran into the stream and jumped up and down a couple of times. "Hi, Rhegan! This is awesome!" His skinny, nine-year-old knees protruded from the bottom of his damp shorts.

"Hi, Adam. Where were you last night?"

"At the Stampede and then Jason's. He has everything. A pool table, a big screen TV. Can I invite him over to see the water?"

"Yes, maybe later, but does he have — ?"

"Don't say it!" Adam looked at Nemit who now stood, pants rolled to her knees, boots and bag clutched to her chest beside her son.

"A urinal?" Nemit and I said together.

"You have a urinal in your home?" Sarah asked Nemit.

"God, I had to have one bastion of male paraphernalia for Adam!"

"Jesus Christ," Sarah said. "Why did you not just teach him to sit down?"

"Mrs. Flett! My mom doesn't like that kind of language — I'm starving."

"Sorry, darling. I was just about to cook something."

"Can I watch?" Adam asked.

"You can help me," Sarah replied. "Come along." We followed her into the kitchen. "What will be done about this water situation?" she asked. She seemed calmer, but kept looking out the window nervously toward the garage.

"Earl said he and a colleague would discuss that with me today. He said sometimes there's a way of draining an aquifer."

"Why is the water only right here?" Adam asked me. He knelt on a chair next to the counter where Sarah was gathering ingredients for pancakes.

"There must be a layer of bedrock or soil under the yard at the back. I think that's what an aquifer is and who knows how far it extends, but it can hold and transmit water — "

"Like a sponge?" Adam interrupted.

I nodded, " — I hope Lakes and Rivers will figure something out."

Nemit smothered me in one of her bear hugs. "Don't worry about the barrel racing tickets," she said. "We won't go."

My mother turned her back to us, and helped Adam switch on the electric mixer.

"No, you should go," I told Nemit. "I have to stay here and there's nothing you can do. Adam can keep me company." No barroom two-stepping for me, I thought. I had a dull ache between my hipbones that I knew would reach my pelvic floor by nightfall. I was disappointed; I had been imagining an encounter with a pretend wrangler for days.

"Sure? I'll come back afterward, collect Adam, and see how things are." She moved off into the living room and picked up the phone there.

"So what did you think of the group yesterday?" my mother asked as she added dry ingredients to the mixture Adam was beating.

"The Monday Tuesday Wednesday Friday bunch? Not bad," I said. "I'm going upstairs to shower and put some clothes on."

"Can I increase the speed now?" Adam asked.

"Just one level," Sarah said. A puff of flour filled the air over the bowl. She smoothed her hands over her polyester blouse. "And the Thursday group?" she asked.

I ignored her question, which was intended to make me comment about Hugh. Instead, I imagined the moisture the blouse siphoned out of her skin, and the feel of the static electricity it would cause under a fur coat.

A while later I heard Earl's voice explaining that bedrock wasn't porous. I listened from the second floor as he told Adam that alluvium, the fine, fertile soil that the river left behind on flood plains, was what really attracted and held onto water in an aquifer.

I jogged down the stairs. "I like the look of you two in my kitchen," I said to Nemit and my mother. They scowled and then laughed simultaneously.

"God. That was a first. I'm off! I'll be back when the barrel racing is over," Nemit said standing up beside the table. She left through the front door, to avoid getting her feet wet again.

I followed her out and said hello to Earl.

"Good morning, Rhegan!" he replied. He was wearing hip waders. "I checked the metre stick I left at the back of the garage and the water level is steady."

"That's good isn't it?" I wanted to feel relieved.

"The less than good news is that your garage is flooded."

"Flooded!" Sarah screamed. My mother could sneak up on me even when I had expected her. She let Adam and me hug her.

"Let me explain," Earl went on. "There appears to be an old vent at the back of the garage."

"For lacquering," Sarah said. "My husband had a rudimentary fan system in the shop — garage — when he built cabinets."

"About two feet above the ground," I said. "The stucco company finished it beautifully when they did the outside, same time as the addition to the house was completed, in 1996." It had taken me two and a half years to renovate the house and shop after my parents moved.

"They didn't seal up the vent."

"Earl let me look in the window!" Adam said.

"Ed," Sarah whispered, "Ed — "

My arm was still around her shoulders. I squeezed. "His tools will be all right — the lathe, maybe the motor for the dory are the only things to worry about. Thank God I left my car out!"

"I've called in the City," Earl said. "They'll cordon off the street. Then we can drain the water in a controlled manner. We'll raise one of the double doors slightly and direct the flow toward the storm drains. But first, we'll line the driveway with sandbags."

We all looked at the steady film of water running down the driveway and out toward the two large grates in the ground, less than half a block away. The water was flowing in exactly that direction as if by intuition.

"The crew should be here soon," Earl continued. "In the meantime, you need to move your vehicles. I'll go door to door, let everyone on the street know."

Sarah said she'd get the keys to the Rover and the MG. Adam wanted to help Earl. I forced my way into the thickness of the lilac, squeezed my foot into the split in the trunk, and used it like a step-stool. I stared through the window, hands around my eyes against the glass. I decided to add the garage door company to my list of preferred services. The weather stripping that was supposed to keep wind, rain, and snow out, was keeping most of the water in. Small cans and jars of old varnish that had been on the shelf below the workbench were suspended in the space below its top. The toolbox was fine. The life jackets that I'd left on the floor were floating, so were the Styrofoam canoe supports. The canoe bobbed about where the MG should have been.

I heard the electric motor that raises the doors start to grind, then stop. I backed out of the bush and stumbled toward the driveway. Sarah sat in the passenger seat of my car. The door was open and she had the controller in her hands, pointed it through the window.

"Sarah, wait!" I called. "Wait!"

She slammed the car door, pressed the remote once more and the garage door went down again. Her first try must have raised the door just a few inches. Water gushed over the ground. I grabbed on to the downspout on the corner of the garage and watched as she pressed again. She held on longer this time and I bit through my bottom lip, tasting blood as the door went up. The noise of the rushing water was deafening. Its weight initially kept the door straight, but once the door was above the waterline, the sudden lack of pressure knocked it off its track; it went up another few inches before the motor ground to a halt. The door hung there, twisted at an odd angle.

The water tumbled in a wave toward the MG, hit the front, and moved the car to the street. At the same time, the canoe, which had been parallel to the door, turned into the flow and thundered toward my mother. I heard her muted screams. The canoe crashed bow first into the grill, ended up seam-to-windshield when the rest of the water poured out, lifting it onto the hood. Cans and jars and containers of varying sizes were sucked out from under the workbench; the life jackets rushed past me in a flurry of colour. The large plastic bin that stood between the two doors tipped drunkenly on its side and rolled on the surface. Some of the garbage that had been inside it floated toward the storm drains. Then the water filled the bin and scraped it along the ground. The drywall behind the bin peeled off in chunks, exposing the vapour barrier and the pink insulation below.

I stood in an eddy behind the wave, feeling the effects of its runoff. I heard a sucking sound as water swirled around my legs, and doubled back on itself. I felt as if I had been standing in the rush and pull for hours.

Earl said the worst of it was over in two and a half minutes. That was when the canoe had rolled over to one side, spilling its contents. The bailer, the teak paddles, and my new camera case were swept under the Rover, where they snagged on the drive shaft and washed up against the transmission. Earl ran toward the storm drains.

I thought that my mother was too shaken to open the door of the MG, because she hit the window with her palms, screaming hysterically until I managed to let her out. At that point, the water on the street wasn't even ankle deep anymore. She ran to the Rover, crouched on the ground next to it, and looked underneath. Then she lay down beside the running board on the street side of the car, extended her arm, and withdrew the camera case. She held it to her chest as Earl helped me take her inside the house.

Sarah lay on the couch in the living room, skirt and blouse soaked, feet and elbows cut, sobbing uncontrollably.

17

I CALLED JANE. SHE ARRIVED SOON after the paramedics, pant legs tucked into a pair of wellington boots. When asked, she said that my mother wasn't taking any medications or hormone replacement drugs, only vitamins. Sarah was given a sedative. When it began to take effect and she was calmed, she let go of the camera case. The paramedics wanted to take her to the hospital, but physically there was nothing wrong. Jane thought it might be best if she took my mother home. When Sarah tried to sit up and tell us that she was all right, they checked her again: pupils, blood pressure, heart rate, pulse, and respiration — almost normal.

"I still think it best if I take her home," Jane repeated. "She'll be more comfortable in her own bed. I'll spend the night and call you if anything untoward comes up."

They decided to leave her with us.

Earl and Adam came in the front door.

"You have a lot to deal with here," Jane went on. "Surely, what I'm suggesting is best for everyone."

"The neighbours are snooping in your garage and there's some people waiting to see who's going in the ambulance," Adam said. "Who's going in the ambulance?"

"No one," I told him. "Everyone is fine."

"Fine," my mother repeated, "breathe in, breathe out."

I smiled.

I let myself survey the scene only after Sarah had been taken care of. The disappointed crowd dispersed. A few people stayed to make sure that there really wasn't a patient. They stood on the street near the Rover until the ambulance drove away. Adam was right, my neighbours were milling about in the garage, leaving their footprints in the sediment on the floor. They had lifted the canoe off the car and set it in the middle of the driveway on the supports that Adam rescued. The Styrofoam pieces had hit the deep curb where the crescent curves, five hundred metres from my place, and flipped up on the lawn next to the largest house on the block.

Adam said the owner had looked out from his turret window, watching him as he picked up the Styrofoam. "Why didn't he come out? Didn't he see the big wave running down the street?" he asked.

"He probably thought that there was just some kind of Stampede barbeque game going on," I replied. "Some people hide when the counterfeit cowboys take over."

He laughed and ran off.

The canoe supports had landed furthest from the house. The life jackets were about three hundred metres away and the things that had been under the bench were either on the storm drain grates or scattered around them. The empty bin was against the back of the Rover.

"Lucky there isn't more damage to your car," my neighbour said to me. His family had planted the row of blue spruce. "Talk to me about the boat you have for sale when you get organized." He and his wife, who was fifteen years his senior, took Ed's long brooms off the wall at the end of the workbench and started sweeping the garage floor in the corner farthest from the open door. The others, who I didn't know, strolled off, hands in their pockets or arms folded in front of their chests. Some yipped their way back to a nearby Stampede party. Others said things such as, "Well, that made Sunday exciting," and "I told you that woman couldn't manage that place by herself."

I opened the second double door, said thanks to the neighbours for sweeping, and padded down the driveway. The MG was wet inside. I knew that the covering on the floor, which curved up and over the metal body behind the bucket seats, would have to be stripped out and replaced. The surface of the seats didn't seem wet at all but the hollow underneath was damp. The material lining the trunk was dry. The hood had a single, long scratch on it that mapped the canoe's slide into the windshield. I looked over the Kevlar, ran my hands along its length, examined the seam at the bow — it was unscathed. I didn't feel any scratches or punctures on the flat bottom. The surface of the stern, which had settled on the driveway, was grazed.

Adam became the Bow Crescent ferryman. He ran back and forth, making a pile of cans and containers near the canoe. The glass jars had been shattered and the City crew, the one that Earl had called, was cleaning up the street, sweeping up shards and using something that looked like coloured salt on a few patches of ground where solvents and varnish had left stains.

"You're going to be billed for the clean up," one of the men told me.

"I realize," I said. I turned and looked for Earl, hoping he would give me some news that would make me feel relieved. I expected to find water still running through the vent onto the garage floor.

He was smiling. "I just checked the metre stick I placed at the back of the garage two weeks ago. The water level is down. I don't think you'll have to evacuate!"

The ache in my pelvis settled in my groin.

Adam explained the whole story to Nemit when she arrived. She didn't know whether to laugh or cry, whether to go home or stay, whether to hold on to her son or to let him go.

Disorientation, I thought, happens on water.

While Adam watched television, I asked Nemit to come into my den. On my desk stood a long plastic box that had been washed out of the garage. Next to it was my camera case. She sat in the chair. The row of tiny silver coins dangling from the low waistband of her Italian jeans clinked together.

"I opened the camera case about an hour ago. I wanted to see if the seal was as good as they said it was, thought that when it fell out of the canoe and got wedged under the Rover that maybe it had ruptured."

"And?" she asked tipping the chair back.

"Take a look."

She opened the case. Her brows furrowed and she stared back at me. "What is it?" She picked up one of four plastic baggies, set it on the palm of her hand, and inspected the contents. "It's doubled," she said, pulling on one of the layers.

"I think it's Ed."

"What?"

"I think it's Ed! It's the only explanation for my mother's behaviour!" I paced between the desk and the door.

She set the baggie down beside the others. "Are you sure? But what about the interment?"

I wiped perspiration off my hands onto my jean shorts. "I'll know as soon as the sedative that the paramedics gave Sarah wears off. As for yesterday's pantomime — my mother orchestrated the entire thing."

Nemit adjusted the collar of her Western-style halter top, "God. She's obviously overcome with grief." She pointed to the other plastic box, this one was labelled, Master Meats. "Another relative?"

I took the top off and showed her lengths of dowel, a small cloth bag containing nails and glue, and a spool of string.

She shrugged.

"It's a box kite," I said, "minus the material. Something Ed and I were supposed to build when I was a kid, maybe a bit older than Adam."

"And these two things are related because?" She skimmed her hands along the inlaid brass strip on the top of my antique desk.

"Because I'm taking them on the canoe trip that my mother agreed to go on with me."

"Even now that she's had such a shock?"

"Especially now."

Half an hour later, Nemit lifted her sleeping son onto the bench seat in her van, pulled the seat belt around him, and closed the sliding door. "We'll take the day off and help you with the clean up — "

"But you're supposed to — "

"Work, yes. I won't take no for an answer! I didn't take parade morning off or go to the all-afternoon company party. In some departments that's compulsory! I was on call. I had a summer student working in the field. The student will be the responsibility of another geologist this week, so I'll take tomorrow off. I'll just tell my VP that I'm hungover, which is a perfectly acceptable sickness after using his infield tickets today."

I waded out to the gazebo just before the sun went down, cowboy boots under one arm, the sombrero Nemit brought from Mexico for me dangling behind my shoulders. It seemed that every man, woman, and child in cow-town had a Smithbuilt. I preferred to stand out. It was still hot, a typical July in Calgary: thunderstorms and rain for eight or nine afternoons, then not a drop on the last day of Stampede. The sun often came out as the tourists left and the downtown people put away their western duds for another year. I slipped my bare feet into my boots and sat cross-legged in the middle of the wood floor with a bottle of cold Viognier and two glasses, and poured myself some.

I hoped that Earl would pick up my scent when he came to do his late night check. He wasn't unattractive. I remember that, based on his hair and skin, I thought he was in his fifties. He was in good shape and didn't have any bulges or rolls shadowing his belt. I wondered if he would provide me with some relief. I unbuttoned my microfibre blouse, exposed my blue bikini top. The straps looked like lasso rope and I cinched them up until my breasts looked firm. I sipped my wine, slid my free hand over my flat stomach, let it rest on my pubic bone, and waited.

Someone did arrive a while later, but he wasn't who I expected. He waded out to the gazebo, mounted the stairs and faced me. Moisture coated the surface of my skin like the residue left by a melting hoar frost. I lifted my hands and allowed them to hover. He thought I wanted to maintain the distance between us. I closed my eyes and my mouth went slack. I remembered other men, other seasons. Domenic's young ribs projecting the odour of Longview. The sweet breath of Jack's self-deprivation and the tongue that tasted of Aspartame. The feel of Raj's strong back below just-washed black hair, freed from a turban. Lynn's chest covered in hair so coarse that I heard it move against a flack jacket. A mark on the back of Thomas' hand that looked like the curve of the Little Bow.

I opened my eyes. The man who stood in front of me was none of those things. Beneath the patterned shirt was a smooth chest, under those jeans a set of well-defined glutes. His back was long and his hair was short. Rows of late afternoon whiskers ruptured his skin, and that breath, I imagined, would taste of the morning we met. His ribs enclosed lungs that had duplicated the movement of a shallow-breathing woman all day, and his skin smelled like a warm hospital death.

"Joan passed today," he said.

I wondered for the rest of the night why Liam said "passed" instead of "died". He poured wine and we sank to the dark floor. He talk-touched me. The ridges on my tongue hardened. His voice was like a low growl that moved around and over and into my body. I listened to the water surrounding us bubble and laugh like the stream in Assiniboine Pass. I watched him and sniffed when he turned away, let my tongue taste the air and the salt on my cheeks.

I told him about Ed, about what Sarah had and hadn't done with my father's ashes, what happened that day. Then I said that there had to be a connection between my father and the water. For the first time in nine years, Liam touched me.

When he lay down behind me and held me, I combed the fur on his forearms, contracted my flesh within the cage of his bones, and relaxed my hips against him.

I felt as if I had reached cover after a long storm.

18

YOU WAKE BECAUSE YOU HEAR A roar coming from upstream. Your head hurts and you are dehydrated. You are amazed considering how much water there was at your daughter's home. You panic momentarily but you know that when your daughter discovers your husband's ashes they will be as safe as they were in your own hands.

"How are you?" your sister asks from the chair in the corner of your bedroom. You cringe because she is wearing her safari suit, the one that has buttons on the rear pockets. The chair and ottoman are covered in delicate Thai silk.

"Lovely," you say. You do not have to explain your actions to your sister. You know that she separated herself from men in a previous lifetime. You ask your sister to put the burgundy walking shoes that rest on your ottoman on the floor, please. Then you wonder why most of her shoes are that colour and why you have not noticed that particular preference until now.

"You should have the second dose of sedatives," your sister says, but you both know that you do not need them.

"Perhaps you would like to sleep in the guest room," you say. You hope that your sister will not ask to lie next to you as she did when your parents died. You cringe when her dry lips meet your forehead and you feel relieved when she disappears down the hallway.

Yesterday your sister chastised your daughter. Jane does not understand that your daughter is a woman of action. You do, and you know what your daughter will expect of you now. You are ready. You have spent the last five and a half months preparing yourself to make another journey. The first one you made with your daughter was masked by your own grief and compliance. Your next journey is planned and arranged — to use your daughter's words. You have worked hard so that she won't have to. Your husband's personal effects, what there were, have been categorized, catalogued, and divested appropriately. You wrinkle your nose because you remember the smell of his business records as they were incinerated. Your sister agreed with your methodology. She helped you burn your husband's work clothes. You think that she will also understand your next and most personal of divestments.

You decide to let your daughter know that you will meet her expectations. You think about how many times you neglected Rhegan's wishes and how many times you shrugged her off. When your husband was alive, you told yourself that he came first. Now that your husband is dead, you evade real conversations with your daughter simply because it is your habit to do so.

Rhegan wants to take you on another trip, canoeing. You are happy because in doing so you will cross another border and reunite yourself with your husband. You will agree to the paddling lessons that your daughter has already arranged at the Bow Waters Canoe Club, but you will insist that she adjust her current travel plan so that you will avoid any danger until your own goals are met.

You watch the sky warm and you decide that your daughter will accept your explanation about absence. You wrap yourself in your Aran sweater, sit outside in the old teak chair at the bottom of your garden, and wait for your sister to awaken. You imagine you hear the soulful moaning of animals in season.

19

I DIDN'T SLEEP AFTER LIAM LEFT. By the time my mother and aunt arrived, I had piled one headpiece, five garters, a veil, a bridal missal, and a Kevlar hunting vest next to the camera case and the kite makings on the family room floor. I was hosing the driveway, washing away the traces of sediment that had swept out of the garage when Jane parked her Fiat.

I hug-held my mother and invited them inside.

Jane declined, said "I really should get home and check up on my place," which meant, check up on Reed.

I stayed on Sarah's arm, squeezed her when she said, "Things look better than I thought they might," and was surprised when she didn't pull away.

The water that still pooled in the yard was behind the gazebo; it had stopped running over the flagstones to the front of the house. The pool that was left was following the grade of the backyard and draining slowly into the river.

I felt some relief, and touched my mother's forehead with mine before we walked toward the house. She seemed pleased. I felt as if I had put her at ease.

Inside, she picked up the headpiece and the missal, the veil and the garters, and examined them one by one. She set down each of them as if it was a china cup in a gloved hand.

I picked up the camera case and set it on my lap. "It's time for us to talk."

"Be careful with that," she said.

"Why?"

"You know why."

"I want *you* to tell me why." I opened the case.

She sat perfectly still.

I held two bags by their tops, waist-high over the floor. "What is this?" I asked. My hands moved rapidly together and apart in a clapping motion as I spoke.

"BE careful!" Sarah said, hands reaching out.

"Man-in-a-sack? What are you planning to do with these remains?" I asked. I threw the bags up in the air and caught them, deciding that I could be just as odd as my mother.

"Rhegan!"

"Now I know why there was no priest at the interment — even you can't lie to one." My hands gripped the bags and the contents bulged around my fingers.

"Watch out!" Sarah yelled. "You will burst them!"

I turned to her with my father still in my hands and embraced her. I whispered in her ear as if we were in church. "Why couldn't you have just kept the urn? Why couldn't we have forgone that whole ridiculous ceremonial charade?"

She pushed me away. I expected her lip to quiver, her eyes to fill, her hands to fly to her face. She was stony.

"I don't understand you!" I screamed. *Easy lassie*, echoed in my head. I dropped the baggies into the camera case.

Sarah closed the top and slid the clasps back into place. She picked up the case and began walking steadily to the front door. "I'll start the Rover," she said.

"Oh, no you don't!" I grabbed her arm. "You are not leaving until we figure something out!" I tightened my grip. Suddenly I was fifteen, but she was me and I was her. "Mum. Mum," I said gently, letting go. "Sit down here, okay?"

"Why did you drag out the veil, the missal, and the garters?" she asked.

"Because I think I should take them on our canoe trip. I have to let go, the same way you have to let go."

"I have. Look here, darling." She held up the camera case. "Here he is. He can be whatever he wants."

"He's contained!"

"Finally, you understand. Your father did the same thing to me all those years. We could have had our own home, but no, he had to keep me bottled up with his mother and her remedies all those years!" She shook. "I loved that man. I only tried to leave him once, remember that?" Then her body convulsed as if her leaving him was the root of her pain. "I did everything for him, everything." She gasped for air. "I — love — him. Why is it that you — you — cannot understand?"

I stood staring at her in the middle of the living room, trying to make my voice soft. "I don't know that I'd want a lover who can take my breath away even when he's dead. I believe that sometimes *love* has nothing to do with why couples stay together."

She crushed the case to her chest.

"I've been married five times. It's not love that keeps people together, or forces them apart; it's their belief system or their fears, or their finances or a thousand other reasons that have nothing to do with *love*." I stroked her thick, short hair, grabbed a tuft, repeating a gesture she used to calm my father. "Let's take that trip on the Bow. Let's take Ed with us."

"I will try to let him go," she said, "in the river."

Later that day, Nemit and I walked shoeless across the wet grass to my property line. "Strange that your mother keeps your father like that," she said gently.

"Maybe," I said. I could understand why Sarah couldn't let go of Ed, but I couldn't make sense of how and where she kept him. I thought about what I kept beyond the boundaries of relationships, what I had contained. I pictured the house in Inglewood and thought about the way Liam still made me feel, but I said nothing about his visit to Nemit. She didn't press me into another conversation. Instead, she gifted me with her quiet reassurance as we sorted through the rest of the cans and containers that were swept out on the wave, hung the life jackets up to dry, and watched the garage man straighten out the double door. Just as he was climbing into his truck, the guy who had repaired the walls in the Parkdale house for me, arrived to assess the drywall. He recommended cutting the gypsum at the four-foot mark and pulling out the insulation.

"I'll replace them," he said, "after the cement floor and foundation are completely dry,"

Moisture had climbed some of the panels in the back corner where the old vent was and the wall behind the maps was spongy.

"We'll have to go to six feet there," he said. "I'll start next week."

When he drove off Nemit and I leaned on the workbench, arms folded. For five deafening minutes, the only noise came from the giant oscillating fans that she had picked up from the rental shop.

As we trudged across the wet ground between the garage and the house, we heard Sarah and Adam laughing.

"They must be in the equipment room," Nemit said, shading her eyes and squinting up at the open French doors.

I stared when we reached them. Sarah wore a long, off-white shift. She jangled fifteen gold bangles and finger-waved a plain gold band at Nemit and me. Her clothes and Adam's clothes were hanging from the wardrobe door.

"You're wearing the wrong jewellery," I said.

"I got the rest right, though — correct?" Sarah replied.

Nemit stared at Sarah's bare feet. "God, yes," she said. "No shoes that time."

"The shift is too long for you, Mum," I said, surprised to discover that I didn't want her to damage the hem.

Sarah looked at me sideways. "This afternoon, Adam is wearing Victorian lace." She used her best London accent. "The traditional, high-necked, long-sleeved dress contrasts sharply with the ruby ring, and complements the square-toed slipp-ahs and the plain-Jane veil."

"I don't really like this dress," Adam said. "The inside is really scratchy."

Nemit stared at me, and raised her eyebrows.

"I want to see you in one!" Adam said to her, excitedly.

"I'm too big for Rhegan's clothes," Nemit replied.

"Not the sari," he said.

I shook my head in disbelief. I never got over the attraction people had to bridal regalia, especially *my* bridal regalia.

"Please? Please, Mom? Put it on!" Adam said.

"I will get you the *right* jewellery," Sarah said, wriggling her hand out of the bangles. "Come on!"

"That leaves two gowns for me," I said, moving to the wardrobe.

Sarah handed the folded lengths of the sari to Nemit, who slipped off the long cotton shorts that she wore.

I sighed.

"Well?" Nemit said to me. "Don't tell me that you're feeling nostalgic!"

I slipped on the taffeta, ballet-style gown Thomas had bought for me. Adam followed Nemit's instructions. He circled around his mother, who raised one arm then the other. She held the fabric in place. "Now help me make a knot." Together they began to pleat the long remaining portion of material.

"Careful! Try not to step on your dress, Adam! Let me do up the hooks for you, darling," Sarah said, turning to me. "Oh, the top ones will not close . . . you have . . . " she held her breath and tried to connect the last two. "Well, never mind. Here is the scarf," she said, placing it at the base of my throat and draping it over my shoulders. "And the shoes!"

I slipped them on.

Nemit tucked the pleated section of sari into her waistband, wrapped herself once more, and draped the end over her shoulder.

"Shall we?" Sarah held up the hem of the dress Adam wore.

"Let's!" he said.

They led our parade down the stairs, through the living room, and outside. Nemit and I followed Sarah and Adam as they circled the canoe. When they stopped, we stood on the opposite side, facing them. We were like brides waiting to take part in a group marriage ceremony. All we needed were willing partners.

"Have you thought about naming this vessel," Sarah asked.

I hadn't. "It's a canoe."

"The last one had *Clipper* scrawled across the stern," she said.

"The bow. That was the name of the manufacturer," I told her.

"The manufacturer?"

"The manufacturer."

"Who made this one?" Nemit asked. "Maybe that could work."

"Same company." I said. "The model is called The Tripper."

My mother and Nemit were shoeless. Sarah stared at Nemit, and seemed to admire the hem of the red and gold sari as it brushed the top of my friend's feet. I thought momentarily about Whitefish and the dream I'd had. I watched the other end of the material float in the breeze, and drift forward over Nemit's shoulder. Sarah caught it and smoothed her hand along the fabric, traced the length of Nemit's back, repeating a gesture I saw her make toward Ed when she didn't think I was watching.

"You could call it Mad River Canoe!" Adam giggled as he examined the bear paddle.

When Adam and Nemit had gone home, Sarah and I discussed our trip for two hours. Afterward, I had been surprised that Sarah left the camera case with me. I thought that I still didn't know everything, that she was holding something back. My mother had agreed to the canoe trip too easily. As I watched her drive off in the Rover, I wanted to believe that my father had been a catalyst, and that both of us had been changed somehow, that we would develop trust in each other. Instead, I was suspicious, and felt like a bear who smells a new foe. I thought about why Sarah was so unhappy, why she was performing again just hours after admitting that she hadn't interred my father's ashes. I decided that holding on made my mother angry, trapped her in a place between head and heart where reconciliation was impossible.

During the time that remained before our canoe trip that thought stayed with me. It wasn't until the day of our departure that I realized Sarah and I had something in common. There was something that I held on to, one set of wedding paraphernalia that I didn't store in the wardrobe or let anyone else try on, that I hadn't included in my selection of disposable belongings. It was the dress that I'd worn for my wedding at Assiniboine Lodge. I stored it in the basement as if that would help me to keep my feelings about Liam underground.

20

I STOOD ON WHAT LOOKED LIKE an outcrop of rock overlooking the gorge below the headwaters of the Bow River. Rogue strands of my hair flew skyward in the updraft. I had to turn the baseball cap I was wearing, peak to the rear, so that it didn't fly off. I was, in fact, in the middle of a natural bridge, on a boulder of house-like dimensions that had been deposited over the chasm formed by receding glaciers and the river. The Parks Department and its volunteers had placed a series of stacked flat rocks on either side of the gorge so that the boulder was like an overpass of the animal variety, the kind that the Federal Government spent millions of dollars building so that fewer bears and elk would become Highway One statistics.

The natural bridge joined the trail to Bow Glacier Falls, with the trail to Bow Hut, one of the Alpine Club's numerous western shelters. Climbers most often used the hut, but local legend said that once it had been used by a runaway Stampede bride. There's proof in the *Giddy-up* belt buckle left behind by the woman who crossed the Wapta Icefield alone, and by the pair of size five Alberta Boot shit-kickers standing in the northeast corner of the hut. The bride had traded them for hiking boots and crampons but the recipient couldn't wear them and left them behind. The story goes that the new husband tried to follow his bride but turned back, too afraid of the deep ragged crevasses he had to cross to get anywhere near her. I had felt like the exhilarated runaway as I stood in the middle of the overpass. The waters of the Bow raged forty feet below me.

Sarah stood at the edge of the treeline, wrapped in a fleece jacket. She was about twelve feet above me on the trail to the falls. Nemit and Adam were below both of us on the hollow sounding ground that lined the gorge next to the improvised staircase. Nemit held on to the back of her son's yellow waterproof jacket while he threw chunks of slate and limestone into the cushion of clear water rushing over a massive pink boulder. I was just able to make out what they were saying.

"How far below the surface?" Nemit asked Adam.

"I can't tell, Mom. I can't hear rock hitting rock. Can you?"

"No, the water is too loud — look for a bigger stone."

Sarah held a small baggie of ashes. The top was open and air currents drew the lighter contents toward the noisy flow, as if my father was once again being seduced by the river. After two minutes, she choked the top closed. I expected her lower lip to tremble the way mine did, or that she would cry, but the only moisture on Sarah's face came from the air.

"Your turn," she yelled.

I took a moment to quiet the shaking in my hands. They held the crown shaped tiara I'd worn when I married Domenic. It rose to a small inverted "V" at its centre and was covered in little white daisies. A comb on the inside had helped it stay in my thick hair. Then I threw my least favourite headpiece over the headwaters as if it was a Frisbee, conservationists be damned. The throw involved my whole body, as if the thing had weight.

"God in heaven protect us!" Sarah said. "Be careful!"

The headpiece seemed to float in the cold air, then it broke through a thermal and came back, hit me in the chest, and landed by my feet. I tried again. This time I threw it downstream. It plummeted toward the flow. It was like looking at a whiteout. I blinked and saw flashes of colour. When I stared hard, I saw the water envelop what I'd surrendered.

"One," I mouthed in Sarah's direction.

"One," her lips said back.

Adam yelled and pointed.

"God — I thought it would sink immediately," Nemit said, laughing.

"Swiss lace on plastic. Nineteen eighty-five," I said, jumping from the boulder to the rock stairs.

"I thought it was wire," Nemit replied.

"Nope," I said, arms out for balance. She caught my hand and steadied me. I imagined the headpiece was already destroyed by the force of the water; the material separated from the plastic cutout, the glue, brittle with age, embroidered daisies bobbing, the plastic vacuumed into a sieve-like strain and drowned in a log jam.

Adam lay down on the hollow-sounding dirt bank. "Aw — it sank!" he cried.

"Adam! Adam!" Nemit screamed. He was prone, hanging over the bank from the waist up. She sat on his legs.

"I can see it, Mom! Please get off!" She did. He jumped to his feet. "Here, Rhegan, look through my binoculars. Look," he said again, pointing. "We can't leave it there."

I crouched beside him. When I focused the binoculars, I saw the headpiece. It was suspended from the branch of a partially submerged tree, fluttering in the spray. Then I watched as the plastic shape edged off the drowned bough, plunged over a two-metre ledge, and disappeared in the souse hole.

"Gone?" Adam asked.

"Gone," I replied. I showed him where to look.

"Why doesn't it come out?" he asked.

"A couple of reasons," I said. "The water might have flipped the headpiece up under the ledge where it could stay — unless the water level drops significantly."

"Or?" he asked.

"Or, the natural hydraulic power will re-circulate the plastic."

"Forever?"

"Technically. If the souse hole is a keeper."

"A keeper?" Sarah asked. She had climbed down from the trail, on her rear by the look of her pants and the dirt on her hands.

"A keeper," I said.

"I like that idea!" she said.

"Is that where Mr. Flett will go?" Adam asked.

Sarah sucked in her breath.

"Probably not," I told him. "You see, ash isn't really porous. It's more like sand."

"I get it. So it'll travel and sink?" he asked.

"Yes. The ashes become part of the river system. When the water goes down, the ash will settle. When the water level goes up — "

"I like the idea of being washed over," Nemit said. "It's comforting."

"I don't know," Sarah said backing away from us, holding the fanny pack that was now a permanent fixture at her waist.

Nemit went to her, and surrounded Sarah's shoulders with one lean, powerful arm; I was surprised when my mother relaxed against her.

"I'll help if you'd like," Nemit said, gently.

We climbed the steep bank up to the trail and began walking toward Bow Glacier. It took forty-five minutes to clear the trees and cross the moraine between the forest and Bow Glacier Falls. When we emerged from the woods, we stood in a natural amphitheatre, its rough walls lined by striations of colour. Further on, we crossed a draw of tumbled rock in single file. It was four hundred feet wide and I knew it would move if conditions were right. We could no longer see any part of the glacier. It was above us and, beyond the draw, the trail was a vague line in the moraine. Parts of it were covered in a thin glaze of running water that spilled over the top of the creek running from the glacier falls to the gorge. Nemit, Adam and I pulled our hoods over our heads and Sarah put on the poncho that was bundled in my small pack, the poncho she had worn when she and Ed visited Niagara Falls. We stayed on the path by looking for the next in a series of cairns, and moved toward each like careful shadows. We were mesmerized by the waterfall that spilled out of the iceberg-filled tarn at the base of Bow Glacier and fell almost two hundred feet before landing near us.

When we stopped, my mother rested her head against Nemit's upper arm. They seemed to glide over pebbles and small rocks to the grey-brown, muck-lined edge of the headwaters. I put my arm around Adam and we followed them, stumbling. We stood as close to the base of the falls as we could without losing our breath in the downdraft.

"My great-grandmother told me that committing her husband's body to the Ganges was an act of pure love," Nemit yelled.

"*Pure* love?" Sarah yelled back.

We huddled together like curious yearlings.

"*Pure love*. You see, he did not live the best life. He did not always treat my grandmother with respect. So, she washed him clean in the original river. Later, when she died, my family did the same for her. In that way she was able to join her husband."

"Just so," Sarah said, clutching her fanny pack.

Her words puzzled me at the time, but I didn't dwell on them or begin to connect them to the uneasy feeling I had when she left my father's ashes in my care.

"But this is the Bow," she continued.

"But here you are at its beginning where the water is uncontaminated."

Sarah turned the little pack until its cargo was in front of her. She removed the contents and unfurled her arms. The small bag rested in her palms as if it was an offering. Nemit gently opened it for her; the outer bag then the inner. The back of my mother's poncho waved in the wind like the ceremonial gown of a priestess in a mountaintop temple. Adam's thin arms circled my hips and his head rested against my ribcage. My breath was ragged, my jaw moved involuntarily, and my teeth slammed together repeatedly, as if I was preparing to charge.

I thought I was in control, thought I was handling Ed's death and my mother's grief. I suddenly realized that I hadn't *managed* any of those things at all. I had submerged them below the surface of my own skin and there they were, trying to escape.

Sarah crouched and submerged the bag. Nemit's hand sat reassuringly between my mother's shoulder blades until she stood, empty bag dripping from her blue hands.

We were all quiet on the drive down the Icefields Parkway. Our destination was Lake Louise. Adam slept for the forty or so minutes it took to get there. I had asked Nemit to stop the van twice before we reached the Trans-Canada Highway so that I could take photographs of Mount Temple. The north face was draped in cornices and the peak melted into the only white cloud in the quintessential Alberta blue sky.

I decided that weather and mood are related. The first time I hiked to Bow Glacier Falls was with Liam and the conditions were changeable. When we started our trek, it was warm. We were happy. By the time we reached the end of Bow Lake we were wearing light jackets over our T-shirts and shorts. We had assumed that we didn't need our stiff hiking boots — the trail was listed as a visitor's route in the guidebook we had. The trailhead was crowded and we had to excuse ourselves through swarms of tourists. When we reached the natural bridge, the tourists were far behind, preferring to photograph each other against the glacial background, the alpine rays touching their umbrellas, hats, and glove-protected hands.

The trail was covered in a treacherous quarter-inch of mud, and my white-and-blue-striped running shoes soon became unrecognizable. We grumbled at each other as rocks dug into the soles of our feet and we stumbled our way over the moraine. The top of the falls was shrouded in fog, but Liam insisted on standing in the spray before agreeing to turn around. We were soaked to the bone.

The descent was worse. Without the traction of thick-soled boots, we slipped and slid, fell and caught each other. We looked like we'd taken a mud bath when we got back to the trailhead. A new wave of tourists whisper-spoke and giggled behind rigid hands, which they held in front of their mouths, wanted a "picture please with Canadian hikers." We declined, but I sensed a shutter volley as I changed out of my wet clothes into dry ones next to the car, felt the eye of a zoom on my hide.

"This place gets under your skin no matter how long you have lived here, do you agree, darling?"

I was startled when my mother spoke over her shoulder from the front seat. I didn't like to be taken by surprise.

"Look at these peaks, think about this day, this place we have come to. Splendid!"

I agreed but didn't tell her. I smiled and nodded, but I must have looked sad because she reached back and touched my knee. I couldn't understand why I seemed to be the one suffering as a result of my mother's secret. Instead of feeling remorse for excluding me from her bizarre behaviour, she had invited me to join her, so that I, too, experienced her heartache. I thought about having to repeat the Bow Falls scene when she spoke.

The place we had travelled to was both a beginning and an end, a false start and an illusory finish. There would be three more such events on our trip before a real ending would take place. She would let my father go as we travelled the Bow River, send him into perpetuity when and where she thought appropriate. Sarah expected me to maintain a stiff upper lip, but I felt like collapsing. If my heritage really was true, technically the femur was the bone that had allowed me to stand up that day. That same bone was the one that allowed some bears to dance and others to show their prey their full height before they attacked. Nemit, Adam, my mother and I hadn't met any bears when we made our hike to the headwaters of the Bow River.

I imagined that we travelled not unlike past inhabitants of the Banff area such as the Whytes and the Simpsons: supported by friends who guided them and helped carry their gear. They had explored and painted in the mountains, had a hand in building the first lodges such as Skoki near Ptarmigan Valley, and Num-Ti-Jah, which sits on the edge of Bow Lake. Liam and I had taken in the spectacular view of Bow Glacier while we ate lunch in the old library there after the tour buses pulled out. My mother and I would also travel through the mountains, transported by the goodwill and presence of friends and vehicles, eccentric diversions, rich food, and bottles of wine. Nemit and her son, Adam, had ferried us in their vehicle, packed our gear in the cargo space, and walked with us toward a glacier. The difference was, unlike our foremothers, we weren't required to wear skirts, the kind that were hemmed ever so slightly so that they grazed the top of lace-up boots. It's nearly impossible to swim in wet, heavy woollens. The difference between those early mountain people and us was that we were travelling to get home, not adventuring to get away. However, none of those things could have prevented what happened near the end of our journey.

Later that night I slipped our yellow canoe between two narrow outcrops of sandy bank and watched it rock gently in the wash of the river.

"Why are we putting the boat in tonight?" Sarah asked.

We were alone on the bank of the Bow River in Lake Louise. Adam and Nemit had driven to Banff and would meet us there on July twenty-third, two days later. "Ritual," I said.

"Ritual?"

"I'm testing the water. I always get the length of the canoe wet before I take it on a long trip. "

"You are joking."

"No. I'm quite serious," I replied. "Liam and I always dipped the hull before embarking on the river."

I had been squatting next to the canoe. When I straightened up and wrapped the stern rope around my hand, Sarah's lips were pressed together in a straight-line smirk. She crossed her arms on her chest, and rocked back and forth on her feet.

The sound of the frigid water lapping the sides of the canoe amplified the quiet. I wondered if Liam had told her that he came to see me. "Okay, let's heave it out," I said, bending and holding on to the nearest strut, but my mother hadn't moved a muscle. Instead, she dug the toes of her white canvas deck shoes into the gravelled bank.

I realized that I had given her an opening, and assumed that she'd bring up her favourite son-in-law. I wanted to talk about Liam with Sarah but, by habit, avoided doing exactly that. My body was tense, my knees were straight, and my knuckles looked white against the black aluminium trim.

"You are going to hurt your back!" she said.

"Then help me!" I fired back.

My mother liked to make me wait because it made her feel as if she was in control, liked to infuriate me so that she had grounds to spar with me. When Sarah finally grabbed hold of the canoe, my straining hamstrings were thankful. Sarah is much stronger than her size suggests. My hand felt incidental next to hers. She helped me ease the canoe from between the lips of earth and we dragged it onto the coarse grass. The bank on the opposite side of the river was heavily treed, but we stood in an exposed area.

"Imagine us carrying the canoe, four twenty-litre waterproof bags, a Honda generator, and a tent across all the portages and man-made breaks," I said.

Our canoe lessons and preparations had consumed us for ten consecutive days before we left. I had insisted that my mother practise portaging with me. Each time she came over, we traipsed up and down the street near my home, canoe balanced over our heads. Often we'd do that two or three times during one of her visits.

"What, not up to it, darling? Honest to God, the people on Bow Crescent must think we are insane."

That evening in Lake Louise, we repeated an exercise we had performed many times. We rolled the canoe up on its side, each of us placing one hand on the exposed edge and one on a strut. Then we crouched and heaved together, lifted the canoe over our heads, strut hands switching quickly to the other edge before resting the struts on our shoulders. We used our hands to balance. Afterwards we walked across an area covered in wild grasses and moved toward the one-track road that circled the campground.

"I have no idea why you will not let me walk at the front," Sarah said, intentionally switching feet so that she was out of step with me.

"You'll be in the front when we paddle."

"Lovely — I will get wet when we go through standing waves."

I was happy to hear that she had read some of the canoeing book I gave her. "Don't worry," I teased, "there's only one set of rapids tomorrow." I wondered if there would come a day when neither of us would struggle for the lead.

None of the other campers paid any attention to us. They gathered around small fire pits or cast their shadows against the inside of illuminated tents. "Stay in step with me!" I sang.

"You're pulling," she said back.

We covered the last fifty yards of blacktop and switched to the manicured gravel that designated our campsite. I stopped alongside the tent. When I said, "Down," we shifted the canoe right, side parallel to the ground, and my mother banged the edge against her shin.

"I have a permanent bruise there!" she said.

I remember her lifting her pant leg, asking why I let Adam set up our tent on a cement pad. I told her that the ground was sopping wet, and that the pad was really for a picnic table.

"I do not see a table," she said.

"Parks took them away. Too many bears," I replied.

"Bears?" Sarah moved closer to me, stood with her back against the tent.

"They want people to use the cook shack out at the edge of the campground."

Sarah stared at me, eyes big.

"Remember the news a couple of years ago?" I said. "Two Swedes were mauled in their tent."

"Here?"

"Yep. In sunny Lake Louise. They probably had food in there."

"Darling," she said. "How about dinner in a restaurant?"

"We're camping."

"We could eat at the Post Hotel." She knew I loved to go there. She milled around, followed me closely as I gathered kindling for a fire.

"Careful, you're going to end up with wet feet," I said. "There's a hole off to the side of the cement pad. Let's get the generator going."

"We can not start *that* up in Lake Louise!"

"Then why'd we bring it?"

I had enjoyed teasing her, and she was quite right. Mountain campers held to a certain kind of etiquette. It would have been bad form to run the generator in Lake Louise, a high country *faux pas.*

"The Honda is for down the river," she said, " . . . for when we get to those obnoxious campsites that border the recreation areas — to keep the dirt-bikers and the power-boat people and the fly-fishermen away." She hated quiet, which is exactly why she searched out and bought the small generator.

I had agreed to take it, planning to use it along the way to keep animals out of our campsite, away from chewable materials like wetsuits, sweaty socks, the contents of our canoe bags and our tent. I pictured us portaging every dam and weir from Lake Louise to Carseland. I felt tired even though there was no doubt in my mind that Sarah was perfectly capable of carrying everything she brought.

I dropped a few logs next to the small fire pit. "Were you serious about dinner?" I asked.

She smiled, confident that she'd won.

As we rummaged in the tent for jackets and a flashlight, I wondered why my mother and I didn't just say what we meant. I had hoped that I might come to understand her better on that trip. Sarah was like a difficult teenager, confidence fluctuating, actions unsure. She jumped puddles on the way to the restaurant, the way I used to when Ed walked me to school.

I hadn't realized then why our roles had been switched, why I felt as if the natural order of things had been altered. But, I did come to understand that the gentle movement of Sarah's hand in her pocket was her way of staying close to its plastic-covered contents.

"I went to a funeral yesterday, a lovely service for the wife of a friend. The whole event was staged — a designer celebration," I said as we took our seats in the Post Restaurant.

"That is not how you saw Ed's funeral," Sarah replied. She shook her head as if her neck was stiff.

I took in the heavy décor with its log walls, pine tables, and duck-patterned wing back chairs, while Sarah rearranged her silverware.

"You're right. What you did today at the headwaters was far more impressive."

My mother smiled at what I said, and touched my hand across the table. She sat back in her chair, swinging her legs freely underneath, the way she could in most restaurant chairs.

I ordered a bottle of Argentinean Malbec, assuming that Sarah would choose red meat, and continued my story. "Joan arranged her whole funeral months in advance. Everything was colour-coordinated: from the clothes she and her family wore, to the flowers on her casket, to the priest's purple robes."

"Let me guess — cancer," she said as she examined a large print that featured the Three Sisters Mountains.

"Yep. Brain tumour."

"There is an epidemic, I tell you. Ed is one of the lucky ones. I want to have a good death. I want to go the way he did. Fast. No warning."

I agreed with her, but I had no idea at that point what she was planning.

Joan's daughter told me that her mother filled a book with instructions for the family. Instructions on how to plant the garden, how the Halloween decorations should be placed on the driveway, where the large Thanksgiving turkey roaster was kept, lists of what went where on the Christmas tree, lists of family birthdays and anniversaries — of both weddings and funerals. Sarah and I agreed that organization was helpful, but decided that my friend had gone a bit too far.

The server opened the wine, poured a small amount, and waited for my approval. She filled our glasses and wiped condensation from the fluted dish that held the candle in the centrepiece.

What Joan did was a waste of time. Her husband had planned to sell everything after her death, and move to a condominium.

As I was trying to leave the wake, he caught me and asked me to help him find one on the river.

Sarah wanted to know what else he said, if he had said anything about missing his wife. I told her he had, not wanting to upset her, because the truth was disappointing. He hadn't said much about Joan. He had a girlfriend waiting in the wings, someone that he'd been seeing for years. Instead, I told Sarah that attending the funeral made me feel strange.

"What do you mean, strange?" she asked.

I explained that the place had been packed when I got there. Both parking lots were leaking cars onto the street, and the foyer was full of people. Then I added that I'd stood through the hour-long Mass with Liam.

"Our Liam?" Sarah shrieked. "He was there and you did not tell me!"

I should have known better. "You know he's in town for a few weeks." That's when I decided to tell her he'd come to see me, but she wouldn't let me get that far.

"Cancel the trip! Forget the canoe!" She thumped her fists on the table, and wine sloshed over the brim of her glass. She never gave up the idea that we would reconcile.

"Everything all right, ladies?" The server appeared immediately.

"What is your name?" Sarah asked.

"Carolyn," she said, sponging the red stain on the white tablecloth.

"Well, Carolyn, I am really hungry. What is the best thing on the menu?"

"Rack of Lamb with raspber — "

"We will have two."

I waited until the server was a few feet away before I continued. "He stood really close to me, laughing at the parts of the eulogy that were supposed to be funny. I felt — " But my mother cut me off again.

"I think we should call Nemit right now and have her pick us up."

"Sarah."

"How could you not tell me this? How could you *go* somewhere with Liam and not tell me? Where is he staying?"

"I'm trying to tell you. He's out at his parents'. We're not cancelling the trip."

"Longview. Longview. The Highwood River, correct?"

"You're conniving, Sarah. We've talked about this before." I found myself wondering if he would participate in one of her schemes and, not for the first time, I thought that might be useful.

"Is he staying there for the whole time? I am going to ring him up. I am having him over. How *do* you feel? Maybe he was happy to see you. Did he leave with you?" She was relentless. "He *knew* you would be there. He mentioned a dying woman when I saw him at the camping place — "

I didn't tell her that I'd seen him since then.

"Did you have lunch?"

"Our friend died. I attended her funeral. He attended her funeral. There is no *we*." I still couldn't tell her that I wished I could have said, *we*.

"What was her name again? Nice service, you said — the casket?"

"The most expensive. Joan."

"Was she buried?"

"Cremated."

"What a waste. Was it open?"

I marvelled at Sarah's fascination with macabre details. "No."

Our dinner arrived and I was thankful for the interruption; it disturbed my mother's momentum and allowed me to re-group. Lamb used to be a favourite with Ed and Sarah on a Sunday. Yorkshire pudding, thick brown gravy, and mint sauce as well.

The server pressed the cloth that had been draped over her arm into the condensation pooling at the base of our wine glasses. "May I bring you anything else, ladies?" she asked.

"No, thank you, Carolyn," Sarah said. "Darling! Think about cutting the time to Calgary — forget about all those hazards. The ledges, the rapids, the wind on the reservoirs, and the currents caused by the dams, I am unsure about all that. Tomorrow we can start early, paddle right into Banff in one day, get Nemit to pick us up at the Boathouse — "

The Banff Boathouse had closed decades before. She meant the canoe rental place. I told her that we shouldn't skip the portage around Bow Falls. We had made arrangements. The Banff Springs Hotel would supply porters because we were staying the night. "Aren't you forgetting the reason we're paddling?" I asked, trying to change the subject. I didn't tell her, but I was beginning to have second thoughts about the stretch between the Horseshoe Dam and Calgary. I knew that section would be difficult.

"No. How could you let Liam go?"

"Why can't you? No excuses, Sarah." I still wasn't ready to tell her that I hadn't let go of him either. She knew of course about the Inglewood house, but I had convinced her, or so I imagined, that it hadn't sold because it was such an oddity.

We concentrated on the meal cooling in front of us. Sarah poured more wine, drank another glassful, and then another before finishing her dinner.

My mother hung onto people tooth and nail while I kept my distance, but we journeyed together to let go, a travel oxymoron.

The server offered to take our plates and bring us the dessert menu, but Sarah scared her off by striking her wine glass with her fork and asking if the roof was leaking. Our tablecloth was damp.

"It's just the sweat from your water glass," I said. Then I thought about the fact that Ed was in my mother's pocket. I swallowed hard. "Drink up," I said sitting back in my chair as if I could separate myself from the strange scene. "We're paddling in the morning."

People take trips to get away, gain experience, collect paraphernalia, and meet new friends. We travelled to go home, to forget what we knew, to cast off our belongings, and disconnect from family — disconnect over and over. We paddled several stretches of river and Sarah took her time. She separated herself from my father by degrees. Why my mother hadn't wanted to leave all of Ed in one place was beyond me then. Later on, I understood why she did that; the shock of losing everything at once causes immeasurable pain.

On the way back to our tent that night, she insisted on holding my hand. I felt like a mother with a dependent cub, one that had tailed its parent far too long.

21

SARAH WALKED DOWN TO THE RIVER. She found the cut in the bank that we had used the night before and dropped the first of the canoe bags and the generator onto the grass. When she came back, the tent and fly lay drying in the morning sun. I handed her a cup of milky tea and she held it against her head.

"Something in it to take the edge off," I said.

"Ed's remedy?"

I nodded and folded up the legs of the one-burner stove, slipped it into a bright blue padded sack. It was six-thirty in the morning; we were the last overnighters to break camp. The tent and the grass across the road shone with dew.

"I only had three and a half glasses," she continued. "I cannot drink anymore."

"You never were a big drinker, Sarah."

"How many glasses did you have?"

"One," I replied, sipping my tea from a speckled tin cup.

"Well at least I didn't go over the top about Liam."

I sat cross-legged on an insulated mattress and opened the valve to expel the air. We both wore full wetsuits with the tops turned down, fleece jackets, and old running shoes.

"I will make another trip," Sarah said, gathering up another canoe bag, the small stove, and our life jackets. She slipped her arm through the two jackets, slung the bag over her shoulder, and dangled the stove from her other hand. The jackets rubbed rhythmically across her shins as she walked away from me.

Sarah rarely felt guilty about bringing up Liam but I knew she felt sheepish that morning. For years I had hoped that she'd let go of Liam, even though she said he was like the son she never had. He dug her garden, painted her fence, drove her out on stormy nights, attended Mass with her every Sunday he was in town. I wondered why I hadn't been able to admit that I understood her feelings about him, even to Nemit.

I rolled the mattress and knelt on it to force the rest of the air out, closing the valve when I was done. Then I slipped the mattress into another stuff-sack and repeated the exercise for Sarah's.

"How much longer?" she said when she came back. "I am anxious to go."

I was surprised. "Let's carry the cooler next, then we'll come back and fold up the tent. That's about it, apart from our own bags."

Sarah took the two rolled-up mattresses and I took the bag containing the items we planned to cast away. We lifted the cooler together.

"Maybe I should take that bag, Rhegan," she said.

"I'll be careful," I replied. "Besides the baggies, I have the makings of a box kite in there."

"A box kite?"

"Remember the frame Ed made for me?" The cooler rocked between us.

"In Guides? You were ten! And you call me a pack rat! What exactly are you planning to do with that?"

"Fly it of course!" I replied.

"There are too many trees along the river."

"I'm thinking of Johnston Canyon and the Ink Pots."

"A hike?" Sarah said.

"We'll want the exercise after sitting all day."

"I suppose," she said, as we set our cargo next to the bags she had already carried. "We have not been there for years."

"The trail will be busy until we reach the first set of falls, but not too many people continue to the Ink Pots and beyond. Game?"

"Game!" she replied. "The fog is lifting."

"Let's get the tent, and the last of the gear, then the canoe."

Sarah ran back to the flattened site. My hips and knees complained when I tried to follow at the same pace. I ran my body marathon-thin five years before that and I never did recover. My mother had better bones than I did.

"Sixty-four," I said, cinching the last tie-down over our load.

"Not until next year, darling! You cannot rush birthdays," Sarah replied.

"Kilometres," I finished.

"Oh — is that a lot on water?"

"We'll be fine. About thirty-six to the campground today and the rest tomorrow."

That morning, her silhouette was missing the fanny pack and the auxiliary bits of Ed that I sometimes saw bulging in her pocket. She looked free. Her thin legs were outlined in black rubber, her yellow life jacket was open in front, and her hair stood up in clumps all over her head.

"Ready?" she asked, teeth chattering.

"Ready steady," I replied. "Remember how to eddy out?"

"Yes." She distributed her weight evenly and stayed low getting into the front of the canoe. She knelt, legs wide, fastened the clasps at the front of her life jacket, and pulled on her gloves.

I handed her the coyote paddle that my father had carved, and an aluminium paddle that we kept near the bags for emergencies.

"Where is the bailer?"

"Should be by your feet — at the front of the gear."

"Ah — got it. Okay, Rhegan, get in!"

"Hang on — the throw bag will sit there, just off to the side of the cooler," I tossed it to her. "And here's the map case." I put the bear paddle in the stern.

We were about fifty metres below the Louise rapids. Before we cast off, we watched two kayakers negotiate their way through the rough, boat-eater chop. The first used her whole body, sank one end of her paddle vertically, swung her kayak around a boulder, and plunged through the standing waves at the end of the hazard. The second kayaker rolled, came up, and grounded himself on a gravel bar. The woman yipped and pumped her paddle over her head, then removed her nose clip and yelled at her partner to stick to the outside the rest of the way.

"I am not sure that looks like fun!" Sarah said.

I smiled, and began to unravel the knot in the line. The woman waved to us and eddied out. She freed the spray skirt and stepped onto the stony bank. Then she lifted the kayak over her head and began the three-hundred-metre portage back to the parking lot west of the rapids.

"Strong," Sarah said.

"Those things weigh less than half what this canoe weighs. Remember what to do if we tip?"

"On my back, feet downstream," she said. "But I will not have to do that, will I, Rhegan? Submerging my body in water this cold will knock me out in less than three minutes."

"Eight or ten," I replied. Then I thought I heard a soft snorting noise, and turned my head in the direction of the cook shack.

"Comforting," she said softly. "Shall we?"

I stood up, hands on my hips, nose into the wind.

"What is it, darling?"

"Nothing." I was sure I had imagined the animal noises. I took in the forward line and threw it to Sarah. She used her paddle to move the canoe away from the bank. With one foot in the canoe and one in the water, I pushed off. Sarah paddled for the middle of the river, bow slightly downstream while I arranged myself in the stern.

"Stop paddling!"

Sarah held her paddle ready while I sank mine and used it as a rudder. The current took the front of the canoe.

"Paddle!" I said when we were almost parallel to the bank.

"Paddling," Sarah said, "paddling!"

We pulled together.

The river flows fast in July and the section immediately east of Lake Louise presents few hazards. Bathed in morning light, we rode the glacial flow through the Bow Valley at the base of mountains that were the colour of West Coast sand. Some slopes were majestic, covered three quarters of the way up with thick, deep green forests. Others were coated in stands of dead trees that had pink-red branches. Patches of rock glimmered in the sun through kilometre after kilometre of blight-ravaged trees. Alberta Forest Management had contained the spread with controlled burns, creating breaks that the disease couldn't cross. Some sections of forest had been sacrificed so that thousands of hectares might survive.

Sarah and I reached the campsite below Johnston Canyon by two o'clock. The rapids I expected to negotiate were only rolling waves at high water. She did well, didn't get wet until we eddied out. "Holy Mother of God!" she screamed, as she stepped into the frigid water that engulfed her from the knee down. "Shit! The current — Rhegan!" She fought to hold onto the front of the canoe, bent over, muscles straining for the seconds it took me to swing the stern parallel to the bank. "I think we should eddy out the other way," she continued when I stood on the riverbed. "Parallel — together — like in the lessons."

I dropped my paddle in the canoe and joined her at the bow. We backed up onto the bank, dragging the front of the canoe out of the water.

"Feet cold, Sarah?"

"Understatement!" she said.

She sat down, took her runners off, and pulled up the legs of her wetsuit. Her skin looked blue, the way my father's had the last time I saw him. "Are you not cold, darling?"

I wiped my hand across my mouth. "Yep," I said. "Let me grab our gear bags and we can put on dry shoes."

She rubbed her hands vigorously up and down her shins, then grabbed one foot, pulled it up chest height, squeezed, put it down and took up the other — the same stretch I used after running. I loosened the tie-downs and pulled out the bags we needed.

"We can camp anywhere here," I said, looking across the small plateau we were standing on. If we had walked directly north through the tall trees, we would have reached a National Park campground.

"I think we should pitch the tent close to the forest," she said, jumping up and down as if warming up for a run.

I carried the tent bag to the piece of ground Sarah paced out.

"Just a few rocks to clear first," she said. I could tell that she was tired. Paddling took more out of her than I thought it might.

"After we're organized, let's have a bite to eat and rest for a while," I said.

When the tent was up Sarah disappeared inside with the mattress pads. I put the fly on and pegged it out, and ferried the rest of our bags from the canoe. I divided the gear between the two vestibules, gently resting the twenty-litre bag on Sarah's side.

"Okay," I said, unzipping the door on my side of the tent.

Sarah was sound asleep, softly wheezing the way Ed used to after a day in the shop, the mattresses still in the long cylindrical bags under her head. I covered her upper body with my fleece jacket, and sat back on my haunches, watching her the way I imagined she watched me when I was a child.

I decided to build the box kite. I moved quietly outside and settled on a rock near the canoe, taking stock of the materials. The dowels that Ed had cut for me when I was a child were still straight. The four longest pieces measured thirty inches, each notched in four places: twice near each end, six inches apart. Sixteen smaller dowels, each fifteen inches long, were cut to fit the notches. I tried to swallow and ease the tightness in my throat.

From the twenty-litre bag I pulled Ed's smallest hammer, a small box of pin-like nails, and a tiny tube of wood glue, the kind used in the balsa planes Ed and I flew over the river at the back of the old house. I began the frame by fitting two short pieces into two long sections, then gently turning the skeleton around. The trick was to repeat the exercise at the other end without the first coming apart. I was unsuccessful. I breathed in and felt a sharp stab in my windpipe.

I remembered the method Ed made me write out and give to Brown Owl when I was about ten. Build side one. Build side two. Join side one to side two, forming side three. Apply glue to each joint. Use nails to secure the joints without splitting the dowel. Use remaining pieces to build side four, close the frame. My eyes began to fill with moisture.

I made three bundles of dowel and held them together with twist ties, squatted next to the river, and submerged the first bundle for five minutes, alternating hands every few seconds. Then I found a flat rock big enough to hold the other two in place. Moist wood was less likely to split when I nailed the frame together. Tears ran down my checks and off the end of my nose.

I built side one: two thirty-inch dowels and four fifteen-inch dowels. The glue held. I set the frame in the grass, retrieved another bundle, and built side two. I took the last bundle out of the water and glued four dowels to side one, holding each in place for some time before moving on to the next. They stood perpendicular to the frame on the grass. I was hyperventilating.

"Do you need a hand, darling?" Sarah asked in a sleepy voice.

"How long — have you been — watching me?" I managed to say between sobs.

"Long enough to see you add the last few posts." She yawned and rubbed my back with the palm of her hand. After a few minutes she sat down, legs in a flat 'V', and held the vertical sections, one at a time, while I attached side two. My tears were subsiding.

"Why did you never build this kite with Ed?" she asked. The wind made her hair dance.

"I locked him in the shop — remember?" My breathing was almost normal again.

"How could I forget that?"

"Don't move!" I left her holding up the side I'd just added and retrieved my camera. When I came back, the frame stood on its own, long edges on the ground. Side three up. I snapped a close-up of Sarah lying on her stomach, looking through the frame at me. It was one of the last photographs I took of her.

After I added the remaining dowels to close the frame, I used the hammer and sank sixteen tiny nails into the joints. Only one dowel threatened to split.

Shortly before five o'clock Sarah started our one-burner, iso-butane stove and set a pot of water to boil for pasta. "How will I heat the sauce?" she asked.

"Pour the water out, add the sauce, and put the pot on the burner for a few minutes," I replied. "I'll look around for some wood for a fire and get back to the kite later."

I made a pile of dead wood and split some of the smaller pieces for kindling. After we ate, I brought out the fabric that I would use to make the two box-like end sections.

"God Almighty," Sarah said. "Is that the silk shift you wore when you married Jack?"

"Yes," I said, "excellent kite material! I've cut it off leaving the bodice and some of the fabric below the waistline intact. Sarah choked.

"No point in completely destroying the dress. I can hem the top and wear it. I only brought the skirt section."

She expelled tea through her nose, before managing to repeat, "The skirt — section," and blowing her nose on a hanky.

I stared, fabric suspended between my hands. I'd decided at home to leave the skirt as it was until I'd built the box-kite frame. Then I'd packed pinking shears, needles and thread in my gear bag.

"I can't believe it!" she said, trying to gain control. She put the hanky into her pocket. "Where do you plan to cut the material?" She coughed again, trying to clear liquid from her windpipe.

"On the canoe," I said.

I expected a rant, but she was quiet.

We took the throw bag, bailer, paddles, and life jackets out of the canoe and turned it over. The hull settled to one side.

"Throw your wetsuit over, inside out," I said. "Make sure it's completely dry for tomorrow."

I laid the dress section on the upturned canoe and cut through the back seam, before folding it lengthwise and cutting it in half.

"My God," Sarah whispered.

She held the fabric taut as I cut eight-inch-wide strips the length of the skirt.

"That does it, Sarah. I'll start the fire."

"Are you sewing tonight?"

"The light is still good. Sun won't set completely until nine-thirty or so. Want to help?"

"Will that start with a match?"

"One match," I said. The secret was in the fire starters, which I broke up and pushed under the small pile of wood. Once the wood caught and I added a few bigger pieces, Sarah and I sat cross-legged with the kite between us, sewing the silk around the dowels near the ends of the frame.

That night when I slept next to my mother, I didn't feel the urge to escape. We started on our sides, backs touching. When I awoke, I was facing her, my body curled against her for warmth.

We left the tent to dry, and hiked to Johnston Valley carrying the kite and a small pack. We followed a dew-covered path though the trees behind our tent, crossed the Bow Valley Parkway, the two-lane mountain road that snakes its way between Lake Louise and Banff, and walked toward Johnston Canyon Lodge. The parking lot next to it was teeming with cars and rented motor homes.

Sarah looked at me in amazement.

"I know!" I said. "I also know that if I'd told you we were this close to a hotel, last night would have been quite different!"

"It was different," she said.

We followed a paved path for about one kilometre to the lower Canyon Falls. The ten-metre drop seemed just as incredible as it did when I was small. "Want to go into the cave?" I asked Sarah. It was behind the waterfall.

"I think not!" she said, shivering in the updraft the plunging water made.

The kite wobbled in my hand. We continued to the upper falls, climbing a set of stairs that took us up and over the canyon lip. I was careful, one hand on the rail, the other holding the kite. I kept an eye on Sarah, who walked in front of me, head down as if inspecting the trail for hazards.

"The area feels as if — it has been tamed," Sarah said, gasping.

She was right. I thought it felt unnatural, and wanted to roar at the few people already encroaching on the trail during their return trip. "By the time we come back we'll have to go through crowds," I said panting for breath. "So stick to the inside wall as much as possible on the lower trail."

We followed the white water and reached the upper falls quickly. Sarah strode along the well-worn path that cut through a stand of Douglas fir and Lodgepole pine. I was almost jogging to keep up, kite in both hands in front of me. She stood in the downdraft, hands on her hips like Peter Pan ready for take-off.

"Twenty minutes!" she said. "Last time we were here you were twelve. Ed and I had to run the whole way to keep up with *you* — Kite intact?"

"In — tact," I managed.

"Want me to carry it? Too heavy for you?"

I handed the kite to her and led the way along another half-kilometre of easy trail to a junction with a narrow access road. I felt the silk stretching off the frame, reaching out of Sarah's hands toward my back.

"How much farther, do you think?" Sarah asked.

"About two kilometres."

My mother la-la-la-ed her way through a forest of white spruce. "Sing with me!" she bellowed.

"I don't know the words!" I sang back off-key. "You're afraid of bears, aren't you?"

"I'm not afraaaid — of what I cannot seeeee!" she wailed at an operatic pitch that hurt my ears. I was glad she sang. Some trees had been stripped of their bark and marked by grooves in a five-claw pattern where the trail narrowed at the edge of the forest.

"Here!" she sang at the top of an incline. "You carry the kite."

"Is that the tune to 'God Save The Queen'?"

"Long live our noble queen!" she continued, marching.

We followed the rough path down into the meadows and stopped once to drink before reaching the Inkpots. Six natural Karst springs gurgled water up out of the ground at four degrees Celsius. We ate chocolate bars and apples while we examined the quartzite around the edges of each spring. The kite, which I had set on the ground, tumbled off like a weed at the first hint of a breeze. Sarah caught up with it easily, and gently grounded the box-frame.

"Time to fly." I took off my pack.

The end of a long veil, which I'd rolled to the size of a volleyball, flapped from side to side. "Let's stand the kite on its end," I said to Sarah.

We knelt. I tied the end of the veil to the vertical dowel just below the top section of silk, twisted it, and wrapped it around the next upright. I did this three times before I let out a length and did the same thing at the bottom section of silk.

"You better tie it off," Sarah said.

I knotted the veil to the base of the frame, then let out the rest to make the tail. The kite vibrated on the ground under Sarah's hands. One by one, I extracted five, frilly bridal garters from the pack, cut them open and tied them at equal distances along the eager material.

"You are amazing, darling!" Sarah watched as the tail waved up and down, jerking at each tie.

"Just the string," I said.

"The wind is picking up!"

Calmly, I fixed four equal lengths of nylon to the top and bottom corners, brought them together and tied them separately to an old metal key ring.

"What? No wedding band?" Sarah said.

"Got to save something for further down the river," I laughed.

I began to knot the main string to the ring. The grass around us looked like it was running away.

"Hold the kite!" Sarah pulled a baggie out of her fanny pack and pierced a hole in the plastic below the sealed top. She cut off a section of string and threaded it through the hole, knotted it once, then tied the ends to the base of the frame next to the tail. She made another small hole in the bottom corner. Grey dust trickled out.

I pictured the deep lines on my father's rough hands, and felt ill.

"Hurry!" she cried. She held the kite down for the last time while I knotted the main string.

"Ready."

Sarah stood with the top of the frame in one hand. The kite billowed out behind her.

I ran in the opposite direction, spooling the line out as I went. "Now!" I yelled.

She jumped and released the kite. The string was immediately taut. I held both ends of the spool loosely and let the wind decide how far the silk and veil would travel. Ed's ashes zigzagged across the horizon in front of Castle Mountain. Then they were gone. Sarah turned to me, white hair dusted with grey, hand over her mouth just as the end of the string took flight.

I had trouble with endings, had trouble staying composed on the hike back. I was in front of Sarah most of the time, not listening to her account of the flight over the meadow. I enjoyed endings that remained whole and undistorted — as they did in fairy tales. When Sarah prompted me for my version, I couldn't speak. I was mortified by the image of my mother with a powdered halo that circled her head like a sundog, haunted by the shadow that clung to her forehead like a thumbed cross on Ash Wednesday.

"Well?"

I exhaled loudly through my nose. "Well, what?" I managed.

"Stop doing that! What about the house in Inglewood?" Sarah asked.

I had completely missed the post-flight report and her question about the Inglewood house.

I did have something to say about beginnings. Beginnings interested me more than endings and whenever Sarah asked me about Domenic or Jack, Raj, Lynn, or Thomas, I stuck to the beginnings, but my mother rarely asked me about those husbands.

The home that Liam and I renovated during our years together was still mine. He and I had managed a beginning while we lived there. "Still not sold," I said. "Watch out for the crowds down there." We descended the stairs and retraced our steps on the paved path to the trailhead. It was impossible to hold a conversation and I was thankful. I ploughed through the mobs feeling as if I was dragging a cadaverous weight. When we got closer to the trailhead, I wished that I could run up the canyon walls and spring through the trees, branch to branch like a racoon.

My mother bumped into me when I stopped suddenly on the north side of the Parkway. Two black bears crossed the road five hundred feet downwind of us. They ran into the woods like a pair of scared schoolchildren who'd been told not to speak to strangers.

"I never thought I would say this," Sarah whispered, chin on my shoulder, "but I think we will be safer in the canoe."

22

YOU UNDERSTAND PERFECTLY NOW WHAT YOUR husband told you about trying something new. When you allow your daughter's friend to help you dispose of the first bag of ashes you feel unsure of yourself. When you commit the second bag to the air, you feel calm. You surprise yourself; you feel a kind of awe, but not because of what you have accomplished.

You saw emotion wrack your daughter's body as she stood next to Bow Falls. You delighted in her tears as you watched her build the kite. You felt a sensation that repeated itself when you realized your hair was thick with ash. You craved more of the same and you felt strangely pleased at the idea that you should run your fingers through your hair. You indulge yourself after you leave the riverbank and the canoe has settled into what you call the middle flow, that subtle v-shape it makes in the water that reminds you of a flight of geese. You switch your paddle from the left to the right side of the bow, and glance back to make sure your daughter is paying attention. You rest the paddle across your lap, touch the ends of your hair as if you just had it set, and then you scrub the fingertips of your right hand on your scalp. Fine particles fall onto the shoulders of your life jacket, graze your bare arms, land on the legs of your wetsuit, and the cargo piled behind you. Your daughter's face shows silent revulsion. You smile at her and you wonder if she will throw up the way she did on the roundabout at the park when she was little.

You consider taking a practise plunge in the river, the kind that Marilyn Munroe took in *The River of No Return*. You ponder the idea for a while, but your lower legs begin to ache at the thought. Perhaps a bear, one of those that you saw on the Parkway, will do for you what you hope to do for yourself.

23

My mother and I got into the water below the Johnston Canyon campground. Twenty minutes after that we stopped to assess the rapids Red Earth Creek makes as it tumbles into the Bow. We decided not to portage.

"They're class three at low water, class two now," I said. "I know we can make it, Sarah. Liam and I have paddled this section three or four times."

"All right," she agreed. "If Liam thinks it safe, it must be safe. I do not relish the thought of emptying the canoe when we just packed it a little while ago."

I checked the gear and we paddled away from the rocky edge. As soon as the canoe entered the deep troughs of the colliding waters, Sarah screamed, blood-curdling sounds penetrated the forest around us. Glacial water poured in over the front of the canoe.

"Paddle!" I yelled. "Sarah, paddle or we'll go right in!"

She stroked, kneeling in a pool of greenish water that was just two degrees above zero.

"Hard! Pull to the inside!" I moved from my seat and knelt as low as possible in the body of the yellow canoe. She pulled hard. If she hadn't we would've gone wide and dropped over a small ledge.

"Rhe — gan! Rhe — gan!"

More water spilled over the bow. For a long second we float-turned as if the waves were smooth, and the canoe was weightless. The water lifted the stern section. Then the bow, suddenly heavy, banged against the surface.

I fought to keep the stern from swinging forward, didn't want the canoe to overturn. We both used sideslip strokes; I pried at the stern and Sarah drew at the bow. She leaned out as far as she dared. Her strong arms kept the canoe on the inside curve. My collarbones rubbed against my life jacket and my shoulders shook uncontrollably. "Eddy right!" I called.

We dug deep with our paddles as if driving a dragon boat in a still water race, and beached the canoe on the gravel outcrop at the end of the rapids. Our body weight flew forward as the canoe hit dry land.

We had attracted the attention of a busload of tourists who were photographing the Bow Valley at Red Earth Creek. The crowd in the parking lot was out of sight from where we landed, but a few people ran along the portage route to see if we'd made it. A man in a uniform and two women holding cameras returned my wave. I breathed hard, looking downstream until the echo of their feet on the hollow ground had stopped.

"Get out, Sarah," I said. She was still kneeling in the bow. I got out and helped her, took her arms above the elbows, urged her to stand. Her lips were blue. The fact that she was quiet disturbed me. I pulled off my life jacket and she sank onto it. Her feet and lower legs had no colour. I rubbed one, then the other until she told me that I was hurting her. I took her pulse. It was racing. I sat next to her, arms around her shoulders until her body stopped quivering.

"F-fuck," she said before standing up and walking around. She shook her legs and arms out like a runner preparing for a race.

I used the bailer to empty as much water from the canoe as possible. I couldn't tip it myself and hadn't wanted to unload and re-pack it again. That's when something caught my eye. I walked southeast toward the low rumble of traffic on Highway One. Partially concealed in the shade of a thick band of spruce were the remnants of a bear kill. The bones of an elk protruded from a shallow pit that had been covered with branches torn from nearby trees. I looked toward the bank on the other side of the river. It was rocky and inaccessible. The hair on my neck stood up and my fight-or-flight responses were doing battle. I felt the pocket of my life jacket for the folding knife that I put there. I told Sarah that we should go.

"Is the gear wet?" she asked.

I stayed calm despite the way I felt. "There's a bit of water left in the middle of the canoe, but nothing inside the bags is wet." I checked the hard plastic case that now contained my camera. "Everything is just fine," I said. "The sooner we go, the sooner you'll warm up."

"Wh . . . what about Ed?" She stammered.

I knelt on the pebbled shore and unfurled the top of the canoe bag, looked momentarily toward the edge of the trees then back at our cargo. "Dry as a bone!" I said. Two baggies stared up at me.

I sometimes forgot that my mother was not my age. I forgot that there were things that affected her body more than mine. She couldn't warm up despite the fact it was sunny and twenty-five degrees Celsius. She shivered sporadically as we paddled under the high bridge at the end of the Bow Valley Parkway and continued toward the lazy slope of Mount Rundle on the south side of the Trans-Canada Highway. In spite of the effort required to cross the deep standstill water of the Bow near Vermillion Lakes, Sarah didn't warm up until later when she immersed her body in a hot tub in the basement of the Banff Springs Hotel.

We saw the limousine pull up while we paddled the deceivingly gentle current that led to Bow Falls. The slow, deep water said nothing of the peril ahead. A line of buoys were strung across the river between two *Danger* signs. Two porters had been waiting for us near the former site of the historic Banff Boathouse. Despite our ordeal, Sarah and I were almost on schedule.

We watched the porters, who wore burgundy vests, light cigarettes and lean against the hood of the black vehicle. I knew that the people crowded around the car weren't locals. Banffites avoid pomp, and resent the attention that some filmmakers bring to town. Tourists crowded the car. They peered at the dark glass, looking for a famous face.

"What is going on?" Sarah asked, pointing her paddle.

"That's our car."

"How do you know?"

"I see the poles of the canoe trailer sticking up behind the trunk."

After we beached the canoe, the porters, Luke and Michel, introduced themselves and welcomed us to Banff, took our arms and escorted us to the car. We sat inside while they loaded the gear into the huge trunk, listening to them marvel over our light canoe. The leather seats were draped with the rough wool of traditional Hudson's Bay blankets edged in red, yellow, and green. Thick covers, purely for show on hot days, but Sarah wrapped herself in one.

As the car pulled out of the parking lot, she waved like the Queen Mother in a carriage, posed like Garbo, and let a woman on Bear Street photograph her profile through the open window. We passed the Whyte Museum and turned left toward the bridge at the end of Banff Avenue, then turned right and crossed the Bow. The car smoothed its way to the entrance of the castle-like Banff Springs Hotel.

"You are like a leettle doll!" Michel told Sarah, as he guided her rubber-clad body into the lobby.

I felt relieved and uncomfortable after we'd settled in. Sarah seemed better, but she still made me uneasy. We sat in the deep pool in the ladies' spa. Two robes and two bottles of French water were within easy reach on the tiled floor.

My mother assessed my body, and watched me as I slipped into the pool of too-hot water. "That was an uneventful day," she said over the low rumble of the water jets, "except for the part where we were nearly killed."

I smiled and put my head back to wet my hair.

After five minutes of silence, Sarah sank under the water. When she came up, she made eye contact with me. "Did you see the look on the faces of the people paddling in front of the canoe rental place today?" A canoe and two kayaks had collided while their passengers stopped paddling to watch us get in the stretched-out car.

"A limousine pulling a canoe trailer is pretty unusual," I said.

She sipped the expensive water and added, "Someone should bottle the Bow."

My face was dripping and my skin was bright red.

She closed her eyes, rested the back of her head on the edge of the pool.

I took the opportunity to get out and wrap myself in a robe. As I stretched out on a lounge, I thought about the time it had taken for us to paddle from Johnston Canyon to Red Earth Creek. I decided that it had been more than long enough for the animal population to take note of us.

As we opened the door to our room, the telephone rang.

Sarah answered and I heard Nemit's shrill voice. "Where have you been?"

"Oh, we were just soaking," Sarah said. "I got you the price list, and the rates for a day in the spa are very reasonable."

I took the phone from her.

"Didn't you get enough water today?" Nemit said. "Don't let Rhegan pressure you into doing things that make you uncomfortable — "

"Don't tell me you're worried," I said. "You know how many times I've been on the Bow."

"Not with your mother! Is she all right? Has she recovered properly? I left a message for you. The desk clerk was supposed to tell us the moment you arrived!"

"She got a little wet at the beginning of the day, but — "

"Rhegan! What room are you in? I'm coming up there."

"She's fine," I said leaning over the wide window ledge and taking in our view of Bow Falls. Despite the fact that it was almost dark, people with cameras lined the trail next to the crashing white water, and the parking lot at its base was full of vehicles. Two women wearing hijabs climbed into one of four large, orange dinghies. They were about to embark on a twenty-five minute float-tour that ends at the Banff Park boundary. They waved at two men who stood on the shore where the Spray

River meets the Bow. The men didn't respond; instead, they climbed into a golf cart and drove across a small bridge, headed for the ninth hole of the Springs course. I watched the two women in the wide watercraft with the single rower standing in its centre. Their bodies bobbed and swayed as the dinghy disappeared around a curve lined by tall rocky banks.

"Rhegan."

"Hmm?"

"We're meeting you for brunch tomorrow, right?"

"Exactly as planned."

"We've brought you a gift," she said, "something very practical that you can take with you for the next section. Unless — haven't you changed your mind about paddling across all those man-made lakes yet? She's too old."

"Nonsense," I said. "She's in better shape than I am." I had already decided to forego paddling the section of river between the Horseshoe Dam and Calgary. "We'll paddle tomorrow from Bow Falls to the Dam. After that, you can drive us back to Calgary. We'll have an extra day at home before we paddle to Carseland."

"Thanks, darling! I knew you would make the right decision," Sarah said, from the telephone in the large bathroom.

The next morning I was pleased and surprised. Nemit's gift was a collapsible canoe trailer. I lifted it.

"Only four kilos," Adam said proudly. "Mom found it in Undercurrents, the canoe shop on Bowness Road."

"It's wonderful!" I said.

"Good for up to one hundred and fifty pounds," he added.

We stood on the cobbled driveway in front of the Banff Springs Hotel, waiting for Nemit's van. Sarah and I were dressed in our wetsuits. My mother held the twenty-litre canoe bag in her left hand. Nemit was between us. She had one arm around Sarah and the other around me as we watched two porters struggle up the stony drive with the canoe. They carried it right side up.

Adam ran toward them, pulling the mini trailer at the end of its long, tie-down straps. He motioned to the two porters. They set the canoe on the padding and watched, arms folded over their chests, as Adam steered the contraption to where we waited.

"Easy!" he called.

"You won't have to strain," Nemit said to Sarah squeezing her arm.

"You are so thoughtful, dear," Sarah replied, repeating a phrase she had often used with Ed.

Nemit and I threw gear into the back of her van while Adam and Sarah started pushing the canoe trailer towards the place where I'd watched the dinghies being launched the day before. As we followed them down the road that curved behind the hotel, I told Nemit that it would take us about three hours to reach the Horseshoe Dam near the town of Seebe.

My mother and I pushed off from the wide area below Bow Falls wished well by a crowd of unfamiliar wavers. Two naked sunbathers watched us from the cliffs a few hundred metres downstream.

We float-bobbed on standing waves most of the way between Banff and Canmore, avoiding trees that hung out over the water and those that swept the surface from below. Sarah was on lookout and when she alerted me, I steered the canoe clear of single waves that crested on rocks in the middle of the river.

The mountains in the east Rundle Range seemed taller than those further west. We became part of that optical illusion as the ground elevation began to fall. We travelled quickly toward the Banff Park boundary, the Three Sisters Mountains and the first part of the long s-bend in the Bow that took us away from their shadow.

When it leaves Canmore, the river flows under Highway One again. Then it meanders northeast toward Grotto Mountain, before curving east until it meets the tumbling white water of the Kananaskis. The two rivers pool and swirl against the ageing wall of Horseshoe Dam near the utility company town of Seebe. The people there lived on a high plateau, which could be reached only by crossing a one-lane wooden bridge over the Kananaskis. Several years after Sarah and I made our trip, TransAlta put the town up for sale, but I couldn't make a bid, my real-estate license was redundant by then, having expired when I did.

As we paddled the canoe towards the Horseshoe Dam, it carried Sarah and me, the twenty-litre bag, the cooler, the stove, an axe, the canoe cart, and our safety gear. Nemit had the rest of our paraphernalia in her van. As we paddled, I wondered why my friend had suddenly become of such interest to my mother, but I didn't focus on Sarah's about-face for too long, deciding that it was just another example of her state of mind. I was soothed by the bubbling downhill water and by the sound of her voice. Sarah sang love songs from old musicals, as if responding to my quiet breathing with lullabies, the way I had longed for her to do when I was a child. I was calmed, and lost in my own thoughts. I used my bear paddle as a rudder when we negotiated the overflow channel from the Bow onto Lac Des Arcs.

My grandfather, Harold Flett, read romance novels when he was eighty-eight. Pored over them with an intensity I'd never seen before. He took the old teak and canvas deck chairs down

MEMOIR OF A GOOD DEATH

to the riverbank, set them up and didn't come in until the book was done. Read one a day every day of the week except Sunday, with my grandmother's chair always in the shade near him. He loved old Canadian stories involving exploration, hard women and vindicated men; he died reading one the day after my granny's funeral.

Harold Flett loved the river, said it reminded him of the ocean that rimmed the dried-up property he quit with my granny in the north of Scotland near John O'Groats. He passed his love of moving water on to Ed. I caught Ed reading one of Granda's novels once. *Signed, Sealed and Delivered* it was called, had a picture of a woman in a buckskin jacket and gloves on the cover. A man kneeling in a canoe filled the background. Sarah said she found that same book in the middle of a stack of *Car and Driver* on her bedroom floor a few months after Ed died.

I thought about the depth of connection people have to each other. Sometimes I looked at Sarah and thought she was free of Ed, and then I'd find her smelling his clothes or wearing his huge watch on her tiny wrist. Two days before we began the canoe trip she built a wall between the end of their bed and the bedroom door, using the magazines she'd kept. Said she found an article on Feng Shui, which advised that the knife-edge of the door should not compromise the bed. I decided that there was a subtle difference between a screen and a wall, and wondered if my mother thought so too.

As the west wind pushed us across Lac Des Arcs, I thought about Granda and Ed, about my grandmother and my Scottish ancestors. I was relaxed. I hadn't seen any evidence of large, clawed animals.

"Ugly, isn't it?" Sarah motioned with her paddle to the scarred mountain to the north of us. She was right. The rock was the remnant of a giant wedge, thrusting up from west to east. Its limestone sheets had been quarried since 1906, and as we gazed over our shoulders, we saw a magnified cross-section of strata, peppered with dynamite holes.

I imagined that her heart and mine had been cut in the same way. "Ugly is an understatement," I said. Smoke had billowed from the stacks in eighteen-minute cycles for many years. I felt like a character in a sci-fi-western, a B-movie, with no director.

The wind changed and came over the port side. We had to lean hard into the inconsistent gusts. Whenever the gale died, the canoe rocked dangerously. I pressed against the mud three feet below the surface with the flat of my paddle. "Stop!" I yelled, trying to centre my weight. "Paddle!"

We were closing in on the end of the lake. The microbursts were powerful and we fought to stay off the rocky shore until we reached the portage. "Draw!" I called to Sarah, but my voice was lost before it reached her. She looked back for a moment, and then completed the move.

"So . . . thought . . . ful," she said, her breath ragged as we pulled the canoe onto the bank.

"Thoughtful?"

"Nemit," she said, holding on to the canoe cart and looking at her shoes.

I threw my life jacket next to the gear, unfolded the cart frame, and snapped the locking mechanisms in place. I was still skeptical about Sarah's softened point of view. "Can we lift the canoe?" I asked, standing back, hands on my hips.

"Let me get the low end," Sarah moved down the slope. "On second thought, the cooler is probably heavier than the canoe! Perhaps we should take it out."

We blocked the wheels with rocks, front and back, and then lifted the canoe onto the trailer. We balanced the canoe and fastened the tie-downs. Sarah put the cooler back, and gently touched the twenty-litre bag, then we started along the bumpy trail.

The wind blew, blustered, and moaned around us. I thought about the way my father's body sighed after he died, imagined that I saw him standing at the edge of the river, smiling, just as I saw him standing in the corner of his room. But, when I looked too hard, he disappeared.

Sarah screeched at the sight of two dozen crows on a tree beside our next launch. "What do you think that means?"

"Probably a dead animal around somewhere, or they may be following hunters."

"I thought the Bow was just popular with fly-fishing types."

"Fishing isn't as popular on the upper Bow because of the water temperature and the silt during run-off."

Sarah looked nervously at the black flock.

"We may see people fishing closer to the Seebe Dam."

She stumbled over the uneven trail, her neck bent at a strange angle so that she could keep the birds in sight. We stopped at the top of a steep bank, blocked the cart wheels, and looked for the best way to get the canoe down to the water.

Bleak images of cold rock and frigid water inhabited my mind that afternoon. Even when the Seebe-Exshaw area is hot, there's a coldness about the place. Maybe it's caused by great gusts of glacial air resident in the gaping holes in the mountains — updrafts from dead-end mine shafts. Perhaps the disruption of the natural flow of the river gives the region a stilted feel. I had hunkered at the tops of a number of Bow Valley mountains. The vistas are fantastic but the wind lets you know that you're not welcome to stay for long. The only place that ever warmed me was Grotto Canyon. In the summer, the rock floor and walls send heat through the body.

I turned, and started. A man with jet-black hair stood at the end of the canoe.

"Never saw a canoe with wheels," he said.

Sarah grabbed my arm. A rifle rested in the crook of his left arm.

"Don't worry," he added, "it's not loaded." The breast pockets of his dark-blue jean jacket bulged with ammunition. "What's it made of?"

"Aluminum," I said.

"That?" he asked, barrel pointing to the yellow canoe.

"Kevlar."

"It's as thin as a skin." He circled the canoe, ran his free hand along the sides. "Stands up to rocks, does it?" He set the gun on the ground, caressed the seam at the front with both hands. "How much's it worth?"

"Twenty-two — " Sarah started before I cut her off.

"Hunting deer?" I asked.

"Fishing."

I gauged the face, the well-known brand of outdoor shoes, and the micro-fiber pants he wore.

"Zip off to shorts," he said. "Never used that option yet. Too many insects."

"Interested in a vest?"

"A vest?" Sarah asked.

"A vest," I repeated. "Kevlar. Just like the canoe, only thicker. Can stop a bullet."

"Let me see, then."

I pulled the twenty-litre bag from our small bundle of gear and retrieved Lynn's camouflage vest.

"Adam likes to wear that!" Sarah said. She took the bag from me and hugged it to her chest.

I held the vest like a coat, inviting. The man turned and put his hands through the armholes. The vest didn't quite reach his waist, but it fastened easily over his lean chest. He sank three fingers into the cylindrical tubes on the front.

"How much?" he asked, as if we were standing in the middle of a car lot.

"Nothing," I said.

"Oh, no!" he said. "Gotta be somethin'." He whistled. A girl, about Adam's age, emerged from the bush carrying a fishing rod and a small cooler. The man motioned to her. She left the rod against a tree and took the lid off the cooler. Two good-sized brown trout stared up out of crushed ice.

"That do?" he asked.

"Very nicely," I said.

Without another word the girl picked up the fishing rod, the man retrieved his gun, and the two disappeared behind the green canopy.

"Mother of God!" Sarah said.

I thought I had made an equitable trade.

We decided to unload the cooler again before we eased the canoe, which was still on the trailer, down the steep slope to the river. The terrain was as good as it could have been, because it hadn't rained in some time. We both stayed at the up-hill end, held on, and skidded down the slope behind the trailer, grounding the canoe next to the water. The next section of river looked easy. It cascaded near Highway 1-A, but I had known beforehand that the wind would take its toll on us.

Traffic was minimal that day. A bright-red truck slowed and stopped at a picnic rest stop. The man who exchanged the fish for Lynn's vest got out. He smoked and watched us. Sarah looked back over her hunched shoulder at him until the river bent away and he disappeared behind dark-green forests.

"So," she said after a while. "Will I ever know why you kept that hunting vest? Or why Lynn left in the middle of the night?"

"I don't think I should tell you, Sarah."

"Why not?"

I didn't answer her right away. I thought about why not, about my attachments to endings and I decided it was time to let the story go. I thought that if I could tell her about Lynn, maybe I could tell her how I felt about Liam. The Kevlar vest was gone and the silk damask I wore the day I married Jack was probably lining an animal den or bird nest. "Okay," I said, looking downstream at her back. "I held a gun to his head."

The canoe rocked violently and Sarah dropped her paddle in the river.

"Just days after we got married he came into the bedroom wearing nothing but that Kevlar vest."

Sarah retrieved the paddle.

"I thought he was playing hunter. We wrestled. I crouched on all fours, then I felt a cold barrel between my shoulder blades. I hadn't noticed the revolver. He'd tucked it in the pouch on the back of the vest. As soon as it touched my skin he lost his erection."

"God in Heaven," she whispered. "If Ed had known — "

"Later, when he was asleep, I stashed the vest and the revolver in the basement freezer and retrieved Granda's old shotgun."

"Mother of God! That is an antique! What do you know about guns?"

"I know that particular model does a lot of damage." I paddled rhythmically. "I stood next to the bed, held it to his head, and waited for him to wake up. He thought it was another game. I told him to get dressed. He pulled on some pants and smiled. I motioned to the bedroom door. He walked through. I followed and nudged him. He skipped down the stairs. I pointed to the open patio door with the barrel. He went out and turned a pirouette on the lawn. I motioned toward the garage. His truck was running on the driveway. He slid onto the passenger seat, moved it back as far as it would go. I watched him open his fly before I told him to leave."

"He didn't ask any questions?"

"No."

"What about his guns?" Her hands gripped her paddle. I imagined coyote shapes printed on her palms. The teak clunked against the gunwale as she twisted in her seat to stare at me.

"Stroke," I said.

She managed two or three before she turned around again. The skin on her neck was so taut, it looked like it would tear.

"I called the police and they confiscated the guns."

"Just like that?"

"Just like that. Every home containing a registered firearm gets a call from the police department. When the gun owner changes addresses, the new place is supposed to get a call. They phoned when Lynn moved in and asked if I felt threatened. If I'd said yes, they could've legally taken the firearms away. The night Lynn *left*, I called the district office."

"Jesus Christ, Rhegan! The non-emergency number?"

"Three officers came and emptied the gun case."

"No questions? You must have told them the *details*. How could you not tell us?"

"One officer stayed in a car about half a block down the street."

"Why did you not call us?"

"The other two waited in front of Lynn's office building. He showed up at home before they were finished, feet still bare. He was escorted away."

"Nemit came to stay."

"Yes."

"We thought she — converted you! We asked Sister Margaret and Father Joe to visit you."

"They did. There's a bend coming up."

She started to paddle again, sporadically. "A few months later Thomas invited you to the farm."

"I went to meet Nemit for lunch one day and he got off the elevator at the same time she did. I recognized him from the beach in Whitefish."

"Why could you not tell me? I am your mother."

"I just did."

Sarah paddled the last few kilometres muttering, "Why . . . Nemit . . . Lynn . . . son-of-a-bitch."

I smiled.

We reached the west side of Horseshoe Dam an hour or so before Nemit, and walked up to the parking area anyway. It was empty. We decided to stay by the river and cook the fish. I collected dead wood, and before I started the fire, Sarah hugged me, held me. It felt as if she was trying to make up for something.

"You are the strongest and also the most stupid woman I know."

"Come by it honestly," I said.

I built a small pyre of twigs, and reached inside the twenty-litre bag. It looked deflated without the kite makings, the skirt section of the silk shift, the veil, the garters, the vest, and two baggies. I took out a bridal missal with a pearl-finished cover.

The pages had gold edges and the tail of a silk ribbon protruded at the base of its spine.

"Jane gave that to you when you married Thomas!" Sarah said, horrified.

"No. When I married Raj," I said. "She objected to his religion, wanted to make a point."

Sarah stomped around, and then banged a small pot onto the stove.

"Won't you need water?" I asked.

She took the plastic jug of Calgary water out of the cooler.

"You could use river water since you're going to boil it."

"No point in taking any chances," she scowled at me.

I enjoyed tearing the page with spaces for the bride and groom's names away from the threaded binding of the missal.

She spilled water on her dry runners.

I crumpled the page and tore out five others before I struck the match. I fed the little blaze with pages until I could add bigger, dryer pieces of wood.

"That's sacrilegious," Sarah said.

"Sacrilegious?"

"Blasphemous!"

I ignored her comment while wondering why she cared. "Rice nearly ready?" I asked. I knew that it wasn't.

She calmed down watching me prepare the fish. I decided to cook the smaller one. It was about two pounds.

I pulled out the folding knife that Liam had given me. I couldn't for the life of me figure out the contradictions that formed Sarah's outlook. When Ed died she temporarily quit the church, didn't go to Mass for three weeks. When she did go back, she went every day for the next month, as if carrying out a self-imposed penance.

I exposed the blade. Sarah tried to get me to go too. Said I had no excuse since I didn't work in the early mornings; I agreed to go with her on Sundays.

I inserted the tip of the blade in the throat. "Head on or off?" I asked her.

"On," she said.

She squatted next to me and ran a fork around the inside of the rice pot. Then she set it on the ground, wincing as if she could hear my knife tearing the delicate flesh. Her body bounced as she adjusted her stance.

"Bones now or later?"

"Later," she said, as she spread a doubled length of foil on the ground and folded in the edges to make a tray.

I submerged the fish in the river, emptied the guts and the contents of the bowels in the flow. Better than dust-to-dust, I thought, thinking of Ed.

"Who taught you to gut a fish like that? Liam?"

"Granny. She liked to use an old ironing board to work on, hated to crouch because she always wore a skirt."

"How could I forget that!"

Sarah smeared butter on the foil while I patted the inside of the trout dry with some paper napkins that I then added to the fire. I laid the fish on the aluminum. Sarah produced dill, lemon pepper, and salt, sprinkled them on the flesh, and filled the cavity with the rice and two knobs of butter. Then she folded the foil carefully around the gashed belly and sealed the ends before handing the packet to me. I placed it cautiously on the grill, which I'd removed from a barbeque in the parking lot. I balanced the packet quickly over the grey, flaking wood so I didn't scorch my hands. I kept the heat steady by adding small amounts of wood to the hottest sections of the fire. Sarah watched me for a while, then walked along the river as far as the worn bank would allow.

I put the condiments and the roll of foil away in the cooler, puttered about, moved gear that didn't need to be moved. I looked upstream. Sarah was praying, head bowed and hands clasped. I split the plastic missal cover with the axe. She looked up at the cracking noise. I strode toward the canoe and retrieved a garbage bag. I couldn't imagine spoiling the fish with the kind of chemicals burning plastic releases.

"Incinerate the whole thing?" she asked when she came back.

I turned the foil packet over using two long branches. "I think the fish will be ready pretty soon; it's not even sticking to the foil."

When I looked up Sarah held a baggie. I watched as she trickled the contents into the fire. The grate moved. Blue smoke swirled. I stretched out my arms and tried to pull the haze to my chest. Rested my hands for a moment, imagined them touching my father's back. I knelt on the ground, watching dust settle against Sarah's legs. The smoke subsided.

"Is it Friday today?" Sarah asked.

"I don't know," I said, quietly. I felt just as emotional as I had at Bow Falls and at the Ink Pots.

"Of course you know! Today is Thursday. So I will not worry about having fish tomorrow."

I thought about the contradictions that mapped Sarah's outlook. I decided that she love-hated the church, my father, and me. I jostled the packet onto a tin plate and opened it gingerly, peering inside.

"They're here, Mom!" Adam screamed, as he ran full tilt down the slope. He threw his arms around my neck and kissed me. "The canoe cart works?"

"It works," I said, play-punching his shoulder. He wiped moisture from my cheeks, held my face between his thin hands, while Sarah walked towards Nemit, and embraced her. The two of them turned toward me. Adam let go of me and poked the fire with a long stick. I felt strangely vulnerable.

After we'd packed our gear in Nemit's van, we drove across Highway 1-A toward Seebe. The Kananaskis raged below the one-track bridge that provides the only access to the plateau town. We parked and got out of the vehicle again, watched Horseshoe Falls cascade over the ledges of rock below the dam before driving to Calgary.

24

THREE DAYS LATER I WASN'T SURPRISED to see Liam's tall frame in Sarah's front window. I knocked and opened the door to their laughter.

Liam looked over at me, said, "Hi, Rhegan," turned to Sarah and continued, "I won't join you for Mass, but I'll see you again before I fly out." He stood and hugged her. "Drove by the old house," he said to me. "Let me take it off your hands."

"You're moving back?" I asked.

"In a month or so — think about it!" He kissed Sarah on the cheek and left.

I pressed bacon crumbs onto my fingertips. "Nice breakfast?"

"Very nice, darling. You should have come." She hadn't invited me.

Although we had lots of time, I asked her to hurry up, and before we drove off, she leaned a worn, leather briefcase against the back of the car seat. For the next hour, I went through the motions of standing and sitting and kneeling. Sarah tried to engage me in whisper-talk, but I resisted.

For nine years I hadn't been able to picture anyone in the Inglewood house, couldn't find the right buyer. That day I pictured Liam — his hair much shorter, his body over-worked to retain its youthful hardness — filling the planters with miniature Arctic willow, stretching for a map, climbing the metal stairs.

"Why so somber?" Sarah asked. "Mass is over, darling. Wait for me in the car. I need a moment or two with Father Joe." She strode toward the business office.

I waited for the crowd to clear before engulfing myself in outdoor light. When I dropped her off she said, "I will be over at seven-thirty tomorrow, as planned."

"Okay."

Her hair radiated a purple glow where the sun penetrated its thickness. She'd applied a rinse, the first she'd used since my father died. "Wait! I'll give you the canoe bag to fill." She jogged inside, briefcase flapping. The MG sputtered and coughed. I revved the motor as Sarah came back. She thought I was in a hurry. The bag was open, and contained one thing — Ed.

"The old house — let me take it off your hands," Liam had said. Just like that. No thought, no careful consideration of what I might feel.

Liam. I stood in the basement of my home, fists clenched, staring at the dress I had designed to include the most critical elements of bridal style. It was the dress I wore to marry him. It had been the only dress I panicked about, fretted and fussed over. I had considered neckline options: off-the shoulder, jewel, Queen Anne, illusion, bateau, wedding band, scoop, V, and sweetheart. Sleeve styles: short, sleeveless, long, fitted, Juliet, and leg o' mutton. Trains: sweep, chapel, and cathedral. Fabric: silk chiffon, crepe, taffeta, damask, and peau de soi. I mulled over duchess satin and tulle. I considered the headpiece: headband, garland, tiara, full and half circle, comb, crown, and hat. The veil: Madonna and birdcage, flyaway, elbow, fingertip, and chapel-length, blusher, and mantilla. I had taken care with the shoes, the stockings, and the lingerie. I wore a merry widow, borrowed Sarah's earrings, and the ribbon trailing from my bouquet had been blue.

The gift for the groom dangled from the neck of the dress form; one sixteen-inch chain and a small oval Saint Christopher medallion in twenty-four-carat gold intended to protect the traveller. I put it on. I examined the dress for stains. The peau de soi was unmarked in spite of the trek I made along the river between Inglewood and Bowness. I had been wearing the dress, hoping to excite another crinoline-driven frenzy in my partner, but that was the night that Liam asked me to leave. The off-the-shoulder bodice was no longer discoloured by sweat.

Sarah had saved the gown, submerged the layers in her bathtub, watched the fabric bubble and float, wore gloves to treat the stains on the hem and skirt, carried it dripping and un-wrung to the basement. I remember the dress hanging from the floor joists by long threads carefully drawn through the shoulders, the waist, and inside the back of the hem. The bodice packed with white plastic bags to help keep its shape, skirt wide as a church bell. The dress, dancing in the artificial wind, whipped up by the caged blades of two large electric fans.

I imagined the platinum wedding band resting on my ring finger. I stared. Technically, the ring only becomes the bride's property after she marries. I didn't own the band Liam designed to incorporate the repeating image of the Celtic cross; he had asked me to give it back. I stood there for an hour, looking for something else to take on the next leg of our journey, unsure about what I could discard next.

I removed the dress from the form and carried it upstairs.

Later that night, I dropped a set of twelve stainless steel forks in the twenty-litre canoe bag. The bundle looked meaningless next to the remaining baggie that Sarah seemed glad to give me. The bag was vacant. I decided to use a small stuff-sack instead. I knew Sarah wouldn't be disappointed that I hadn't included any rings. They are, after all, the one component of wedding paraphernalia that can be worn again without causing a stir. I thought once more about giving her the diamond from the Jack ring, if I ever found it. I remembered a woman, a friend of Auntie Jane's, dyeing her tulle wedding dress emerald green, wearing it to a Christmas party, and waiting six months for her skin to shed the shade it left. I wondered about the shadow a white dress made. I breathed in, placed my open hand on my ribcage against the bodice of the one I was wearing, relished the snug fit.

To that point, I had cast away the headpiece I wore when I married Domenic, the garters I wore at five weddings, the veil I wore when I married Liam, part of the silk shift I wore when I married Jack, and the missal I carried when I married Raj. I thought Raj left me because the prayer book insulted his grandmother, but I was never sure. I felt good about Lynn's vest. The man we met at Seebe would use it properly.

I had been home for three days and I managed to make two decisions: one about forks and the other about underskirts. I considered making a sail out of my granny's underskirt. I wore it below my dress when I married Thomas, but the cotton was so thin I knew it wouldn't trap air. Now I love to remember the feel of crinoline against my legs.

The answering machine in my office had played back four messages from Nemit. Each reminded me of something related to Sarah's well-being. I erased the last without listening to everything she said. Six people inquired about new river listings. I set up appointments for each, scheduling them for a week later, but I wasn't able to be at any. There were several messages from the designer who viewed the Inglewood house. I called and told her I'd decided to keep the property, and rent it to another vendor. She was abusive again. I said, *goodbye*, politely, and hung up.

The first thing I had noticed when I got home from Seebe was the absence of water in my yard. The lawn was firmer when I walked the fence line. Only the bike path was still covered in a thin liquid coat. The second thing I noticed was the note taped to my patio door by the Rivers and Lakes man. He'd been reassigned. His note invited me to spend the weekend in his fire lookout, and included an excellent map of how to reach him.

At the kitchen table, I turned my attention away from my dress to focus on a chart of the next stretch of river Sarah and I would paddle: Calgary to Carseland. Nemit would be ecstatic. The total distance was seventy-five kilometres and the overall grade was one .

I knew that Sarah would love that section of the trip. Weight wasn't an issue because there was nothing to portage. I thought that we might even use the generator, and decided it was too bad about the underskirt. My fishing rod would've made a great mast.

I made a note of items to add to our gear, and wrote *dining tent and small folding table with stools.* I added *pillows and bug light*, thinking that Sarah would be pleased. I included *2 bottles Pinot Gris*, and chewing the pencil, wrote *trowel*. There'd be no bathrooms on this stretch of the river. Sarah would pack the cooler, include two lunches, one supper, one breakfast, and a multitude of fatty snacks. I cringed when the metal surrounding the eraser touched a filling, added *chocolate* at the top of the list. A heavy rain began to fall. I looked over at the pile of gear on the family room floor where I had thrown my waterproof, hooded jacket. The arms were spread out, and it looked like a person floating face down in water.

I had slept for three hours before I heard Sarah in my kitchen. I looked at the clock — six forty-nine. She assumed I would be asleep and let herself in with the key that I gave her for emergencies. I rolled off the bed and ran into the bathroom. I had fallen asleep wearing my best-loved wedding dress. I slipped it off and rolled it up, put it in the linen cupboard, and jumped in the shower before the water warmed up.

"Don't worry about the weather!" Sarah said a few minutes later as she threw the glass shower door open and bounced it off the commode. "The sun is breaking through and the forecast is dry for the next three days!"

I glared, said, "Do you mind?" My head felt dull.

She closed the door.

I stood in the stream of pulsating water. I had spent the better part of the night drinking wine and trying to come to terms with feelings that were resurfacing, feelings about Liam. I thought I could relax a bit, and that Sarah had gone downstairs, but I heard her open the linen cupboard door.

I felt as if I'd been tagged.

25

NEMIT DRIVES YOU AND YOUR DAUGHTER to the southeast end of the city. She uses Sarcee Trail and Glenmore Trail, crosses the reservoir that holds drinking water for Calgary's southern inhabitants, passes Rockyview Hospital and Heritage Park, drives on the outskirts of Pump Hill, skirts the edge of Canyon Meadows Golf Course, goes past one of those franchised funeral homes, and parks at Bankside in Fish Creek Park. Adam is still in bed. Nemit kisses you full on the mouth, then rushes away to wake him for a baseball game. You feel remorseful at the thought that she will have to console your daughter at Carseland.

When the canoe is loaded and ready to go, you disappear into the vaulted provincial building. Your daughter finds you in the washroom and rolls her lips in on themselves when she sees you.

"What is the matter, darling?" you ask.

"There's a dead bear lying in the water upstream of the canoe launch."

Your daughter expects a response, but you do not repeat what she says.

"Not a mark on the chest, the abdomen, the arms, or the legs. I've called the Park office; they'll look after recovery. They asked if we could wait until they arrive. They might want us to fill in a report."

You know that it is not unheard of for bears to come out of the mountains and into the city. You wonder if the bear is female, if she, too, lost her mate, or if she simply lost her way.

"I once read an article in the Banff *Crag and Canyon* about a similar find near Mosquito Creek," your daughter goes on. "The bear had simply died of natural causes."

You wonder about the attraction of the dying to flowing water and you speculate about which local and provincial departments are called when the body in the river is human. Tears sting the back of your eyes.

"It's okay, Sarah. The bear can't harm us." Your daughter puts her arm around your shoulder, but she hardly understands your thoughts and impulses.

You have considered jumping into the Bow from one of the bridges near downtown Calgary. You rode your bike from Bowness to Tenth Street and walked out to the middle of the low span. Even during the month of May, there simply is not enough water to warrant an attempt. You decided quickly that a jumper might seriously injure herself on the rocks covering the riverbed. The last thing you want is to be confined in a living shell because you broke your neck or back as the result of a dive into a too-shallow stream.

You give yourself up to your daughter's compassionate side as she walks next to you. Together you go through two doors, across a bike path, down a rough slope, and across a grassy ledge to the river.

You stand next to a man and his dog. You listen as your daughter tells him that she has already reported the bear. You look at the dead animal and take in the hooded eyes, the open mouth, the exposed teeth, and the lolling tongue covered in flies.

You watch the river water wash over matted fur, which becomes sleek like the coat of a submerged seal. You are suddenly unsure about your plans despite the fact that you are well prepared. You left important items with your favourite priest.

Your daughter talks with the man who is nervously looking about for another animal. "There can't be another one anywhere close," your daughter says to him. "Your dog is too calm."

You listen to the man as he points toward tracks which he says lead away from the scene. You feel afraid.

Your daughter turns to you and wonders why you look upset. Your answer is a whisper. "So sad," you say as you watch the man move away and take up a post at the edge of the parking lot to look for the warden. You recall the sensation of water burning your skin. You shiver.

Half an hour later, you are glad when your daughter is distracted by the arrival of the Provincial Park officials and the Alberta Wildlife people. You watch the men in the rubber boots wade into the shallow water and begin their examination of the bear's remains.

You pull yourself together and walk to the canoe. You have made plans. Father Joe has an envelope containing your will and the smallest bag of Ed's ashes.

26

SARAH SAID NOTHING WHEN WE EDDIED out and made a rough turn into the current, nothing fifteen minutes later about my directions to stay to the middle of the left span of the Highway 22-X bridge. She knew from our lessons that we should navigate the centre span of a bridge whenever possible. She had still said nothing when we left the city limits, and paddled numbly wherever I directed her. At the time, I could only wonder about what was really upsetting her. I steered us almost perpendicular to the flow, into the tip zone, then let the bow swing downstream. None of that provoked a reaction. I maneuvered the canoe down a narrow, weeded branch of river until it was grounded near the Cottonwood Golf Course clubhouse. Sarah reacted only when the four men on the first tee took off their shoes and socks and waded in to help us.

"I think we are — lost," she said. She didn't complain about getting her feet wet up to her knees.

Six of us muscled the full canoe off the mud hump. The men laughed and threw out their names as we paddled away, inviting us to come in for a drink on the return trip.

"Why in God's name did you put us in there?" Sarah finally asked, as we reached the main channel again.

"For fun!" I said.

"Not funny!" she replied managing a grin. "The man who got his golf glove wet reminded me a bit of Thomas." She was right. The youngest of the four men had a rugged look and sandy hair, looked as if he should be wearing ropers instead of golf shoes.

I decided to tell her about Thomas. I thought that if I added to what I had said about Lynn, I could work my way up to talking about Liam. I told her that I had made a conscious decision when I married Thomas. Told her that I hadn't seen him for years, and that I had trouble remembering why I should recognize him when I saw him. He'd been standing next to Nemit in the lobby of an oil company office. It turned out they both worked for the same multi-national. I heard the elevator ding. Then I remembered forced air that sounded like a flute, and Thomas next to a frozen lake, his face ruddy and cold, my limbs Whitefish weak.

"My legs are asleep, Rhegan," Sarah interrupted. "Can we stop for a while?"

"Switch up to the seat, that'll help."

"I *need* to stop," she said.

I scanned the banks ahead. The Cliffs of Doom rose a hundred or so feet above us on one side. A brand-new sport utility vehicle, roof crushed, lay partway down the slope. "There's a gravel bar up ahead. Draw right," I said.

Her knuckles shone white around the top of the coyote paddle.

After we landed, I watched her hands shake as she took the top off the cooler. I was puzzled. Until that morning I thought she was in control of herself, however bizarre her behaviour had been.

Sarah munched mixed nuts and raisins. "I'm just going over here for a bit," she said, wandering into a clump of poplar. When she came back, she sat next to me in the grass and I continued my story.

I told her that when I separated from Thomas, it was for sound reasons. He had been protective and practical to excess. He helped me disconnect from Lynn, who helped me forget about Raj, who rescued me after Jack. Thomas had been well prepared for the future and he was past the point where he felt the need to raise children. I left him because he was habitual. "At the time, I took a portion of the only wedding gift we accepted," I told Sarah, "stainless steel flatware from you and Ed. I took the forks. The tines were marked by his teeth. I hardly ate when we were together for meals, couldn't stand the sound of enamel on steel." I was lounging in the long grass, a stalk suspended from my lips. "Are you okay, Sarah?" I asked.

"Take that thing out of your mouth, darling."

"I mean you seem sort of — " I dropped the green stalk after its bitter juices contacted my tongue.

"Sort of what?"

"Quiet?" I licked the palms of both hands then ran them up and down my thighs.

"Rhegan, that is disgusting! What were *you* thinking about all that time — besides hazards?"

"Thomas Phillips." I scratched the surface of my tongue with my fingernails.

My mother gave me a hanky and a look that said she knew me better. "That poor man was devastated when you quit him. He left his job and moved to the homestead. I think that he has lived down there ever since."

I scrubbed the cloth over my tongue, and gave it back to her. "He was ready to retire," I said.

She took it with two fingers and put it in a small plastic garbage bag tucked next to the gear in the middle of the canoe. "He is what? Twelve years older than you?"

I spat. "Thirteen."

"You could have stopped working and sold the house in Bowness, and the Inglewood house, and just settled next to that little river. You could have lived off the income from your rental properties." She rinsed her hands in the river.

"Too dry and windy."

She stood up and turned toward me, shaking her hands. "He was very good to you. I even saw him folding your laundry! How could you let a man like that go? I tried to talk to him, but he was far too proud. I think he was the sort of man that found it difficult to confide in a woman."

I had let all my men go, except one. "It was because you were my mother," I said.

"Maybe, but that has not prevented Liam from talking to me."

A group of five canoes heavily laden with camping gear floated toward us. There was a single paddler in the lead canoe. Each of the others had two paddlers. One contained adults.

"Any trouble, ladies?" the lead canoeist called out.

"None!" I yelled back. I watched the canoes float-bob. "Must be an instructor from the Bow Waters Club or maybe from the university," I said. I stood up next to Sarah and waved.

"Sounds Australian. Why did we not have him during our lessons?" She crossed her arms over her chest.

"All right, boys," he said, "back paddle — slowly, Scott! With your partner, Evan. Okay, spread out a bit. Sheila — you're too close to me."

Two canoes collided.

"My name's not Sheila!" one of the paddlers called.

"No mate, your name *is* Sheila when you can't get on a simple move like that one!"

The whole group laughed.

"They look about sixteen," Sarah said. "Lovely, just what we need."

"Okay, blokes, remember how to ferry? We're now going upstream so that we can join those ladies," his paddle waved in the air in our direction, "on that nice bank over there for a bite of lunch."

There was low chatter as the boats huddled slightly downstream. The group watched the instructor demonstrate the technique.

"Front ferry, boys! Stern in the current. Keep the angle shallow, don't let the current," he paddled with more effort, "take the bow straight, or you'll just — go downstream. Notice I'm paddling forward, Sheila."

The group cheered when he raised his baseball cap to us.

"Show off," Sarah said. "That was not very difficult."

"Boy Scouts," he winked at me. "Run for your lives."

He paddled downstream of the group and hovered in the middle of the river. "First canoe!" he called. "Let's go, Scotty!"

"Good idea," Sarah said. "Let's go."

"Don't you want to watch?"

"Not really. One boy is fine, but six, plus the leaders, plus instructor? That is a small herd."

We pulled on our life jackets. I sat in the stern while Sarah pushed us out and hopped in. She said nothing about the water temperature.

"Catch up with you later," the instructor drawled, as we paddled past.

"I hope not," Sarah said, switching sides.

"Pivot turn!" I called.

"Oh, for heaven's sake," she said, but she knew the move and drew on the starboard side while I drew on the port side. We completed the spin. I waved to the instructor who laughed, and we headed down the Bow toward its confluence with the Highwood.

I had been amazed the first time I paddled to Carseland. I was with Liam. I couldn't stop taking photographs of the birds. Great flocks of pelican and stork stood in the shallows, covering whole islands. It had been hard to imagine the dry towns and highways perched out of sight on the prairie above; there was only lush vegetation along the river.

Sarah and I approached a stretch of cabins, dubbed The Mansion Run below the small town of Indus. I'd arranged for three sales there, made the Carseland trip eight times after that, and never saw people in those places. Maybe those clients just wanted bragging rights. Some ranches and a few campgrounds bordered the river along the next stretch we would come to, but it would be quiet. Powerboats were rare.

We passed two float boats and four silent fly-fishermen, chest-high waders keeping their red plaid shirts dry. I wondered if the shirts were standard issue by the tour company, or if they came free with their expensive hats. Sarah blew them a kiss.

"Ma'am — little ma'am," the tallest one said.

"How much do you think a weekend of fly-fishing costs?" Sarah asked.

I didn't know. The river curved against a high sandy cliff, and seemed to move slowly as it deepened.

"Does Liam's dad still run that outfitter's cabin on the Highwood? That was the reason Mr. Richards said he could not come to your wedding," she said, "remember?"

"I remember. He said they'd been having trouble with a black bear. Truth was, he didn't trust or approve of me, was afraid that his land would end up in my hands. He had willed it to Liam." I held my paddle in the water like a rudder as Sarah pulled us along.

"What about his wife?"

"Bypassed her completely."

"But how could he do that? I mean legally, is it not *theirs?* The marital home? Where would she live if he died?"

I began paddling again as the river straightened out. "Completely up to the son. Made her sign something before they married. Light years ahead of his contemporaries. Probably designed the prenuptial agreement Liam brought to me. Land's been in the family since the great-grandfather came over from Stirling."

"It is a good thing then that Liam likes his mother." Sarah pointed to a sweeper on the left. We both pulled right.

"Liam's from a run of men who were property heavy."

"Property heavy — now that would be you." She stopped paddling, turned to look at me.

"I still believe that investing in land is the best thing a woman can do. Every husband but my first, Domenic, signed away his right to my business. When I married Dom, I didn't own a thing. When I came home after my post-pubescent adventure, I still didn't own anything."

"Ed thought Domenic was too young for you. I thought you were in love." She sat up on the fiberglass seat, placed her paddle across her knees.

"I *was* in love," I said without telling her with whom. "I did like-love Dom and Jack and Raj and Lynn and Thomas."

I was surprised that my conversation with my mother ended there, thought that maybe she was just biding her time, striking the names of my husbands off a list in her head, patiently waiting for me to get to the one that mattered. We had just touched the tip of the Liam iceberg and neither of us had engaged in a conversation about him. I began to think that perhaps she was tired, and had given up thinking that I would ever discuss Liam with her again. The truth was, whether Sarah responded to me or not, she had the power to punctuate the conversation.

I used to wonder how my mother could hold me at word-point. It wasn't her knowledge or intellect, or her personal strength, or even her voice that established her rule. It was the annoying way that she knew me better than I knew myself. I had been a small part of the whole that she was, the part of herself that she allowed to escape from the birth canal into the main stream. When I was pregnant, I wondered if the process of heredity was involuntary, or if the body of the mother was in control. I believed that it was the egg that drew the sperm toward it. Rather than survival of the fittest, the laws of attraction and selection were in play.

"Rhegan, I think we should take our lunch now." My paddle was at rest and hers stroked twice on each side of the bow. "What is the key to choosing a place?" she asked over her shoulder.

"Anywhere that you think looks good," I replied. I followed her lead. She chose well, spotting an eddy on the left where there was a small strip of damp earth and a six-inch step up to a grassy ledge. We went in bow first. Sarah drew left, cross bow. I drew right and the stern swung around so that we faced upstream. She was relaxed and didn't seem to mind the small jolt the canoe made when it crossed the eddy line.

"I think I would like to try steering next," she said. "Today may be my only chance."

Sarah had taken the time to prepare before we left. Lunch was fish wrapped in parchment. She took the paper bundles from their plastic box and baked them in a deep skillet, lid on, over the stove.

"You told me no restrictions and this lunch is light." She thought my face showed scorn instead of surprise, when she handed me a plastic wine glass.

"It's fabulous!" I said. "Gourmet! What's for dinner?"

"Our last supper will be cranberry pork tenderloin, new potatoes roasted in a Dijon paste, vegetable medley, and pie."

"Pie?"

"Pie. I researched reflector ovens," she said.

We were enjoying the fresh tomatoes, red and yellow peppers, and seasoned halibut with a Sauvignon Blanc when the Scout group floated past, their five canoes tied together like a large raft. The adults and the instructor snoozed. Four boys paddled from the outside corners. The centamaran turned large, slow circles midstream.

"Sleep," I said. "What a good idea." I stretched out in the shade near some skinny birch trees after I finished my meal, drifted into an afternoon haze.

When I woke up, Sarah was writing in an embossed, hardcover journal. I lay on my back, life jacket under my head, watching. I had no idea that she ever wrote anything down. Her pen seemed to dent the page and I felt as if I was eavesdropping.

I stretched and yawned but she stayed focused on the book. I crawled to the canoe and took out my camera case. There were two shots left on the black and white roll. I captured the intensity on her face with the first and zoomed out to include her whole body with the second. *Mother Below Tree*, I thought as the film rewound.

I wondered if I had been wrong about how Sarah was dealing with Ed's death. Maybe she had been journaling and working things out on her own — she had refused the idea of the bereavement classes I'd proposed when we came back from our trip to England. I had even offered to go with her.

She closed the book and said, "I have one last thing to do before I will be ready to leave." She put the journal in her clothes bag. Then she took out the trowel I had packed and tried to dig near the tree she sat under.

"Here, let me help," I said. I sliced into the earth with my knife several times, loosened the tangled roots of wild grass, and ripped out the stalks.

My mother scraped a hole in the ground that had no particular dimensions, and trickled what I had thought were the last of Ed's ashes into the space. We used our hands to cover the ashes with dirt. She held up the small stuff-sack, asked, "What will you do with these forks?"

I took two, stuck the tines in the earth, and let the handles rest together. They formed a triangle with the surface of the ground. I lashed a small, wavy branch to the sharp angle at the top, using half of the drawstring from the stuff-sack.

Sarah sang one verse of, *The Lord is My Shepherd* before she made the sign of the cross and stood up, a rosary in her hand. "I prayed for entrance into heaven," she said, touched the crucifix to her ears, her eyes, her nose and her lips, held it between her pressed-together palms.

I couldn't speak. My throat was constricted and my face was wet, stayed that way no matter that I swabbed my tears with the backs of both hands. I thought about devotion, the kind my father had to my mother, no matter what.

"Is that Liam's Saint Christopher you are wearing?" Sarah asked.

I tucked the medallion back inside my wetsuit.

"J-stroke," I said from the bow of the canoe. "Your paddle is the rudder." The canoe was off centre in the middle of the river. The banks were treed on both sides.

Sarah laughed and I did a cross-bow draw to straighten us out.

"Why the Saint Christopher?" she asked.

"Patron Saint of travel."

"Do you think something is going to happen?"

"No," I said. "Not unless you don't straighten us out."

"I cannot quite get the feel of the stroke," she said.

"Persevere! Turn your hand over so your thumb turns in and down at the end of the stroke."

"But then I will pry."

"Then you'll pry," I said.

"Tell me why you are wearing that medallion."

I took a number of deep breaths until I thought I would hyperventilate, then confessed. I told my mother that Liam and I had almost slept together in the gazebo the night of the garage flood.

"Everyone knows that you never really got over Liam," she said. I continued to compensate for our erratic course.

"What I mean, darling, is anyone who matters to you: me, Ed, and Nemit. We know that you care for him. Mother of God, you still have the Inglewood house! Not even a place without a roof would take *you* nine years to sell. You must be careful where he is concerned."

"I won't hurt him again." I went on, "I don't know how I feel now, it's something inexplicable, not love or desire."

"Maybe it is a kind of yearning that you feel — for what? I think for the kind of relationship he could never give you," she said, while trying not to squash her thumb between the stern and her paddle as she struggled with the J-stroke.

I was stunned. I'd always imagined that my mother thought Liam was perfect for me, and that she still thought I had "missed the boat."

"Be honest," she continued. "Your independence scared him. Oh, he loved you — fiercely — but that was not enough. Your sense of self made him anxious. I think you unnerved him from the very beginning. Today, I am more concerned about you. I hope that you realize what happened in the gazebo was simply two people reaching out to each other in stressful times."

I couldn't immediately digest what she said. Her approach was foreign and unfamiliar to me. My mind reeled. Liam had talked to her. My mother already knew about his visit. In her way, she told me that what almost happened meant nothing to Liam. I stopped paddling.

"Darling, you have to straighten things out. I cannot seem to get the hang of this stroke and I am concerned about hazards. By the way, I told him that we would be camping overnight on your little island near the junction with the Highwood."

I groaned and hoped that he wouldn't care. "There aren't any rapids to worry about, so unless we are sideways on a rock, I'm not concerned about falling in. Keep trying," I said. I paddled again but the effect was counter-tempo to Sarah's strokes. I felt as if I'd completely lost my sense of rhythm.

Sarah did try, tried for another kilometre or so. As we left the cover of the trees, the river became quite shallow in places. "This is not working," she sang.

"Okay, we'll just paddle straight on opposite sides, but we'll have to switch every ten strokes to stay in the middle."

After three quarters of an hour of silent zigzagging through gravel bars, we pulled out to change positions. I didn't want

Sarah to be at the helm when we reached the Highwood. There weren't any significant rapids there but the standing waves had to be negotiated head on. Each river folded in on the other at the conjunction like ingredients suspended in a mixing bowl.

Before we got back on the water, Sarah held me, and I let her. I had often wondered how it felt when a mother deferred to her daughter. That day the opposite happened. I had given in, and told my mother my secret. I realized that I had lost the kind of control I only thought I had — over my life, over the lives of others. I had imagined Liam was like the Inglewood house: empty and alone. I was wrong about that as well.

I began to understand the necessity of letting go, especially when I had no other choice. Until then, I had refused to do that. My mother, on the other hand, had not. She had achieved something I hadn't, despite her strange methods. I felt the same way I did when I used to watch her separate the yolk from the egg white using only her fingers — frustrated because the outcome could be happy or sad and either way you could never hold on to the contents of the shell. She had almost always separated the fluid mass without bursting the yolk. I knew that I hadn't been capable of the same thing.

"Do you think Ed is happy where he is?" Sarah asked after we were on the water again.

"Happy?"

"You know, content."

"Where is he exactly?" I used to be suspicious of people who believed in ghosts. I thought that they were hiding something. "I don't think I know," I continued. The terrain changed; the banks were covered with a thick thorny brush and bushes covered in berries. The river began to run gently downhill. The water was full of small waves that were caused by the uneven, rock-strewn surface of the riverbed below us.

"Ed's in Heaven, of course," Sarah said. "He did not lead a bad life, so he is not in Hell. He did not take his own life, so he is not in Purgatory."

I had wondered how long it really took to die, how long it took to separate the mind from the body, how many levels of unconsciousness there were before the brain stopped functioning. I decided that the process involved degrees of separation and that the death of a relationship necessarily followed a similar course.

"Darling, when I am dead, promise to pinch me?"

"Your cheek?"

"Both!" she said. "Strangest thing, I could not find Ed's ring this weekend, and you know how long it has been on the bedside table. Then I found it in my pocket."

"You must have put it there, and forgot."

"This pocket," she said, motioning to the Velcro topped version on the front of her life jacket.

I thought we were both losing our minds. A cold draft blew upstream toward us.

"I hear loud water!"

"Don't panic, Sarah. We're coming up on the Highwood."

She turned, looking afraid.

"Don't worry," I said. "The water is much warmer here!"

"*That* is terribly comforting," she yelled back, as we began to bounce through the tall waves the two rivers made where they met.

We pulled out onto an island a short distance from the confluence, and set up an elaborate camp.

Wearing Ed's ring on the thumb of her left hand, Sarah busied herself inside the dining tent, and set up the small folding table. Then she expanded something that looked like the end of a heating duct. It was a four-sided, open metal cube that she said was an oven. The fire was burning strong, and soon Sarah was cooking pork tenderloin and potatoes. The pie she'd built at home sat on top of the cooler in an old stoneware dish. I couldn't believe she was going to such great lengths.

"Twenty-five minutes," she said. "Make sure we have a enough wood, please."

I traced my way through the stand of skinny poplar and birch in the middle of our island, stopped on the bank of the shaded, narrow channel that divided us from the nearest ranch. If the water had been lower, a few dozen steps would've taken me across. On the map, we were between the towns of Indus and Langdon. I walked downstream checking the far end of the island for the Scout group. As I emerged from the poplars, I saw that they had made a giant shelter with their canoes and a series of tarps. Nine canoe bags of varying colours hung from a large branch that stretched out over the Bow. A tent stood about fifty feet away from the canoe structure, and a cocoon hammock was suspended between two trees close to where I stood.

"G'day," said a voice from behind the mesh.

"Hi!" I said back. "How small does that contraption pack?"

"To about the size of a water bottle, my lovely," the instructor said, slipping out between the nylon bottom and the bug net. He was shorter than I was.

"Thought your group might have camped at McKinnon Flats."

"Naw — too many other people there. Usually no one else on this island."

"I know," I replied.

"Jake," he said, extending his hand.

"Rhegan," I said. "Come and visit us later. Got to get back."

I heard Sarah's voice in conversation as I came full-circle to our camp. When I got closer, I saw the red hull of an overturned kayak crowned by two spray skirts. I dropped wood by the fire next to another pile that Sarah must have asked Liam to collect.

"In the neighborhood?" I asked.

He stood next to a woman who was barely five feet tall. "Sort of," he said, laughing. "Just tripping down to the flats from Dad's place. Sarah said you two'd be here. Thought we'd stop in. Rhegan, this is Maria."

"Nice to meet you," I said hands on my hips.

They were sipping chocolate from steaming cups that Sarah had prepared. She handed me one. The ache in my pelvis returned; it felt unbearable. "Didn't expect to have company," I said to her, through a smile.

"I was surprised too, darling!"

"Well I've invited others as well," I said, as if I was thirteen. "The Scouts are at the other end of the island." I tuned toward the fire, poked at the wood, and tried to replace Liam's musky scent with the aroma of the food my mother was preparing.

Sarah and Liam ate and joked as if we were sitting at the diningroom table at home and Ed had abandoned us to finish up something he was building in the shop. Maria joined in, spoke about the joint project she was working on with Liam. I sat on the cooler, ate in complete silence, unsure of myself and of what I'd say if I let myself go.

Liam told Sarah that his sister had just given birth to a son.

I downed my third cup of wine. "That's great," I said. "Now your dad won't have to worry about his land."

The Scout group found us just as Sarah decided that the pie was ready. She divided it into chunks and the six boys filed past her with their troop cups outstretched as if collecting alms. I delighted in telling them to keep the forks, which I pulled one by one from the stuff-sack. The boys chewed the tines long after the pie was devoured. I shook off the feeling of metal on enamel, imagined instead, my teeth skimming Liam's shins.

The leaders admired the reflector oven, which Sarah explained in great detail while the instructor worked to hold my attention with stories of the Nahanni River.

"Excuse me," I said, when I saw Liam pulling on his thin, yellow gloves and stepping through the rubber spray skirt. "Have to leave so soon?" I touched his hand.

He stiffened, and stepped backwards. "Dad's picking us up at McKinnon Flats in about twenty minutes. I want to be off the river before dark."

Maria smiled and pulled the kayak toward the water.

"Well, tell him I say hello, and tell Christine I say congrats."

I tried to focus on the conversation that Sarah had with Liam as he helped Maria with the kayak, tried to listen to his answer to her question about partners. I mouthed, *Bye*, when he turned, and let the instructor fill my cup with more wine.

"You could have told me that you'd invited *her!*" I said to Sarah later. The generator hummed, the light outside crackled with dying bugs, and Sarah's little stereo played pipe music.

"I did not know!" she fired back. "*You* are drunk." She turned the music off.

"So what, I've had a long day." I had no idea how many glasses of wine I'd consumed by then, but I remember Sarah opening the bottle that Liam had brought. "Going to pass judgment on me now? Lecture me about what a *good* husband Liam would've been? Tell me that I didn't *have* to marry all those other men?"

"Give me a cup, will you? I told you earlier what I really thought."

"Well, I have no excuse!" I said, passing her one. "Except that I've been brainwashed."

"What do you mean?" she asked, draining the bottle.

"What Nemit says. Lots of women buy into the most widely popular brand in the world."

"I am not following you, darling."

"The wife brand."

"Do you mean like a brand on a cow?"

"No, but maybe we can patent that idea, turn it into a subliminal sign, and sell it to some of the ranchers around here. Let them burn it into the hides of their calves. Then we can have the last laugh."

"I think you have had too much." She tried to take my cup, but I hugged it to my chest, spilling half of the contents on my fleece. She dabbed at it with a tea towel. "I think you are cynical," she continued. "Look at Ed and me. We have been together practically all of our lives, until now." She drank.

"It's catch twenty-two and you know it."

"What *are* you talking about?"

"Don't be coy with me, Sarah. You know exactly what I mean. When you wear a wedding ring there's always someone looking to see how big it is, or asking you where you live, or what your husband does. And when you don't have a husband — "

"People think you of you as a threat — "

"Exactly!"

"Do not trust you around their husbands and sons."

"That's happened to you?" I spilled wine on the ground trying to centre my weight on the three-legged stool.

Sarah covered the puddle with her sandal-clad foot. "Almost immediately after Ed passed away. It is perfectly clear that the Tai Chi wives do not want me too close. Betty next door actually thinks I *like* her scrawny Stan, and Jane, my own sister, looks at me sideways when her drunk of a son is in the room."

"Let's have more wine," I said.

"We are drinking the last of the Pinot," she replied. "I cannot believe you are still conscious."

I threw up my hands. "Everyone either wants to be a wife, or to have one. Who thought up the idea? It's brilliant!"

I remember laying my head on the table, but not how I took off my pants or how I got into my sleeping bag.

Despite the emotion I had felt when I saw Liam with Maria, I knew that I had covered significant ground with my mother. I imagined that if we were bears we would each head off for our own high summer meadow, and had a strange feeling that it would be all right to be apart from her despite our new closeness.

27

I WOKE UP STRUGGLING AGAINST WHAT I had thought was a veil. It was the wall of the dining tent. I was on the ground, my body completely off the sleeping pad that Sarah must have brought inside for me. The smell of coffee and bannock weighed me down.

"How do you feel, darling?"

I cradled my head in my arms as two ultra-lights flew overhead. They sounded like a stereo version of my neighbour's lawn mower.

Sarah jumped up and down, waving. "I see you, Liam! I see you, Fred! Rhegan! Rhegan!" she shrieked. "Look at them!"

"I am definitely not selling the house to Liam. He can damn well rent it!"

"Come on! You are going to miss them!"

"You're burning the bannock," I managed, as I rolled into a ball. I un-zipped my sleeping bag from the foot up and stumbled outside, hood over my head.

Sarah threw the skillet on the grass and turned off the one-burner stove. "Here they come!" she called. "Look! Look!"

The drone built to a whine and then a loud buzz. Liam and his father seemed dangerously close to the treetops. This time one of the pilots dipped a wing and dropped a huge water balloon near the canoe.

"Did you see that? Did you?" She ran toward me from the riverbank. "He certainly went to a lot of trouble," she said, as the drone faded. "Maybe I was wrong."

"Probably not," I said, as I sat on the ground.

She had already collapsed the tent and packed it. Her canoe bag, the table and the stools, the generator, the bug light, her stereo, the reflector oven, and my camera case were all stacked neatly waiting to be loaded.

"Nemit and Adam will have to wait if we do not start soon," she said. "I will make more bannock. Maybe you will feel better after we absorb some of that stomach acid. Here — something for your head." She handed me Ed's remedy: milky tea laced with Drambuie. She also gave me two pills, and a neoprene bottle full of freezing water.

I swallowed the pills dry and wrapped my hands around the hot tea.

She nattered about Liam and insisted on brushing out my hair. I tolerated the strokes; my skin pulled away from my eyes with every draw of the brush. I let her make a long braid, and tried to remember the last time she did that. I think I was seven.

Her voice echoed when I went into the trees to squat. I thought I heard another motor, imagined Liam hovering. I had explained to my mother about camping etiquette, and knew that she brought her own trowel, so I didn't expect my nostrils to be assaulted by her leavings. I wrinkled my nose, looked to my left, and saw a fresh pile of bear scat dotted with raspberries. I wondered at the fact that our cooler was untouched. I thought about Liam's experience in the Yoho Campground, felt the same apprehension I had when he and I met. I stood up, then scoured the area until I found the telltale paw prints — they led toward the channel between our island and the nearby ranch. Bears were good swimmers. I imagined the one that had left the evidence behind was a shy black bear. I decided that it must have followed the river out of the mountains, stayed concealed in riparian forests, and that the animal would turn back as soon as the poplar and birch gave way to prairie brush and fewer berries. I thought that the ultra-lights had scared it away. I was wrong; I should have been more alert, the way I had been near Red Earth Creek. Instead, I breathed a sigh of relief and walked back to our campsite. I took two more pills to dull the sound of my mother's shrill voice and loaded the canoe in record time.

The Boy Scouts were landed at McKinnon flats when we paddled by. Jake called, "Your numba — you didn't give me your numba!"

"You are not!" Sarah said, looking back at me.

I managed a grin. I couldn't wait to get off the water, couldn't wait for the silence of alone to engulf me, comfort me, soothe me. The last section of river was tedious and slow and wide, ever branching towards the dirt road that wound down from the cliffs near Carseland. A while after we started the last part of our journey, we began steering left, moving into smaller channels to avoid the weir that crossed the main stream. The water was deep and moved slowly. Everything was deceptively calm. I lay on top of the gear while Sarah paddled in the bow. It was blistering hot.

I fell asleep wondering about the rosary wrapped around her wrist, dreamt that my mother and I cliff-jumped. The white of her legs and the red of her suit hovered above me, my breath trapped in my inflated cheeks until their insides burned. I smiled, felt saliva dripping from the corner of my mouth, something that Sarah found incredibly unattractive when I was a baby. I remembered the way my father loved me when I was little, the way he helped my mother bathe me. I imagined the feeling I had when he wrapped me in a towel that he'd warmed using Granny's old space heater. It wasn't the gear that I felt below me, it was my father's lap, where I sat while my mother fluffed my curling baby hair with a soft brush. I dreamt about the way they dressed me in clean pajamas and tucked me into bed, about the way my mother sat beside me, listening until the sound of Ed's voice read me to sleep. I'm unsure why I had that particular dream while Sarah paddled alone.

I awoke to the sound of Sarah yelling obscenities. Half asleep, I stayed where I was, stretched out over the gear, imagining she was in the throes of a final letting go, that she was yelling at the sky. When I looked over the side of the canoe, we were closer to the riverbank than we should have been.

"Slanted son of a who-er! Bugger — you!" The canoe rocked because she pumped her arms over her head while she hung onto the coyote paddle. She was sitting on the seat rather than kneeling.

"Sarah," I began. "It's all right. I'll help you paddle to the middle again."

"GET BACK, GET AWAY!" She screamed. Then her voice lowered an octave, "Jesus in Heaven — protect us!" Her paddle slapped the water.

I covered my eyes with my hands, wishing she would stop. "Sarah," I said again, "What are you doing?" As I sat up, a sleek black object entered my line of vision, reached out of the water, and pulled me cleanly out of the canoe. It swam underneath the yellow Kevlar while I struggled up. I willed myself not to cough, and took a deep breath as I broke the surface. The large shape made contact with my legs. I kicked and punched, whirled

around as it dove under me, shook my head to clear my eyes.
My life jacket held me up.

Sarah knelt in the bow of the canoe screaming my name.
I turned toward her, spluttering as water coursed over my
head. She crouched, arm across her face, just as the black bear
engulfed me in its forelegs from behind. The bone of its penis
pressed against my calves; I thought about Liam. My shoulders
were pressed forward until my clavicles broke. I barked in pain,
was pulled under, and almost blacked out.

Above me, my mother was like an apparition wavering
behind a mirror, arms flailing. I saw the paddle break the surface
of the water and knew she was trying to paddle upstream.
The canoe rocked dangerously and I prayed to God that she
wouldn't fall in. I heard her muffled voice as I kicked my heels
into the bear's genitals. Water stung the gashes that he'd made
on my scalp. I smashed my head against my attacker's snout,
then stopped, almost out of air. I was released. I tried to pull
with my arms, bawled at the pain that flashed across my chest,
and took in water as I frog-kicked to the surface trying to get to
the canoe. It looked huge from underneath. My face emerged
just feet from the stern, mouth open for air. Sarah smashed her
paddle against the back of the bear as it dove again. A second
blow ripped through my thigh and dislocated my right knee.

A blood-curdling scream penetrated the air. I didn't realize
immediately that it was my own. For a moment, I was on the bank
of the river watching. The canoe travelled downstream faster
than I did, my mother was shrieking, "Rhegan! Rheegaan!" She
threw the bug light and the stove, then the two stools at the
bear's head, but missed him completely. She was floating away
from me. She beat her paddle against the gunwale, not realizing
she was issuing a challenge. When he roared and turned in her

direction, she dove over the gear, lay flat, her feet spread apart gripping the edges of the canoe behind her.

I kicked the bear's back with my left leg and almost lost consciousness from the effort. My right leg dangled. "Front ferry," I whispered. Red drool covered my chin as the current swept me along. I saw small fish.

I was pulled under again. Claws grazed my vertebrae. The bear let go, and my back burned against my wetsuit. Flesh and bits of rubber floated up. I cried out. My body, still wrapped in its yellow life jacket, made an involuntary move for the surface. I thought too soon that I could breathe in air; my mouth filled with water. I thought about beginning my journey with my mother, the headwaters, the natural bridge, the noise of the rushing white water. I thought about the riverbed, the elements lifting and moving below me, about the flow that carried my mother away from me. I voided — avoided — the flash of an idea that I was about to expire suddenly, the way my father had. In the same instance I imagined the curve of my mother's back as she'd tried to revive Ed, and I knew that her spine would make the same shape as she looked below the water for me. The large teeth in the bear's lower jaw dug into my buttock; the upper set pierced my pelvis between my navel and my hipbone. The ache I'd been nursing was suddenly released.

I was pulled upwards, the bear still holding me in its mouth, until my body was partly out of the water. Then he shook me. My flesh tore from my breaking bones. With a toss of his head he threw me, and I landed in shallow water. My jaws clicked open and shut while my arms and legs convulsed. I thought about playing soldier with my cousin Reed.

I saw the canoe and my mother's torso through a white haze; they were upside down. I heard her voice. Profanities poured from her lips. I couldn't see her face. I wondered how she would manage without me.

The bear towed me upstream. The life jacket and the back of my head grazed a gravel bar, then my body floated again through deeper water. I saw hilltops and tree branches. I imagined lifting my upper body and facing my adversary, imagined treading water, imagined punching at the air between his face and mine, remembered that my knife was still in the pocket of my life jacket. I yelled at him. The bear turned and the next bite ripped away my left arm. The water around me changed colour.

I let go. Warm excrement filled my wetsuit.

I knew Sarah would pray. I had seen the rosary wrapped around her wrist before I fell asleep. "It's going to get shallow soon," I had said. "I'll need you to stroke."

I heard a tongue lapping, but felt nothing except warm breath on my neck. I willed my mother to take up her paddle, and imagined the crucifix pressed into her hand between the carved teak handle and her soft palm.

The bear roared and I answered with my own low growl. The last hard blow to my head crushed my nose and cheekbones, took away my sight, separated my scalp from my body. The bear sank its teeth into my neck and shook me once more. Saint Christopher fell to the riverbed.

I sighed.

28

WHEN YOUR DAUGHTER'S BROKEN BODY IS dragged from the river by her attacker, you paddle forward. Your reluctant hands stroke on each side of the stern because you have no other choice. Your movements are spasmodic.

For years, you tried to separate yourself from your daughter's smell, her sound, the taste of salt on her cheek. You resisted the feel of her touch on your arm.Now you ache for those sensations. You stroke water instead of your daughter's hair. Your eyes are dry. Your knuckles look as if they will explode from your skin at any moment. Sobs escape your lips.

You steer the canoe as if your paddle is a rudder. You move toward the main stream because you want to get away from the shore. You remember that you saw two bears travelling together near Johnston Canyon; you recall the image of the dead bear in Fish Creek Park. You scream out loud and try to break the paddle over your knee. You recoil in pain from the force of your own actions.

The water does not gurgle anymore; it laps silently against lush banks. You are shocked by the contrast between the dark green next to the river and the tinder-dry coulees and hills that rise to the prairie floor near Carseland; life and death are presented to you in a single image. You wish you had Rhegan's knife.

You pull harder. The green-edged banks on the north side of the river melt into prairie colour as if the artist who painted the scene ran out of forest and bush-tinted oils. Further on, the north banks look dusty and seem to be lined with gravel between clumps of dried scrub brush.

You know you are moving the canoe closer to the weir. The pressure in your throat turns into a sound and emerges as something that you cannot control or stop. Your chest tightens unbearably then something inside you fractures, shatters, and breaks. You try to stand, but you end up on one foot and one knee. "There is no Christ, God, or Holy Ghost!" you scream. "No Mary Mother of!" Families of ducks scurry into the reeds on the south bank. "Sons-of bitches! Who-ers in Hell! Fuck wits and pricks and consecrated cunts!" You fall onto the gear, crying.

After a while, you push yourself up to kneeling. You realize that you are holding onto the blade of the teak paddle; blood runs into your palms. You take hold of the shaft and you hammer the handle against the gunwale until bits of carved coyote break off. You raise the thing over your head a hundred times, beating and smashing until your hands are numb from holding on. You drop the paddle in the water. You open and close your fists until you feel the cuts in your fingers. You pull at the gear. Your nails tear from ripping off the remaining tie-down straps, which you throw in the river. The tent goes overboard following the reflector oven, the table that looks like a portfolio with a leather handle, the map, the bailer, the empty cooler, the rolled mattresses, the sleeping bags, the dining tent, the wine bottles, and the garbage bag. Your daughter's camera case and the cooler are the only items that float.

You scream as you hold Rhegan's clothing to your chest. You continue until your throat is raw and only muted sounds come out of your mouth. Your chest convulses. The canoe, which is slightly diagonal in the water, travels forward as if on autopilot, following the deep flow in the middle of the Bow River.

You do not know or care how much time has gone by. You loosen the strap of the waterproof runner's watch that Rhegan loaned you and hear a plunk. You see large warning signs on the bank to the right. In the distance, a row of brightly-coloured buoys dances in the air on a rope that crosses the water. Earlier you had felt unsure about your plan to drown yourself in the river. You have no doubts now.

You sit on the fibreglass seat in the stern, open your own gear-bag, reach in, and pull out your blue pillbox hat. You put it on. You drop the open bag over the side and take off your life jacket. You move the waterproof sack containing your daughter's belongings and hold it between your feet and lower legs. You take up your daughter's paddle and drive the yellow canoe forward, aiming for the centre of the river. You dig the paddle into the water and use it like a rudder, then you lift your arms over your head. The canoe stutters across the cable lined with buoys suspended on the surface. You drop the bear paddle in the river and watch it speed toward the ledge. You are calm; you place one hand on your hat, the other on the gunwale. Hundreds of pelicans with bright-orange bills bob about on the water beyond the base of the weir. You have seen them before on the page of a calendar entitled *August*. You cross yourself, say, "In the name of the Father, the Son, and the Holy Ghost."

29

I USED TO WONDER ABOUT THE moment of my own death. I was carried into this world on a whorl of my mother's waters, gasping for new air. As I left, I drowned in a vortex of my own thoughts. Sarah told me she thought a good death was fast, no warnings. My version of that included doing battle. I refused to let go until letting go was the only option I had. On one level, I was separated from what I loved at the moment I sensed my heart's last beat. On another, I am bound to what I know and those I love.

The bear dragged my body from the river, and laid it in a shallow hole carved from the hard ground. My body reclined there, head to one side, my remaining arm flung out, draped, just as it might be if I were at home in the bathtub. After he disemboweled my body, the bear feasted on my entrails, then covered my remains with dirt, sticks, branches and moss. Later, he rested on top as if he'd made a nest.

He was predacious; he had stalked Sarah and me under the cover of the treed banks and tall brush, slunk into the river unheard. Investigators initially thought he could have got that close to the Parklands by following the Highwood from the mountains, but they knew it was unlikely that he could have done that completely undetected. The bear travelled down the Bow following a centuries-old migratory route, sleeping in hidden dens during the day, and moving great distances at night, until he reached our little island.

The bear was well fed; ungulate remains were also found in his gut. He wasn't interested in the remnants of food in our cooler. He had his eye on a surplus kill. I was one of three people he stalked before he was shot and killed. Two rancher's children were also found in the same lush wooded area.

I became Sarah's worst nightmare, the one in which she was a ghost destined for Purgatory.

30

THE SIGHT OF THE FLOCK LANDING on water crosses your mind when the bow of your daughter's canoe wobbles momentarily in the air over the curvature of the Carseland Weir. You let go of your hat and spread your arms as if they are wings. The seam of the canoe, caressed by the black-haired man at Seebe, disappears below the dangerous rush of the perpetual motion machine. Wings beat. Your head fills with white noise.

You hear Rhegan's voice behind you. It has the same tone it did on the day you exhaled into your husband's mouth. You whisper, "I love you," and the words are launched into the air.

You close your eyes and hear a loud groaning. The Kevlar bends. You think about your sister, Jane, and the card game she made you play repetitively when you were a child. *Snap!*

The canoe uncurls and you fly forward. You open your eyes. You are a projectile skimming the surface of the green-black water beyond the pull and crush of the white water that lines the river below the weir. The pelican roost is behind you. A few birds, undaunted by your appearance, float in the area just below the observation deck. The blue netting of your pillbox hat disappears from view. You close your eyes before you drop below the surface.

The frigid water rushes up the legs of your wetsuit, engulfs your chest and abdomen through the sleeveless top. You think about your daughter's idea of letting go while you are carried away from the large souse hole. You hold your breath and open your eyes. You are shocked when they do not sting. You close them again because you cannot see anything.

You try to scream when a metal barb tears its way through your right nostril. You remember the day last year when your then thirty-seven year old daughter came home with a diamond stud in her nose. Water fills your ears, nose, and throat. You feel it permeate your chest cavity. You black out.

31

WE WERE SUPPOSED TO LAND IN the sharp elbow of the river that defines the pullout, an area that curves three hundred yards away from the water upstream of the weir. We planned to get out of the canoe there on the north bank, and walk up fifty feet of hard-packed dirt to the gravel track that divides the portage area and ends at the observation deck.

Nemit had driven in and out of the area near the Carseland weir twice. She thought she was in the wrong place, and drove over to Wyndham Provincial Park. No one fishing there had seen my mother or me. Nemit didn't tell Adam, but she knew something was wrong. She parked her van near the end of the access road that snakes its way down from the prairie to meet the gravel track.

They waited for us on the cement observation deck. A high fence surrounded it.

Adam stood on the low wall, leaning into the steel mesh that rose twenty feet in the air. He looked over the weir and the river below it. "Is that a keeper?" he asked.

Nemit stood near him, one hand on his calf. She watched two men casting lines in the water downstream of the weir. "God — it's not a keeper, it's a weir," she said. "Come down."

Adam was trying his best to convince his mother that he should scale the fence when Sarah came into view.

They watched, speechless, then ran hand in hand down the long slope on the downstream side of the gravel track. They ran toward the fishermen who were now in the shallows near the boat launch five hundred metres from the weir. One was on his knees and the other was yelling into a cell phone. He dropped the phone, hitched up his waders, and pushed his way into the water. Sarah was carried, floating on her front, toward the boat launch by the outward fan of the river below the weir. He used a boat hook to grab onto her wetsuit and pull her nearer to shore. Nemit waded in to help him. They turned Sarah over and floated her partially up the slope. The second man held Sarah's head in his huge hands.

Nemit began artificial respiration. She pinched Sarah's nose and tilted her head back. She placed her mouth over my mother's lips, which were white and parted. Tears streamed from Nemit's eyes and landed on Sarah's skin. She began breathing into my mother's mouth while Adam looked on.

The fisherman, who had lost his graphite rod when Sarah was caught up in the line, took over. He pulled Sarah out of the water, onto the boat launch, and performed CPR until her neck bulged and her body convulsed. Nemit helped him; they turned Sarah's head to the side and rolled the rest of her body in the same direction, placing her upper knee on the ground. Sarah vomited a pool that smelled like the sea. Nemit sank to the ground, face in her hands while Adam stroked the back of

Sarah's neck. My mother was denied what she'd been hoping for since the day my father died.

Sarah was taken to hospital in Calgary. Forty-eight hours later, her sister, Jane, helped her leave. For the next week and a half, Jane slept on the silk-covered chair in my parents' bedroom, held my mother close each time she awoke crying. Five days after that, they claimed what was left of my body.

After I was cremated, my mother didn't wait; she took me up to Assiniboine and poured my ashes and the rest of my father's into the stream that runs toward Lake Magog.

32

My mother and Liam met at the Inglewood house exactly one year after my death: July twenty-seventh, 2002. Sarah wanted to discuss the terms of the purchase agreement I wrote. They crossed out my name and replaced it with Sarah's, deleted the section that covered first right of refusal. Afterward, Liam asked Sarah if she was sure about giving up that option. She said that she was. He did something I rarely did; he covered her hand with his. After scanning the rest of the pages and finding nothing to debate, they signed the document. Liam spoke about filling the planters, and settling into the old map room again. He told Sarah that he would disarm the line to the security firm; he was more concerned about escaped animals from the Calgary Zoo than he was about rogue robbers.

They climbed the metal stairs, and sat on the floor at the top. I imagined my body cradled between theirs. I knew that I'd have to accept the feeling of being just out of reach; it was the same sensation that Sarah had understood and reconciled herself to for most of my life.

I watched her put her arm around the shoulders of the man who was never really her son-in-law. The stairs absorbed Liam's emotions. He told Sarah that he wanted to make a confession. He said he wished again and again that he'd forgiven my Whitefish ways, and the loss of the child.

His face had changed. He no longer wore the protective mask that he used to save for me. The expression that I had seen the last time we met, the one that suggested he neither looked for, nor expected, my embrace, was gone. I remembered the way my skin felt the last time he was close to me, the way my body ached.

Immediately after my death, the police psychologist suggested that Sarah deal with the pain and the guilt that she felt, and deal with it soon. But her sadness had nothing to do with guilt. My mother doesn't wonder about death, no longer wastes her time hanging on, romanticizing, or constructing alternate endings; she knows I hated endings.

Three years after that, my mother sold her house and mine. Nemit wandered through Sarah's condominium as she packed up, admired the porcelain figurines with wings. Sarah told her that she was giving them away. Nemit asked if she might give them to the nuns at Saint Bernard's. Together, they demolished the *Car and Driver* wall. Nemit took the entire collection of old magazines *and* the paperbacks that Granda loved so much to Adam's school.

Before she locked the doors for the last time, Sarah stood next to the teak chair where the whirlpool used to be. Gently she folded it flat, waded into the river, and set it afloat. It didn't go far before it was submerged in the rush and pull. She gave the house keys to the realtor and drove away in her new car. Her hands were steady on the steering wheel, her fingers and wrists decorated with the rings and the bangles I used to store in the old wardrobe.

I didn't leave any specific instructions but Sarah kept my holding company active and maintained the Findley registration as long as it was needed. She still collects rent from the other properties.

My mother moved away from the river to another Northwest neighborhood. Her house perches on a dry hill that looks west to the foothills and the Rocky Mountains; from there she nurtures our shared love of beginnings.

ACKNOWLEDGEMENTS

Memoir Of a Good Death has been supported by a significant number of people. In its earliest days the seeds of this book were nurtured and provoked into being by Aritha van Herk, who supervised my creative masters thesis, *Altar Ego*. During that initial phase, my work was also graced by the careful readings of Athene Evans, Marika Deliyannides, and Jackie Honnet, and by the sharp eye of Gisele Villeneuve. A number of colleagues from English 598 at the University of Calgary, including Lesley Battler, Mark Giles, Adrian Kelly, Natalie Meisner, and Sam Pane also gave helpful critiques: many thanks to all of you.

Later at the Banff Centre, I continued to grow this novel while studying with Audrey Thomas, bending the ear of Edna Alford, and spending a wonderful stretch of time in the Hemingway, Leighton Studio. For funding while at the Banff Centre, I thank The Alberta Foundation for the Arts and Red Deer College (Faculty Professional Development Program).

Profound thanks to Robert Kroetsch who gave careful and generous consideration to this work, both during his time as the Markin-Falnnigan Distinguished Writer In Residence at the University of Calgary, and later at the Sage Hill Novel Colloquium. For its support of the time I spent at Sage Hill, I again wish to thank The Alberta Foundation for the Arts.

In the latter part of its development, my immediate and extended family, close friends, and running companions wondered, a) how I could spend so much time on one book, and b) when it was going to be published. I thank all of them for their patience and constant support, especially my daughters, Kim and Stacey Budziak, and my dear friend, Claire Verner. I also want to thank Tom Wayman for his selfless sharing of time and for his warm encouragement.

To my husband, Bob Hallett, I give my love and heartfelt thanks. You have been on this journey with me every step of the way, shouldering much so that I can continue to write. Thank you for loving me and supporting my work, no matter what.

For the initial cover concept submitted to Thistledown Press, love and thanks to my daughter Kim Budziak. The stunning image was her suggestion. And, many, many thanks to Barbara Cole for her kind permission to use *Flutter Kick* on the cover.

For her inspiring adoption of Al Purdy's lines from "In the Beginning was the Word," as they appear in *The Antigonish Review* (Spring 2010) in her poem, "The Unbounded Cartographer," I thank Angela Waldie.

To Harriet Richards, editor, words are not enough! Your tireless effort, careful reading, discerning eye, and objective approach to *Memoir* helped to make this novel whole. Its successes are your successes.

Finally, I want to thank Thistledown Press for believing in *Memoir of a Good Death*. Al Forrie, Jackie Forrie, and the group of people who work with them are extraordinarily passionate about what they do; I am a privileged recipient of their patience and dedication.

An excerpt from *Memoir of a Good Death* appeared in *Other Voices*, Volume 18, Number 2: Winter 2005. The first draft was published within the monograph, *Altar Ego: Gender, Property, and the Culture of Marriage* by VDM of Saarbrücken, Germany in May 2008.

ANNE SORBIE was born in Paisley, Scotland and she lives and writes in Calgary. Her fiction has appeared in literary journals such as *Geist* and *Other Voices*, and her poetry, in the 2009 anthology, *Home and Away*. *Memoir of a Good Death* is her first novel.